"Sultry, sexy, s̶... ...ng for hot vampires. . . . ...dark!"
—*New York Tim... bestselling* author Kerrelyn Sparks

"*Afterlight* is a book every paranormal lover is going to fall in love with. . . . Ms. Jasper penned a winner. . . . This is a must-read paranormal book and it comes highly recommended." —Night Owl Romance (5 stars)

"There's a certain thrill that goes with realizing you might have discovered the best book you've read in a long, long time. . . . *Afterlight* is beautifully written, with mind-numbing possession over the reader. It's edgy and modern, with just the right amount of good versus evil. . . . The most absorbing, enticing, and unique paranormal world I've read [about] in years."
—Romance Junkies (5 blue ribbons)

"A fast-paced thriller starring a kick-butt heroine whose unique blood proves more in demand than her unique tattoos. . . . Elle Jasper's rendition of the vampire Everdark underworld of Savannah provides a welcome addition to the subgenre blood bank." —Alternative Worlds

"Darkly atmospheric and steamy." —*Booklist*

"A steamy journey into the world of drugs and magic, sex and blood. . . . Fans of J. R. Ward, Gena Showalter, and Adrian Phoenix will love it." —Bitten by Books

continued . . .

The Dark Ink Chronicles
by Elle Jasper

Afterlight
Everdark

Eventide

THE DARK INK CHRONICLES

ELLE JASPER

A SIGNET ECLIPSE BOOK

SIGNET ECLIPSE
Published by New American Library, a division of
Penguin Group (USA) Inc., 375 Hudson Street,
New York, New York 10014, USA
Penguin Group (Canada), 90 Eglinton Avenue East, Suite 700, Toronto,
Ontario M4P 2Y3, Canada (a division of Pearson Penguin Canada Inc.)
Penguin Books Ltd., 80 Strand, London WC2R 0RL, England
Penguin Ireland, 25 St. Stephen's Green, Dublin 2,
Ireland (a division of Penguin Books Ltd.)
Penguin Group (Australia), 250 Camberwell Road, Camberwell, Victoria 3124,
Australia (a division of Pearson Australia Group Pty. Ltd.)
Penguin Books India Pvt. Ltd., 11 Community Centre, Panchsheel Park,
New Delhi - 110 017, India
Penguin Group (NZ), 67 Apollo Drive, Rosedale, Auckland 0632,
New Zealand (a division of Pearson New Zealand Ltd.)
Penguin Books (South Africa) (Pty.) Ltd., 24 Sturdee Avenue,
Rosebank, Johannesburg 2196, South Africa

Penguin Books Ltd., Registered Offices:
80 Strand, London WC2R 0RL, England

First published by Signet Eclipse, an imprint of New American Library,
a division of Penguin Group (USA) Inc.

First Printing, March 2012
10 9 8 7 6 5 4 3 2 1

For my best friend, Kim Lenox, for always believing in me

Eventide

Part One

SEIZED

From my grave, I've watched her. Watched her in turmoil as a child, then transformed into the tenacious, alluring woman I crave today. Riley is in my mind constantly, and my need for her is excruciating. Sometimes, I can taste her, smell her; I close my eyes and I . . . feel her. I love her. She belongs with me. And I'll do anything— anything—to make her mine forever.

—Victorian Arcos

I can still hear the human screams inside my head. Demented, painful screams of pure torture and desperation. Behind my closed eyes, the slaughter at the Tunnel 9 Club rages red with human blood. It'll stay with me forever. All of this will.

With my strength weakened—even the tendencies I've acquired from being bitten by vampires aren't enough right now—I can do little more than open my eyes and rest my forehead against the window of Victorian Arcos's Jag. Pitch blackness stares back at me. We're on I-16, heading north out of Savannah to Atlanta. A sign that says DUBLIN, NEXT THREE EXITS flashes by, so I know we've been on the road for about two hours. Is that all? Seems like a lot longer. There's nothing to look at except billboards, so I stare blankly into the night. My other tendencies are still present, like my sense of smell, and I can detect the burnt grease from a truck-stop grill permeating the air. The pungent musk of perfume wafts on the wind. And it must have recently rained because the scent of hot wet tar rises to a choking pitch. I concentrate and turn my high sense of smell off. It irritates me. Right now, everything irritates me. Victorian has me under his control. I've been taken against my will. So I do nothing but stare mindlessly into oblivion. It seems to help.

Time passes. Everything becomes a blur. I want to throw open the door and jump, but my limbs are numb, limp, lifeless, as if I've sat in one position for too long and they've fallen asleep. He's incapacitated me with his freaky vampiric mind control, and it royally pisses me off. There isn't a damn thing I can do about it, despite my own powers. I still try to move other parts of my body; nothing works except my head, my eyes, and eyelids. Involuntary muscles, like the ones for breathing, work to keep me alive. I am totally paralyzed. And not at all surprised.

Victorian's knuckles brush my jaw, and his hand lingers against my skin in a caress. I want to slap it away. But strangely, it comforts me. "I'm sorry," he says, and his voice is so heavy with regret, I almost believe him. "I don't like holding you against your will, Riley." I look at him, and he glances at me as the headlights of an oncoming vehicle flash across his beautiful young face. "Truly. Nothing would please me more than for you to come willingly. To trust me. But you're as predictable as you are beautiful, I'm afraid." He smiles, and his teeth radiate an inhuman whiteness in the shadows of the Jag. Only the fluorescent glare of the stereo illuminates his features. "Besides. I have to drive."

Victorian Arcos. Moving my eyes in his direction, I stare at him. Sharp, aristocratic features and long black hair pulled back into a queue remind me of someone who'd once dueled with pistols long ago. I want to hate his guts. A centuries-old Romanian strigoi vampire, he and his brother, Valerian, were once entombed in a grave by my Gullah grandfather's ancestors. Now they're free, thanks to my brother, Seth, and his rowdy friends, who inadvertently set loose the dangerous vampire brothers. Valerian is pure evil, and he's taken Savannah and Charleston by murderous, bloodlust-fueled storm.

Vic, though . . . He's a bit different. I don't particularly trust him, but he's not a psychotic killer like his brother. And for some reason, even though Victorian has used his strigoi mind powers to force me to leave with him, I can't hate him. I know that he's trying to protect me.

I left behind pure carnage at the club. If Victorian

hadn't come for me, I would have stayed and fought. I left behind a lot of loved ones, left them to fight without my help, and I feel like shit about it. I should've been there. Period. But Victorian wouldn't hear of it.

Why would Victorian want to protect me, you ask? I still don't know the answer. There is a connection between us, live and palpable, and he knows it as much as I do. I think it goes beyond the DNA we share. He and Valerian bit me and injected me with their toxins, connecting me to both of them. It's what gave me these tendencies. Their rare strigoi vampire bloodline makes me even more unpredictable than your average human with tendencies. Don't ask me to explain it any more than that. All I know is that I now have crazy superhuman powers, which Preacher, my Gullah surrogate grandfather, says will evolve over time.

"How'd you get a Jag, much less learn to drive?" I ask, curious.

"I taught myself. Not much to it really. As for the car, I obtained it the same way that I got you to sit so polite and still," he answers. "Power of suggestion."

I glare at him. "You stole it."

Victorian sighs and gives a single nod. "I stole it."

A few moments pass in silence. I try to move my hand toward the door handle. I summon all of my strength, so much that I shake inside, but it's no use. Still paralyzed. The thought crosses my mind that Vic-

torian could totally take advantage of me in my motionless state. He could touch me, rape me. No, wait.
He possesses the power of suggestion. He could make
me want to have crazy nasty sex with him, and I'd do
it. He could even drain my blood. Yet, he doesn't. Why
is that? Why is he taking me away? And more to the
point—where? I'd asked him earlier, and he'd simply
said, "When the time is right, I'll tell you." Those questions and more pull at my brain as weariness overcomes me. The world fades away as my lids close over
my eyes. For a while, I rest. As I drift off, I feel Victorian
smoothing back the hair from my face.

I don't know how long I sleep before the visions take
over, but they, too, trap me just as easily as Victorian's
mind control. Behind my closed lids I lie awake, once
again envisioning the macabre bloodbath we'd left behind hours ago at Tunnel 9. With a forceful jab, my
senses kick in, and in my dream state I slip under just
enough to return to that place of horror. Just outside of
my dream state, I can hear "24" by Jem filtering faintly
from Victorian's stereo through my auditory senses.
Soon the music shifts within my dream state, my body
seems to float, and I know the music now comes from
the surround sound at Tunnel 9. It's sifting through the
hazy room filled with humans. They dance, moving to
the music, rubbing their bodies seductively against
each other. Invisible, I look around. Most are high as a

frickin' kite. Some are just sex-crazed, hormonal twenty-something-year-olds trying to get laid. Others are partying, drinking. All are being hunted. I am nothing more than an invisible bystander. Watching.

The first drop of blood is shed as a newling attacks a human. Newlings are nasty, out of control, brand-new vampires with a voracious appetite. They have no decision-making skills and zero self-control. With an involuntary inhalation, I smell it. Taste it on my tongue. I even lick my lips. A scream breaks through the music, and I turn to see the owner of that first drop of blood. A not-so-young guy, maybe thirty. Pale skin, black eyeliner. That's as far as I get in my inspection because his head is now literally hanging on by a flap of skin at the side of his neck. He just stands there, teetering, alive but not, his body in shock after a newling chewed through his throat, spinal cord, and bone to get to his artery. That's the thing about newlings. Inexperienced. Starved. Fucking messy. They haven't learned yet to go straight for the heart.

All hell breaks loose then; newlings filter through the crowd of partiers. The humans try to fight at first. More blood is shed. Newlings rip into their victims. The heavy metallic scent hangs in the air like fog, thick with fear and hunger. The humans scream, run. There's so much blood; arterial spray on the walls, on the humans, pooling on the floor. Deep within me, a pang takes me by surprise. I feel all warm inside, then scorching hot. The sensation fires from my core, down both arms to my fingertips, down my torso, legs—to my toes. It claws at me. It is need. It's so fierce, so vicious, I cry out.

Why am I reacting like this? I'm not a vampire. I'm not a newling. I'm a human with tendencies. I may have taken on some of the traits of vampires when Victorian and Valerian bit me, but I'm not like them. This sensation, or whatever it is, scares the hell out of me. Yet something pulls at me. Unfamiliar. Desperate. Horrifying.

My eyes fix on a human; I don't see male or female. I smell only the warm blood coursing through their veins. As I breathe in, I can taste it on my tongue. I want it. Need it. Will do anything to get it.

I lunge.

In reality, my body begins seizing. I shake, shudder, convulse. Slowly, the screams fade; the metallic scent weakens. My need is still strong though, and I struggle to bring the scent of blood back. In the darkness, I can no longer see the humans; the club has disappeared. I'm on my back on a firm yet soft surface. I now smell pine, fresh cut grass. Slowly, I open my eyes.

The sounds and smells around me bring me back to the present. I'm no longer in Victorian's Jag. I'm lying on the ground next to a parking lot; cars and semitrucks whiz by on the highway, unevenly, at various speeds. A can dispenses through a soft-drink machine. Laughter echoes in the distance. A stereo system blasts Twisted Sister, one speaker blown in the back. My vision clears as I fixate on what's before me. Victorian is straddling me. He has my arms pinned above my head. Holding me still. My eyes scan past him. We're at an interstate rest stop. Concrete buildings with restrooms and drink machines.

I find my voice, and I struggle against him. "What are you doing?"

Victorian studies me. His grip on me tightens and he frowns. "You don't remember?"

For a second, my brain races. I don't remember, and I don't lie still enough to try to make myself remember. I buck—hard. Victorian's grip breaks, I leap up, and take off. My legs are weak, though, and no sooner do I make it ten feet than I'm down again. Struggling, I manage to find my footing and take off. Slices of light from several tall lamps illuminate the side of the concrete building of the rest area; I avoid it and run straight for the shadows and the trees beyond. My body jerks, and my knees give out. Once more, I force myself up and try to run. Strength floods my body so intensely, I can feel it, as though strength itself is a liquid and someone has poured it straight into me. With arms and legs pumping, I fly through the darkness. Speed is one of my tendencies, and I'm fast as hell. I don't care who sees me. It's not like there are a lot of people out at the rest stop at two a.m. In seconds I'm sifting through dense pines, and because I'm still wearing the same gauzy skirt, tank, and Vans I had on at Tunnel 9 hours before, brambles grab my bare legs and scratch the holy hell out of them. I don't care. I have to get away. Ease the craving now gnawing at my insides—

I jerk to a sudden stop. Confusion webs through my mind, and my memories race wildly. Craving? I crave only Krystal burgers and Krispy Kremes. Sugar. Greasy food. Those are my cravings. So what the hell is—

A body rushes mine and I am once again flung to the ground. Without looking I know it's Victorian. Sharp pine needles and cones littering the wood dig into my skin as his weight presses against me. My face is smashed into the damp leaves and moss.

Quickly, my hands are tethered together.

"Sorry, love," Victorian apologizes. He binds my ankles together, too. "You can't imagine how I hate this, but somehow"—he helps me stand, then looks at me—"you broke free of my suggestion." His head cocks to the side as he studies me, and the moonlight shooting a slender beam through the trees glances off his face. "Intriguing. I've never met another who can break free of my suggestion."

Rage fills behind my eyes, pounds in my chest.

"Well, now you have. So now what? What are you gonna do now, Vic? Throw me over your shoulder like a sack of dog food and haul me to the car?"

The slightest of smiles tips his sensual lips upward. "That's exactly what I'm going to do." In one move, Victorian bends his knees, and in the next instant, over his shoulder I go. He keeps his hands secured around my calves. God only knows my skirt is probably up around my waist, booty to the wind. We move out of the woods and start across the lawn of the rest stop, past the concrete picnic tables and restrooms. No one is around. Only a few semitrucks, their drivers more than likely sleeping. It wouldn't do any good for me to scream; Victorian would simply suggest to anyone who heard that I was really okay, and they'd believe. So I keep quiet.

Until I hear the lock click and the Jag's trunk open.

"No way," I say, my voice only a little uneven, unsure. "Victorian, do not put me in there."

He puts me in there. Lays me gently on a soft, down comforter. Had he expected to have to use his trunk to contain me? Warm brown eyes look down at me with obvious regret. Almost makes me forget what he is. "I apologize. I truly hate this. But for you to break free from my suggestion?" He shook his head. "You're stronger than I thought—than you even think you are. You're a danger to yourself, Riley. I can't let anything

12

happen to you." His stare bores into mine. "I couldn't live with it." The trunk starts to close.

"Wait!" I say frantically. He waits. "Where are you taking me?"

Lowering his hand, Vic grazes my jaw with his knuckles. "Somewhere safe. Somewhere I can help you."

Without another word, he closes me in. The moment he does, I hear another voice rise.

"What the fuck are you doing, man?" a deep voice says, full of shock and anger. "I saw you put that woman in there."

"Perhaps you'd be better off minding your own business," Victorian warns evenly, gentlemanly.

A heavy thump hits the back of the car. "Perhaps you'd be better off shutting the fuck up and opening the motherfucking trunk," the stranger says. "Now."

Silence.

I have a bad feeling. Why isn't Victorian using his suggestive powers to make the man walk away?

"What the fuck—"

The only noise I hear is a choked gurgle.

The car door slams, and in seconds, the purr of the Jag's engine rumbles around me. I know without having seen what just happened. Victorian fed. In his defense, he tried to warn the guy. In the guy's defense, he was trying to save me. It's all so messed up. Victorian

13

shifts gears and roars up the interstate. We're on the move. To where, I have no clue.

The one question I have right now is where the hell did a centuries-old vampire get friggin' tie-wraps? I jerk my ankles and wrists—no go. That thick, hard plastic won't budge even a fraction. In fact, they tighten. So I relax and try to forget I'm in the back of a trunk, bound. And that back at the rest stop, a man lay dead in the parking lot, his blood drained. I close my eyes, the sound of the road and the Jag's engine a respite. Everything seems so messed up now.

I think of the one thing in my life that calms me right now: Eligius Dupré. An ancient vampire from Paris, he and the Dupré family have been Savannah's guardians since the 1700s. After making a pact with Preacher's Gullah ancestors, who inhabited the isles off Georgia's coast, they became the city's protectors from rogue vampires.

Never did I think I'd fall for a creature of the night. Or that he'd fall for me. I'm not cutting myself down, but seriously. I'm not everyone's type. I'm taller than most women. My back and arms are covered in wicked dragon tattoos, along with a dark angel wing inked at the corner of my left eye. I have pink highlights. And my past is far from stellar. As a teen, I got into everything a kid could. Drugs. Gangs. Ditching school. Luckily, with the help of Preacher and his wife, Estelle, I cleaned up my act. Went to school, became a successful tattoo artist with a shop in the historic district called Inksomnia. Still, I'm damaged goods. Eli overlooked my past, though, and only sees *me* now. Shocking, to say the least.

Eli is different. Actually, his whole family is different. They're . . . real. They love one another, like humans. I can't put it any other way. I've grown to care for Eli's papa, Gilles Dupré; his mom, Elise; his brothers, Séraphin and Jean-Luc; and his baby sister, Josephine. In all honesty, they helped save my life.

As I drift between sleep and awareness, a vision of Eli crowds my mind; his face, his jaw, his eyes. Ebony hair against alabaster skin. Blue eyes so clear, it almost hurts to look at them. Protective nearly to a fault, Eli is always conscious of my surroundings and cautious of any outsiders. The way he touches me; his lips against my skin. The sex is incredible. Mind-blowing doesn't fully describe it. More than the sex, though, is how he makes me feel. If Jerry Maguire hadn't said it first, I'd tell Eli, "You complete me" and sincerely mean it. Yet I can't admit even to myself, much less to him, that I love him. How screwed up is that? The last words Eli spoke to me as Victorian drove me away from Tunnel 9 resonate inside my memory.

I will come for you.

I believe Eli. But how will he know where we are

headed? The look on his face as I drove off with Victorian had been one of anguish—betrayal—then determination. All in about five seconds. It's not in Eli's nature to give up. I think he probably was that way, even as a human. Before vampirism. It's definitely a quality I like.

Time flies by. I drift in and out of slumber. So much has happened since the night my baby brother, Seth, and his pals inadvertently released Victorian and Valerian Arcos from their entombed graves. It was then that I learned that Preacher and his mystical Gullah ancestry were responsible for putting the Arcos brothers away in the first place. The Gullah are direct descendants of the African slaves brought to the Americas. They grew to be a proud, strong culture as they gained their freedom and claimed the outer islands of Georgia and South Carolina. Preacher's forefathers had bound their families with the Duprés in an effort to protect Savannah and its surroundings by, well, taking the savagery out of them. The Gullah supplied the blood Eli and his family needed in a humane and safe way. No lives were lost, no newlings created.

The biggest vampiric threat to Savannah and the Gullah had been Victorian and Valerian Arcos. They raided the city and countryside in the eighteenth century. All those who supposedly died from yellow fever in Savannah's history? It wasn't the fever that took them all. But you won't find that in any book.

Vic was more or less forced on this rampage by his overbearing brother. But once they were entombed, the city fell quiet. Peaceful. Until they were released. Seems like a long, long time ago. Now I'm in the middle of it all. The same vampire who ravaged the city centuries ago wants my ass.

I'd be a liar if I said Valerian Arcos didn't scare me. He does. Truly.

The back of my legs and back are sweaty atop the down comforter, and quills are poking through the material and sticking into my skin. I wish I could get a small breath of fresh air. I don't know how long we've been driving, but I've reached my limit. With the flat of my Vans, I start kicking the side of the Jag's trunk interior. I kick for maybe five minutes before the car comes to a stop. Victorian's door opens and closes; the trunk pops. The scents of rubber tires and motor oil fill the cool air. I look around. We're in a large underground area—one that echoes. Concrete walls and pillars fill my vision. Vehicles are sparsely parked. There's an exit sign with an arrow pointing to the right a few yards away. It hits me. "Why are we in a parking garage?"

"Are you all right?" he asks, ignoring my question

and pushing my long choppy bangs from my face. He traces my sooty angel wing ink on my cheek. Concern is etched in his face.

"You mean besides not having any air to breathe and being hot as hell? Not to mention I've had to pee for the last hour. Sure. I'm great, Vic." I glower at him. "Get me out of here."

The corner of Victorian's mouth lifts in a slight grin, which quickly disappears. His face hardens; he glances around. "We've got to hurry." Easily, he lifts me from the trunk and sets me on my feet. "Are you going to make me carry you again?" he asks.

"Nope," I say. "But as soon as we get to where we're going, you're telling me everything."

He nods, and produces a pair of wire cutters from his pocket. In a few quick snaps, my ankles and wrists are free.

"Let's go," he says, slamming the trunk and grasping my elbow. He leads me through the parking garage that is slightly lit and mostly empty. A sign catches my eye: WELCOME TO HARTFIELD-JACKSON ATLANTA INTERNATIONAL AIRPORT. My stomach plummets. "Vic, where are you taking me?" He's putting me on a plane? To where? I don't have a good feeling about this. Not at all. And I have to pee. Bad. "Vic. Bathroom?"

Again, he is silent. But we walk toward the stairs,

and thankfully, a set of restrooms are there. "Make it fast, Riley," Vic says. "And please don't try to run."

The bathroom is empty. I duck into a stall and make hasty business out of girly business. Flushing the toilet with my foot, because public bathrooms are just the grossest of gross, I step to the sink and turn the water on.

"Riley, come on," Victorian says. Impatience edges his voice.

"Give me a sec, okay?" I answer. I suds my hands and rinse. The paper towel dispenser is empty, so I dry my hands on my shirt and head out. Victorian is staring at me. "See? No running," I say. Silently, he takes me by the elbow and leads me onward.

We make it to the elevator, and Victorian pulls me inside. I know he's using all of his suggestion to keep me restrained because I try to break free. This time, I can't. He presses the button for the main floor. Just as the doors begin to slide together, I catch a scent. A familiar scent. I can hardly believe it. Eli's here.

Suddenly a hand appears in the narrow divide between the doors, and with my next breath I am literally snatched out of the elevator by my arm and flung to the ground. I land with a grunt on the concrete floor of the parking garage, ten, twelve feet away, on my side. Eli's brother, Séraphin—Phin for short—is there when I stand. Confusion and surprise squeeze my insides. He helps me up. Rather, he yanks me up.

"Are you okay?" he asks. His hands are everywhere, checking me for injury. As I knock him away, my eyes search for Eli. The moment I see him, I leap for the elevator.

"Riley, stop!" Phin yells, as he makes a grab for me but misses.

I don't listen. I can't listen. Because I know Eli.

He'll kill Victorian.

Not only does Vic represent a heinous order of vampires from Romania, he is also in love with me, and Eli knows it. Bad combination, despite the fact that he isn't an evil bloodsucker and I definitely don't return the passion. Vic and I do share a connection of sorts, but it's not love on my part. Eli doesn't care. In his eyes, Victorian needs to die. Especially since Vic's DNA is now bound with mine. To Eli, Victorian Arcos is a deadly threat, through and through. I don't blame Eli. But I have to defend Vic.

Just as I hurl myself at the elevator, Eli and Victorian fall out of it. In a mass of growls, grunts, Eli's French expletives, and Victorian's Romanian curses, we all hit the ground. Eli morphs into his vampiric state—fangs dropped, face contorted, eyes white with a pinpoint scarlet pupil. It's a frightening sight. Victorian's appearance also changes; even now, it's unlike anything I've seen. His skin is ashen, almost . . . dead looking. Not just white. His eyes are bloodred, his fangs long and jagged. With one hand, Eli shoves me away and I hit the ground again. With a violent curse, I jump up, but Eli and Victorian are already thirty feet away. They're tangled, snarling, throwing one another to the ground. I run as Phin tries to grab me. Just as I reach them, I stop. With one hand around Victorian's throat, Eli takes his other hand and tries to fling me again. I slap his hand away.

"Eli! Stop it!" I yell, and throw myself between them. It's like being in the middle of a pair of fighting pit bulls. "Now!"

"Move, Riley," Eli growls, his voice inhuman, nearly inaudible. He once more tries to hurl me.

I cling to Victorian, but my eyes are fastened onto Eli's. "No, damn it! Stop and listen to me!"

"Phin!" Eli shouts. "Get her the fuck out of here!"

With as much emotion as I can summon, I hold Eli's gaze. "Please, Eli. Don't kill him." I'm not used to begging, and it doesn't sit well with me. As a matter of fact, it sort of sounds stupid. But in this, I have no choice. "Please."

Phin's hand is on my shoulder, and he pulls. I resist.

Eli's inhuman white glare freezes onto mine. "Why?" he asks, his voice deadly smooth, even, quiet. I can tell he is confused—hurt. Angry is a given. I don't blame him.

Behind me, Victorian's body shudders, but I keep my eyes trained on Eli's. "I don't know," I answer honestly. "It . . . just doesn't feel right."

Eli's sharp gaze flicks to Victorian. It's filled with hate. "Doesn't feel right, Riley? He abducted you." His grip tightens on Victorian's throat. "He almost killed you."

Yeah, I already know all that. It doesn't matter. "He isn't the monster his brother is," I say. "Please. Trust me."

Eli literally shakes with rage. The scarlet pupils widen, like a cat's eyes adjusting to darkness. He knows Victorian's brother wants me dead. Valerian is, in every sense of the word, a monster. There's no telling how many he has either killed or turned. He's the most feared of predators. A serial killer who cannot die. At least, not easily. And he's got a personal grudge against me. Why, I don't know. Maybe because I'm the one who got away. I beat him, and he hates that. Maybe because his own brother cares for me. But I know Victorian isn't like Valerian. And I don't want him dead.

"Eligius," I say calmly, and he looks at me. "Move."

Pure white eyes stare at me in silent debate for what seems forever. Without looking at Victorian, he manages to say, "Not until he tells me what the *fuck* is going on."

Moving from between them, I turn to Victorian. Bloodred eyes seek mine. I keep my hand on Eli's arm for support and give Victorian a nod. My stomach churns with anticipation.

Victorian simply breathes for several seconds, head bowed, collecting himself. His shoulders, broad but slim, rise and fall with air I'm certain does not circulate within his lungs. When he lifts his head, the only remnants of his vampiric morphing are his eyes. They remain crimson and fixed on me. "Riley has too much of my brother's strigoi DNA. It's . . . changing her." He glances at Eli. "Changing her in ways even her dark brethren cannot cure." His Romanian accent is heavier at times, like now. "She is beginning to crave. I've seen it." His voice lowers. "She will kill."

"I will what?" I ask, shocked, staring back at Vic. "Are you friggin' crazy?"

"Bullshit," Phin says, and his angry voice echoes off the concrete walls of the parking garage. "She went through weeks of cleansing."

"You underestimate the power of a strigoi," Victorian replies.

"Fuck you," Phin returns.

"We underestimate nothing," Eli says quietly, deadly. Threatening. "You're wrong, Arcos."

"She broke my power of suggestion," Victorian argues, flashing me a glimpse. "Started growling, convulsing." He glances at me, then to Eli. "Nearly jumped

23

from my car going eighty-five. I had to pull over and restrain her physically, and even then she briefly overpowered me. I had to chase her down as she tried to escape."

"So where were you taking her?" Phin asks. His voice does not sound like his own; he is getting impatient. Out of character for Séraphin Dupré.

Then again, the flashes I'd had while running through the woods behind the rest stop had been out of character for me. Those weird cravings. What the hell was that? I convince myself it was nothing more than a residual effect from the trauma at Tunnel 9.

"Where?" Eli states. His patience is going fast, too.

Victorian's unholy gaze settles on mine. "To my family home in Kudzsir in Romania. To my father."

I blink, and Eli's body flies in front of me. By the time my vision finds them, Eli has Victorian crushed against a wall. "So you can turn her? Have her for yourself?"

"Eli!" I yell.

With his face close to Victorian's, Eli growls, "I'll fucking tear your limbs from your body and burn them myself before I let that happen. And I'll start with your goddamn head."

"No!" I run now, because Eli's looking like he's about to dismember Victorian right where they stand. Someone grabs my arm and I jerk to a jolting halt. I turn and glare at Phin. "You'd better turn me loose."

Phin just looks at me. Tightens his grip.

Just then, a beam of light arcs over the gray concrete walls of the garage; an SUV pulls in.

"Eli, let's go," I plead. "Now. Just forget about this. I'm all right. I'm with you."

At first, he ignores me—nothing new there. Then he flings Victorian across the parking lot, storms toward me and grabs my hand without breaking stride. He doesn't say a word. Electricity seems to sizzle around him. If anger causes that, he's got an aura of it.

Victorian has more balls than I credit him for. In the blink of an eye, he is standing directly in Eli's path. "Know this, Eligius Dupré. Only a powerful strigoi like my father can cast out the evil growing inside Riley. And you will soon see—it is definitely there. You'll not like it, I promise you that."

Eli stares at Victorian for a split second, then takes his hand and shoves him out of the way. We continue on through the parking garage. I turn and watch Victorian.

"You will soon see," he says, standing in place. He speaks to Eli, but his eyes are on me. "You'll bring her back to me. I will be here, waiting."

We round a corner, and Victorian is no longer in sight. I find it strange to think of how Victorian, a vampire himself, considers vampirism evil. Maybe he dislikes what he is as much as the Duprés do. He has a good heart, despite the fact that it no longer resides in his body.

We reach Phin's black Ford F-150 in tense silence. In the distance, I hear a door slam and an engine start up. I guess it's Victorian's Jag. Phin hits the lock release button on his keychain and Eli opens my door. As I put my foot on the side step to climb in, he stops me.

With both hands on my face, he kisses me—long, ungentle, desperate. I breathe in his scent and return the kiss. Unlike most members of the undead, Eli's lips aren't icy cold, but lukewarm, full and sensual as they devour mine. Then, he pulls back. With startling blue eyes, he inspects me from head to toe. At my exposed thigh he lingers, lowers his hand, and grazes a large scrape.

"Must've gotten that at the rest area," I say, and although his features are cast in shadow, I know he studies me with ferocious intensity.

"Let's go home," he says, and climbs in beside me. No smile. Eli is still angry.

Phin starts up the truck and exits the parking garage. It's not until we hit Peachtree Street that I realize Victorian and I had made it all the way to Atlanta.

According to the digital clock in Phin's truck, it's close to four a.m. Traffic is nonexistent as we weave through the tall buildings and intertwining interstate dissections of downtown and make our way back to

Savannah. Before we hit the interstate, Phin pulls into a BP and fuels up. I run inside and grab some drinks and a bag of Chic-O-Stix. Eli's gaze is locked onto me the entire time. We settle in for the drive home.

Even with Eli's body crowding mine in the cab of Phin's truck, his hand protectively on my thigh, one thought pounds through my brain; one thing needles me and doesn't let go.

Am I truly turning evil? Am I going to kill?

Will I crave blood?

Goddamn, I hope to hell not.

I'm sleepy again—why, I don't know, but I feel like I haven't slept in days. I close my eyes, and slumber soon takes over.

Part Two

TURMOIL

Dat girl ain't right. I noticed time dey brought her back home. She got a mean look in her eye dat don match her face, or her mouth. I've seen it before, on odders, a long, long time ago. I know what it is, too. It's evil, dat's right. Pure dead evil. I don know if I can save her dis time, but I'll die tryin'.

—Preacher

I feel different. Ever since I returned home from my wild ride to Atlanta in Victorian's trunk, I can feel it. And that was over a week ago. It could be nothing more than my own imagination messing with me; it could be something else entirely.

Victorian's shocking words that night rattled me. I may not have shown it, but they did. And Eli hardly leaves my side now, even less than before. As a matter of fact, right now is the very first time since we've returned that he's left me alone for more than an hour. Eli did not go easy. But Preacher needed his and Seth's help next door repairing a leak in the attic, so I'm taking full advantage of the situation and chillin' in a hot bath. It's Sunday evening, there's finally a chilly bite to the mid-October air, and the shop's closed. I'm relishing this time alone. Need this time to myself. Desperately.

Resting my head back against the air pillow, I sink deeper into the hot suds and close my eyes. How long ago it seems since Seth and I discovered everything Preacher had tried to shield us from. After our encounter with the Arcos brothers, sweet Seth's personality totally changed. He wore stupid shades over his eyes all the time, slept all day long, and stopped eating. We didn't know what was happening until we saw Seth hurling himself out of his top-story window, only to hit the ground running. The image will be emblazoned in my memory forever.

He'd nearly turned. But Preacher and his Gullah brethren, skilled in the cleansing of vampirism passed down by their ancestors, saved Seth. Saved his pal Riggs. Saved me, too. I know I wouldn't be in the bathtub right now had it not been for Preacher and Estelle.

Like me, Seth and Riggs have tendencies. Mine are the strongest of all. Preacher warned me that my powers would change constantly, but the feeling growing inside me is unexpected. It leaves a bad taste in my mouth. I just hope Seth isn't going through the same thing. I'll tell you now: I'd die if something happened to my brother.

My thoughts return to Victorian's words. Eli's actions. Ever since our encounter with Vic, Eli's been more intense. The fact that he won't leave me alone is a definite sign that he thinks something really bad is up, too. He knows I can handle myself, but lately he treats me like I have zero abilities. He's everywhere. Being protective is one thing. Not giving me space to breathe is another. But I have to be sympathetic. I know, long ago, that Eli accidentally killed a young woman he'd fallen in love with. He'll never forgive himself for it, and I'm pretty positive he's scared the same thing will happen to me. It won't. But there's no consoling him. Eli still worries he'll lose control with me. So he's careful. Extremely careful.

His image comes easily to my mind; his chiseled face, full, firm lips, clenched jaw. His disturbing blue eyes are always locked on me. And his expression? Painful. Like he's in absolute physical agony. Kind of like when we first met.

Eli's siblings are around a lot more, too, always in the shop. Phin, intense and always so deep in thought. With his short-clipped dark blond hair and crazy-clear Dupré eyes, he's an attention getter to be sure. And he's on my ass just as much as Eli lately. Eli's other brother, Luc? He and Phin could pass for twins, but Luc's hair is longer, with wild curls. He's definitely the clown of the three brothers, although I've seen him turn pretty stinking mean in a vamp fight.

My best human friend and business partner, Nyxinnia Foster, has claimed Luc's attentions of late. I didn't think I'd like it, their coupling, but I do. Nyx is totally crazy about Luc, and he is just as into her. Nyx, with her sweet, loving, and annoyingly trusting behavior, is an easy target for Valerian and his gang of newlings. She's a Goth princess and sticks out like a sore thumb. Luc protects Nyx. I feel comforted knowing that. I love Nyx like a sister.

Speaking of sisters, there's Eli's youngest sister, Josie. She looks like your average teen, with skinny jeans, Converses, and long, light brown hair nearly to her waist. She wears it parted in the middle with her bangs pinned to the side. Sweet as peaches, you might think. I know better, though. She can fight like her brothers. Trust me when I say it's weird as hell to watch her kill. But she's free-spirited and a kind soul. Unfortunately, she's forever trapped in her fifteen-year-old body and is crazy about Seth. He'll age. She won't.

I'm surrounded by people I love, so I'm usually on my best behavior. But these days, I have to think about my next words, my next move, my next interaction with anyone I come in contact with. My fuse is shorter. Even when dealing with clients, I catch myself before saying something awful. It doesn't take much to set me off. It's like there's this shade of irritability that lies just beneath the surface, ready to unleash. Luckily, I can sense it. It's like . . . I can feel this thing clawing at the lining of my insides, trying to escape—digging, scratching, whispering. Almost like an entity, living inside of me, separate from my own self. I have no idea what keeps it locked up, other than my own will. But it wants out. I can tell. Weird. Just . . . weird.

Sometimes I wonder if Eli detects it, too. The way he stares at me? It's beyond intense. His eyes go deep into mine, searching, perusing. I swear I can feel him inside of me. He can read my thoughts and is constantly in my head now, yet he still can't pick up Victorian's voice in my head. I wonder if he can sense this other thing? Because I swear, I feel like it's alive inside of me. It's like Eli . . . knows it's there but just waits. Watches. I guess he trusts me to let him know when I can't control it anymore. I hope to hell and back that day never comes.

The clicking of paws through my room alerts me to my dog Chaz's arrival. He pushes the door open with his nose and peers in at me. He whines.

"Hey, boy," I croon. "Wanna go for a walk?"

His back end wags, just before he lets out a single bark. And I swear, he smiles.

"Okay, okay, I'm coming," I say, and climb from the tub. Quickly drying off, glad I'd pinned my hair up instead of washing it, I change into a pair of sweats, long-sleeved Inksomnia T-shirt, and my black Adidas sneaks, pull my hair into a ponytail, and head downstairs with Chaz. He lets out an excited yelp as I grab his leash and hook it to his collar. We head outside.

The chilly bite sinks into my skin and we take off up the merchant's drive. As Chaz inspects every little thing, I scan our surroundings. We're all alone. I allow my hearing to open full blast. At first chaotic, with sounds and voices and music all overlapping, soon it filters, becomes selective as Eli has taught me. I listen for anyone who signals distress—a tinge of panic in their voice, or excited talking, pleading. All I hear is swearing, ice clinking in glasses, idle chatter, a fight between angry guys. Drawing in a lungful of air, I taste the inhalation. Allow it to settle against my tongue. Newlings, I've discovered, have a unique scent. Slight though it may be, if I concentrate, I can detect it. It's not smelly, or pungent, but it's definitely different from anything else. Tonight, I smell nothing. So far, anyway. I have no idea of the distance my wolflike capabilities and senses are able to travel. Guess I'll eventually find out.

Chaz takes care of his doggy business, but I'm in no mood to head back inside. Something pulls me, something inside of me. The crisp night and unusual tranquility of the city lure me, and we cross Bay Street and head into the squares. There are scattered tourists on benches or strolling along the walk, a few locals. Time slips by—how much, I don't know. It has become unimportant. Along with the crispness of October, there is dampness in the air that suggests an approaching storm. Soon, the crowds thin. Loud, drunken laughter spills from The Boar's Head on River Street. Although I'm on Broughton, it sounds as though I'm right in the bar. I can feel the heat from the patrons' bodies. Smell their cigarette smoke, their breath, their sweat. Almost taste the alcohol they've consumed emanating from their pores on my tongue. Irritation and disgust consume me, and I try to tune those senses out. It doesn't work. The sounds of the city, the scent of humans, suffocate me. Wait, I'm still human. Aren't I? Hell if I know what I am anymore. All I know is that I'm unsettled. Confusion makes my brain hurt. I begin to run. To escape.

For a block or two, it's a slow run, and I'm still vaguely aware of Chaz on the other end of the leash I'm still gripping. At some point, though, I drop it. He follows for a while, but soon he can't keep up, and I feel glad to be alone. As his single bark echoes off the brick buildings surrounding me, I slip farther into the shadows, away from Broughton Street, away from people. The night envelops me, swallows me up like some ravaged beast, and for a brief second the Eagles' "Hotel California" plays in my mind. *They stab it with their steely knives, but they just can't kill the beast.* For some reason, that line has always freaked me out. I like it. It's my favorite verse.

The sharp blast of a car's horn sounds to my left, and for a second I jolt out of the weird subconscious state that I'm in. A Ford Explorer has slammed on its brakes to keep from hitting me. I can't make out the driver's words. He flips me off. I make eye contact with him and keep on running. Soon, in the shadows of tall live oaks and wispy moss, I slow to a jog, then a walk. The sounds that plagued me earlier are now a dull hum, and within minutes fade to nothing. Have I run so far that I've escaped the city? People? Am I finally alone?

Then, a heartbeat. Not mine. Someone else's. Steady. Strong. Ahead of me.

I follow.

The small town of Thunderbolt. That's where I am. As I move beneath the sparsely spaced streetlamps, I watch ahead of me. Male. Young. Early twenties. His tall, lanky figure casts a long shadow as he jogs. A rain begins to fall. Light at first, then more steady. It lifts the jogger's scent and wafts it to me. I inhale deeply. Sweat. Soap. I inhale again.

Blood.

I grow closer. Twenty feet. Ten feet.

A strong hand encircles my arm and jerks me to a stop. I'm aware of very little around me, save the jogger getting farther away. Rain slides down my cheeks, drips off my nose, plasters my hair to my scalp. My eyes remain fixed on the jogger.

His scent remains fixed in my nostrils.

"Riley!" an angry voice growls in my ear. The grip tightens on my arm. Shakes. "Riley! Look at me!"

When I don't, the hand belonging to the voice grips my chin and physically turns my head. Large hands grasp both sides of my face, tilts it up. Uses his thumbs to brush the water from my eyes. He's standing close, intimate. I'm staring, but not seeing. All I can hear is the sound of a heartbeat growing farther and farther away. It fades to nothing, and for a split second, my mind goes totally blank.

Slowly, the sounds of the city, the scents surrounding me, filter in. The blankness lifts. A horn blasts. A door slams. Somewhere, someone is whistling. I blink several times. These sounds are familiar.

"Riley?"

Eli's face comes into focus. Dark brows pulled together, the streetlamp's shine winking off the silver hoop. His face has hardened in anger. Or is it worry? His hands caress my face, so I guess it's worry. Why he's in that state, I haven't a clue.

"What's wrong?" I ask.

Eli's look is . . . invasive. I know he's probing my mind. Yet it seems he struggles this time. "What are you doing out here, Riley?" he asks. "Chaz showed up at Inksomnia alone."

I glance around. How'd he get away from me? I shrug. "Went off chasing a squirrel. Yanked the leash right out of my hand. He's done it before." I give Eli a reassuring smile. "See what a smart boy he is? Went straight home."

Eli's frown deepens. "You're out in the rain," he says, "your mind is blank and you're stalking some jogger." He peers down at me and a wet hank of shaggy midnight hair falls across his eyes. "You weren't aware of your surroundings, Ri. Or of me walking right up on you."

Again, I shrug. And chuckle. "So now I'm a stalker? That's just crazy, Dupré." I sigh and give him a long look. "I'm fine, Eli. I was just lost in my thoughts is all." I play-punch him in the arm. "You worry like an old lady."

Eli's eyes don't leave mine. Even as we both stand in the rain, he studies me. "Did you know that guy?" he asks.

I glance around, my eyes seeking the dim streets beneath the lamps. I see no one. "What *guy*, Eli? I was just out for a run. Nothing more. Nothing less. Can we get out of the rain now?"

Eyes on fire search mine. The black T-shirt Eli's wearing clings to his body from the rain, and every muscle there is perfectly etched beneath the thin cotton material. I look at him. He looks at me. His eyes narrow.

Finally, he drops his hands, lets my face go. "Home. Now."

Home. Eli has pretty much moved in, and it's worked out so far. We take off at a jog in the now steady drizzle, Eli purposely one step behind me. Within minutes we're crossing Bay and easing over the cobbles to the merchant's lane, then to Inksomnia. As I move to open the door, Eli stops me. I look up at him.

"What?" I ask.

After several silent moments, he shakes his head. "I'm having trouble reading you," he says. A frown still tugs at his mouth.

I smile. "And that's a bad thing? Hmm. I get my private thoughts back. How . . . ordinary."

With his knuckles, he skims my jaw. "I don't like it."

I grab his hand and lace our fingers together. His are, as always, lukewarm, steely-strong. "Tough." I open the door and pull him inside. Chaz is there and immediately barks. Next, Seth and Josie are in the foyer, right behind him.

"What happened to you?" Seth asks. "Why'd Chaz come home without you?"

I shake my head. "You too? What is this?" I glance from Eli to Josie, then back to Seth. "Twenty questions?

I went for a freakin' run is all. Chaz yanked the leash out of my hand. I knew he'd come back here. Jesus." I said that last bit under my breath. I was irritated. Tired of being drilled. "Last time I checked I didn't have to wear an ankle bracelet."

The look on Seth's face caught me right in the gut. Hurt. Surprise. And I wasn't used to it. But damn—I couldn't help it. I was tired of being interrogated. "Chaz got away from me. That's all. Now can I go take a shower please?" I don't wait for an answer from anyone. I push past Seth and Josie and head upstairs. In my room, I kick off my sneakers, pull my shirt over my head and fling it onto the floor. I peel off the wet pants I'm wearing and go straight into the bathroom. After a moment of nothing but hot water, the room fills with steam. The water pelts my back and shoulders as I stand there, thinking.

That *was* what happened, right? I had Chaz on the leash, and then . . . he wasn't there anymore. We were jogging. He . . . pulled loose. I decided to finish my run because I knew he'd head on home. Then Eli appeared and freaked out. We came home. End of story.

They, I decide quickly, are all fucking nuts.

It's slowly happening, isn't it, love? The changes? I warned that barbarian you keep company with, but he wouldn't listen. Please, Riley. You must leave. Come back to me. I vow, I'll do everything in my power to help you.

I rub the water from my eyes. Victorian still has the ability to communicate with me through my mind; it's annoying and comforting at the same time. Can't explain it, not at all. It is what it is. *Leave me alone, Vic. There's nothing wrong with me. And holy hell, you too? I just got reamed by my brother and Eli. I don't need it from you, too. Get out of my head and let me shower in peace.*

Christ, woman. You're naked? In the shower? Why do you torment me so? Never mind. I can still see remnants of tonight's events in your mind. You're getting confused, aren't you, love? It will only get worse. Trust me.

I am not confused, damn it. Now go away.

I continue to bathe—wash my hair, scrub my skin, rinse. I can still feel Victorian's presence. How, I don't know. But I do. *What are you doing, Victorian?*

After several seconds, he answers. *You don't want to know.*

Yes I do. Why are you still here?

I can't stop thinking of you naked; your skin wet, slick with soap. It easily places . . . images into my head. I can't help myself when that happens, Riley. I—

Yeah, yeah, never mind Loverboy. Don't wanna know. Later, Vic.

For a certainty, my love . . .

After drying off and pulling on a pair of soft sleep pants and a tank, I brush my teeth, hit the lights and climb into bed. Exhaustion makes my bones heavy, my skin ache, and just as I slip into sleep, Eli's strong arms pull me against him.

"Rest," he whispers against my temple, and despite my sleepiness, the feel of his lips moving across my skin makes me shiver. "I'll be here when you wake up."

"Oh, God," I mumble, sliding my arm over Eli's chest and snuggling close. "Have we become that old couple that doesn't have sex anymore?"

Eli's chuckle rumbles against my ear. "We had sex this morning."

"Okay," I say, already being pulled into slumber. "Sorry if I was a bitch earlier. I don't know what's wrong with me."

Again, Eli's lips brush my skin as he kisses me, and his arms tighten around me. "Everything's going to be okay, Riley. I swear to God, it will be."

That last part I barely hear, but it slips into my subconscious, where I keep it safe. Keep it all safe—Eli's arms, his strength, the brush of his lips across my skin. Somehow, I know that I'll need those reassuring words, those memories. Later. For now, I sleep.

It's raining. Still dark outside. Streetlamps throw an amber hue over the wet cobbles. Close by, a tire hits a pothole and water splashes against the fender. Footsteps slap the sidewalk. A heartbeat echoes off the brick walls. *Human.* I blink and listen, then I look around. Why am I outside? Didn't I just fall asleep, warm in my bed with Eli's arms wrapped around me? I know I did. So why am I here? How did I manage to get away from Eli?

I look around, but see only a long shadow at the end of the lane. The shadow's moving and it matches the footsteps I hear. They're quick, sure—not like those of a stumbling drunk. More like . . . someone who is frightened. I hurry toward the sound, the long-moving shadow. The heartbeat grows louder, faster, and the pungent scent of fear clings to the brine of the Savannah River that perpetually hangs in the air. I am closer now, the heartbeat reverberating off the damp stone around me. Now, only that taunting beat sounds in my head. Nothing else. The human senses me. Hides. The scent of blood hovers like mist in the air.

A craving quickens inside me.

Silently, I edge along the shadows toward the hiding place. Closer. A whimper reaches me, then a strangled cry. Just as I ease around the corner of the alley, I see them. There are two. They're young—one male, one female. Newlings. Suddenly, I'm confused. I react. I leap.

"Get her," the male says. His voice is calm, hateful, determined.

The female newling lunges at me just as I leap at her, and with a growl, we clash and drop to the cobbles. I grab her by the throat and slam her into the wall. Immediately, she's up and lunging at me again. I duck. She hits the opposite wall and I follow her. I have her arm jacked upward behind her. I have the strength to tear it from her body, and I almost do. Until I hear a cry, and I glance down.

"Help me, Riley!"

My blood runs cold at the familiar Filipino Dagala dialect.

The male, fangs dropped, is biting the human. Only then do I notice the short black bob, small stature, wide, frightened brown eyes rimmed by a pair of glasses. It's my neighbor, Bhing, who owns a chic clothing boutique next door to Inksomnia called SoHo. I throw the female newling several feet away and she crashes against the steps. I lunge at the male and yank him off of Bhing. She scrambles backward.

"Bitch," he grinds out, and with more strength than I credited him for, grabs my throat and lifts me. Eyes opaque, one small red pupil in each center, he glares. No mercy. No pity. Only rage and hunger. "Don't fuck with my kills, freak," he says. The streetlamp light shines off his jagged fangs.

With lightning reflexes, I wrap my legs around his waist and jam the heel of my palm into his throat. He turns me loose, and as he drops to the ground, I crawl toward him, yank the silver blade strapped to my lower back, and plunge it into his heart. He seizes, and

I jump off him. I glance up; the female is running toward me. In one fluid motion I pull the blade from his heart and fling it at the female. It embeds to the hilt. She drops and begins to seize.

The craving returns. I turn for the human.

But the alley is empty now; Bhing has disappeared. Out in the street, I search. Empty, all except for a stray cat perusing the trash cans. Bhing's gone. It's only then that I realize why I killed the newlings.

I wanted their hunt. Their prey.

I wanted Bhing's blood.

With both hands, I grasp my head and stumble back into the alley. What's happening to me? Dizziness swamps me, and I drop to my knees, gulping in large breaths. Nausea crashes over me, and I fight to keep whatever was trying to come up *down*. With hazy vision, I notice two piles of ash on the ground. The only thing that can kill vampires is pure silver. Or another vampire.

I'd killed them with my silver blade. But had I done so to get to Bhing—or to save her? My head spins, and I push myself against the wall. Confusion grabs me by the throat, squeezes, chokes. Blackness crashes over me, and I see nothing, hear nothing, smell nothing . . .

"Hey, sleepyhead," a graveled, slightly French accent whispers in my ear. "Wake up."

My eyes flutter open. Uncertainty and disorder web

their way through my memory. Where am I? The room is hazy, with the barely there early-morning light filtering in through the gauzy curtains. My bedroom. I fix my gaze on the figure leaning over me, weight supported by one elbow, chiseled face staring down at me. Eli. I'm in my room, with Eli.

His eyes bespeak volumes. I know he immediately senses my confusion. He frowns. "What's wrong?"

Pushing up on my elbows, I sit up. "Had a bad dream," I said, trying to recount how I'd gotten from the alley to my bed without Eli or Seth knowing I'd left the apartment—if I'd left at all. Suddenly I wasn't so sure. I look at Eli. "Have I been here all night?"

Eli's eyes narrow. "Why would you ask that?"

Frustrated, I jump out of bed. "Damn it Eli, stop answering my questions with more questions." Pulling the curtains back, I stare out over River Street. "Have I been in bed with you all night?"

"Yes," he says, and moves behind me. Wrapping his arms around me, he pulls me against him. "Tell me."

I relax. "Damn, it was so realistic. I . . . was out in the street, at night, and I saw Bhing from next door getting attacked by two newlings. I killed them. Bhing got away." I turn and stare up at his concerned expression. "Then I felt, I don't know. Sick. Dizzy." I shrug. "Next thing I know, you're waking me up."

"Want me to go check on Bhing?" he asks.

I sigh and move out of Eli's arms. "No. I will. If it really happened last night I'm sure I freaked her out. Besides, I want to go visit Preacher and Estelle before I get ready for work anyway." Preacher and Estelle keep a store, Da Plat Eye—a Gullah herbs and concoctions parlor—right next door. They live upstairs, just like I live above Inksomnia.

"They're not there," Eli says. "Ri, they left Monday morning to go visit Estelle's sister in Charleston. Don't you remember?"

Slowly, I turn and look at Eli. My insides turn cold. "Today is Monday."

Eli's face is drawn, worried. "Today is Wednesday."

I close my eyes, push my fingertips against the sockets. What's happening to me? I'm now losing chunks of time? I scramble in my memory, trying to remember. I recall going to bed, then suddenly being outside, fighting two newlings over Bhing's blood. The last thing I want to do though is freak Eli out. The *very* last thing. I chuckle, shake my head. "God, I'm getting old. Dream must've sucked the life out of me." I glance at Eli. "No pun intended." Glancing at the clock on my bedside table, I stretch. "I'm starved. Think I'll go grab some Kremes and coffee. Wanna go with?"

"Absolutely," Eli says.

I don't think he plans on letting me out of his sight anytime soon. It already pisses him off to no end that he can't read my mind like he used to. The Arcoses really did a number on my DNA. Since it keeps changing, I have no idea where I'll end up. Me. Riley Poe. What's left of me, anyway. I can't bullshit Eli for long about my loss of time. Don't want to. It scares the shit out of me, truth be told. I'll try to handle it first. See what Victorian can tell me. Maybe I can learn to control it like I have my other tendencies? I hope to God so.

"Hey, bro, running to KK," I say. "Want anything?"

Seth glances at me, his usually bright expression dull. "No thanks."

"Something wrong?" I ask, perplexed.

Seth's gaze lingers on mine for a second or two, almost as if he's waiting on me to guess. "No," he finally answers, and pulls on his jacket. "Nothing's wrong."

"Where're you going?" It's not like Seth to be so sullen with me, but lately, we've both been through so much crap, we've learned to give each other a little space.

"School, Ri," he answers. "Mrs. Dupré likes me there early." Elise home-schools Seth and Josie.

I nod. "Okay. Later."

Seth, silent, walks past me and out the door. I try to ignore the hurt I feel and look at Eli. I'm pretty sure the smile I paste on my face looks fake as hell. "Ready?"

"He just worries about you, you know?" he says quietly.

I grab the Jeep keys from the hook and head out. "Yeah. I know."

The moment I step outside, I see Bhing at the Dumpster. She is heading back into her store and she spares me a single look and a wave. Her silky black hair, cut in a shoulder-length bob, swings with her every movement. She stares at me through her glasses. I wave back. So, she's safe after all. I wonder what she's thinking?

We make it to Krispy Kreme and back in thirty minutes. I eat four glazed doughnuts and sip my sugar-and-cream-loaded coffee while going over a few ink designs I have scheduled for the day. I can tell my head isn't in the game, or in the food, and both tick me off. What's more frustrating is that I don't know what to do about it. Sometimes it's worse than others. These feelings are relatively new. Eli knows my irritation; he watches intently as I dress for work in a pair of ripped, faded low-rider jeans, a black Inksomnia long-sleeved tee and a pair of worn boots. Pulling my hair into a high ponytail, I brush my teeth and head downstairs to open shop. I feel anxious. Unsettled. Maybe it's because I haven't seen Preacher and Estelle. I just can't figure it all out.

I hear Nyx a full three minutes before she enters the shop.

Rather, I hear her heart beating.

For a split second, just before Nyx opens the front door, my vision blurs. The sound of Nyx's heart thumping inside its cage reverberates inside of me. Her blood whooshes through the vessels as it races to and from the organ. I can friggin' *hear* its resonance. I shake my head a few times, take some breaths, close my eyes, clear my head. Rid my brain of it. Goddamn it! What the hell?

"Riley." Eli stands next to me, his hand on my shoulder, his voice stern, steady. Almost as if he knows my inner turmoil. I glance briefly at him. My mind begins to clear.

"Riley! Good morning!" Nyx greets as she steps inside, and I turn my attention to her. Luc is right behind her. Gene, the Welcome Raven—appropriately named after Gene Simmons—crows above the door. For some reason, both sounds annoy me. Nyx drops her oversized pink handbag with black skull and crossbones at her station and crosses over to me. She pulls me into a tight hug. In the span of a few seconds, she assesses me. "You didn't get much sleep, huh? Poor thing. You look tired."

"Gee, thanks," I say, and move to the iPod station. "Isn't that the same thing as saying I look like shit?"

Nyx yanked my ponytail. "Yeah, pretty much. So get some more sleep. I know you don't need as much anymore, but a little more couldn't hurt. You have dark circles under your eyes, Ri. You've lost all the color that you got from Da Island when you were rehabilitating and between your pale skin and dark circle eyes, you actually look like a, um. You know."

I glance over my shoulder at Nyx, who passes a single look to first Eli, then Luc.

"What? You mean a vampire?" I ask. I almost laugh.

"Yes! But more like a Hollywood version. Dracula. You know?" she replies.

Luc approaches and grasps my chin with his hand, turning my face left and right. His eyes, the same shade of cerulean blue as all the Duprés, study me with intensity. "Damn, Poe. You do look like shit."

I jerk away. "I gotta get busy." Feeling like some Freddie Mercury, I select "Killer Queen" and start work. I tune out Eli, Luc, and Nyx, as well as my own bad mood as I sift through my designs. Without looking up, I feel all of their eyes on me. Eli's gaze is burning into me like a branding iron. This morning I simply don't care.

My first appointment arrives. I'm freehand outlining a fairly large spider over the ribcage of a lanky young dude. Not an ounce of body fat on him. "Take off your shirt and get comfortable," I say, and point in the direction of my table. "You okay with an audience?"

The guy shrugs. "Sure, no prob."

I nod and flip the switch to the Widow, my beloved

tattooing machine. Or, as Estelle calls it, the Black Engine. As I'm setting up the ink pots, I glance at him. "How's your pain tolerance?"

Again, he shrugs. "I'm good."

I again nod. "If you need a break just let me know." I thumped his ribs. He didn't even budge, which was a good sign. "You have zero body fat. It's not gonna feel great over those bones, dude. Promise."

"I'm cool, I'm cool," he assures. "I can take it."

"All right then," I say, shaking my head. I'm not in any mood for a crybaby today. I scrub his side with antiseptic. "Lie with your arm resting above your head on the pillow and let's get going."

The kid's good. He doesn't even flinch as my needle moves over his bumpy ribs. The hum of the Widow mixes with Freddie Mercury's unique pitch and blessedly pulls me into the zone. All is going pretty well for a handful of minutes. I feel like my old self. I sense my old life, before vampires, newlings, and tendencies. Before the Arcoses. I'm in there, barely hanging on by a thread.

I lean close over the kid's ribs, freehand sketching the body of the spider that is approximately eight inches in length, six inches in width. I move with my needle, wiping the blood with a four-by-four-inch piece of gauze. I wipe. Blood. Wipe. Blood.

Blood.

Queen's "Another One Bites the Dust" is now fading away in the background, and becomes muffled until it is nothing more than a soft hum. Nyx's happy chatter fades. Luc's constant flirting fades. Eli's totally silent. Only one thing remains.

This kid's heartbeat.

Thump-thump. Thump-thump.

I take a deep breath, shake my head, and continue.

The needle penetrates the skin in rapid-fire shots as I move along, creating the outline of the spider. My gaze fixes on the beads of blood, and I wipe with the gauze. I continue. More blood. Not a lot. Just beads. But there are a lot of them. The more I stare, the more I concentrate. What was a line of ink with whelps of blood turns into filleted skin as my needle plunges three inches into the kid's side. Blood pours out. I jerk back in horror.

"What?" the kid says. His voice is shallow, as though it's calling from a deep tunnel. He peers over his ribs at where I'm working.

I glance at him, and his face is concerned, but nothing more. When I look back at his side, it's perfectly normal. I blink, shake my head. Sweat breaks out across my forehead and I wipe it with my forearm. "Nothing. My needle jammed is all," I lie. "I'll change it fast. Just relax."

"No prob," he says, and lies back.

I turn to change the perfectly good needle, and Eli's at my ear. "What's wrong with you?" he asks quietly. Even his voice sounds muffled, and I know he's mostly speaking inside my head. He sounds far, far away.

The whole while, I hear that kid's heart beating.

I draw another deep breath. "Needle jammed," I say. "Everything's fine."

I glance at Eli's face to reassure him. He's not reassured at all. His face is pulled into lines and sharp planes of worry. He says nothing. Only watches. Behind him, Luc does the same. Both irritate me. But Eli's constant presence seriously annoys me. I try to block him out.

I continue with the spider and the kid.

Focusing on my work, I try to block the thumping of his heart. It takes such strength to manipulate the sounds around me that sweat again breaks out across my forehead. It's almost what drug or alcohol withdrawals feel like, and I can speak from experience on that one. Your body craves, and turns itself inside out to fight off that craving. It feels like a thousand ants are crawling inside your skin, trying to break free. I try to ignore the feeling, try not to rush, take my time, making the legs of the spider design angled, defined, and structured. I'm almost finished. Thank God. Just a little more.

Thump-thump. Thump-thump.

I glance at the kid's face, and I gasp and stumble back. His eyes are missing, sockets are deep and black, and his face and skin have a bluish-white hue. The area over his heart is filleted open, and the organ beats before my eyes. Beckons.

My mouth goes dry.

"Riley."

A hand tightens around my upper arm, squeezes hard. I blink and wipe my sweaty brow. When I look at the kid, he's okay. Normal. Staring at me.

I force a smile. "Okay. All done." I set my needle on the stainless steel tray. "You did good. Didn't even flinch going over all that bone."

The kid, thankfully, is oblivious to my turmoil. He smiles proudly. "Thanks." Cocking his head, he stretches and looks at my work. "Ah, freak! That's sick!"

My insides are still shaking, and his heart is still slamming in my ear. "Glad you like it. Let's cover it up now."

He lies back, and it's all I can do to apply the antibiotic ointment and cover the area with nonstick gauze. I tape the edges. "You're good to go."

"Sweet," he replies, and hops off the table. "When can I come back for the color?"

"It has to be completely healed," I say, and I wipe

my brow again. "No scabs, no raw places. Let's set you up for four weeks and see how it looks."

The kid nods. "Cool."

"Here," Luc says. "Meet me up front and I'll give you instructions and ointment samples." He glances at me, and I give a half smile. He inclines his head and leads the kid up front.

Only now do I realize the crowd that has gathered in Inksomnia. It's not an unusual crowd. It's not at all strange for a large group to gather at the picture window and watch us work, or a group to stand inside and look through the design books. Inksomnia is sort of well-known, especially in the tattoo world, and I've made quite a name for myself as an artist. People have traveled far just to have me ink their design. People who've never even heard of me gather at the window to watch the tattooing process. It's not weird to have a crowd nearly every day. It's not strange to have people ask to take pictures with me.

It's strange that I didn't know they were here in the first place.

I feel sick. Nauseated. Out of control. Adrenaline soars. Heart sluggish. Sweaty.

"Ms. Poe, can we get a pic with you?" someone in the group asks.

"Just a sec," I say, nausea choking me. I head to the back before I toss Krispy Kremes everywhere. When I glance at the crowd, their faces are all gruesome: eye sockets black, white-blue skin, and the hearts are all beating so hard I see it through their shirts. I stumble. What's going on?

Eli catches me just before I fall and eases me onto the steps of the staircase. I sit, elbows on knees, head hanging between. I gulp in air.

Kneeling in front of me, Eli pushes my escaped bangs from my face and holds them to my head with one hand. "Riley," he says, and I hear the urgency in his voice. "What is wrong?"

I shake my head. "I don't know. Maybe I'm coming down with the flu?" That's such a damn lie and I know it. Eli probably knows it too. I don't know what else to say. The truth? *Human heartbeats are consuming my thoughts. I smell their blood. I'm starting to crave.*

No friggin' way can I tell him *that*. Victorian already did and Eli didn't believe him. Thank God he can't hear it in my head, nor does he recall his own torturous turning. I breathe deeply and give myself a pep talk. *Get a grip, Poe. It's just your wacky DNA morphing again. Gilles said this would happen. Don't be a baby! Talk to Vic. He can help. It's part of him inside you anyway. You can handle this. Breathe . . .*

The slow, rhythmic strokes of Eli's fingers over the back of my neck, along with my slow, controlled breaths, ease the cravings, lessen the noise, dissipate the nausea. I don't know how long I sit there on the steps, but I start feeling better. Finally, I raise my head and meet Eli's worried gaze.

Worried and angry gaze, I should say.

"Thanks," I graze his jaw with my fingertips. "I feel better now."

The penetrating stare tells me Eli doesn't believe it. Not one word.

"Promise," I say, and stand. "Come on. I have a pic to take."

Eli says nothing as I pass by and head back to the front of the shop. His brother is equally grim; Luc studies me as I make my way to the crowd of guys gathered for the pic, and I slide him a quick look and then fasten my attention to the ink fans. Someone pulls out a digital camera, I stand in the middle of the crowd, and several pics are taken.

"Can we see the dragon?" one younger guy asks.

"Ah," I say, "you caught me on an off day. Nothing underneath here this time," I say, pointing to my shirt. "Summer is the best time to catch that." People who know or have heard of me always want to see the dragon inked on my back, courtesy of Nyx. In the summer, I wear clothes that easily show most of it, or I wear a bikini top underneath my shirt so I can take off whatever I'm wearing and show off for the onlookers. It's become sort of my trademark. Today, though, I'm not into it.

A few groans go through the crowd, and Nyx waves to them. "Hey! We have a few postcards over here with Riley and me. You can see the dragon perfectly!"

Everyone moves to the sales counter, and Nyx shows the rack of postcards. She glances at me, and I mouth *thanks*.

I don't understand it, but the rest of the day passes smoothly. I have no further episodes. No further cravings. Heartbeats recede. Only normalcy.

I don't break for lunch but work through instead. By six p.m. I am wrapping up my last client: a Savannah College of Art and Design, better known as SCAD, student with a dainty black butterfly arm cuff. Her arm is as big around as a pipe cleaner, so it doesn't take me long. I apply her ointment, cover with gauze, and give her instructions. In the fading light falling on Savannah, she walks down the sidewalk, happily chatting on her cell, stretching her arm out and admiring her art through its gauzy cover.

My memory skips back to the past, when Nyx inked my dragons. I remember not being able to stay away from mirrors, I wanted to look at them all the time. To me they meant struggle, conquering demons, strength. Empowerment. I was so proud of them. I *am* proud of them.

A ping of envy hits me. I used to have a normal life, where a little body art made my day, made me happy beyond belief. I enjoyed Sundays with Seth, with Preacher and Estelle, and chillin' on the floor of my living room with Nyx, sketching designs. Cramming slice after slice of pizza in our mouths. Taking Chaz for walks. I want it all back. I want it all the *hell* back.

I'll *never* have it back.

"How are you feeling?" Eli asks. His hands move to my shoulders and he squeezes gently.

Moving out of his grasp, I start cleaning up my station. "Better. Are we heading out tonight?" Meaning, *are we tracking newlings*.

"Are you up for it?" he asks.

I glance at him. The lines of worry mean he really doesn't want me to go. But I'm going anyway. "Absolutely."

Nyx's client leaves and she shuts and locks up the shop behind him. My friend, dressed in the style of a street mime from the fifties with black skinny jeans, black loafers, and a white and black striped shirt, minus the white painted face, turns to face me. Her high ponytails on either side of her head swing with the movement. "Riley, are you sure? I don't think you're well. You could"—she waves her hand in the air as if trying to imagine something—"fall from a building or something if you have an episode."

"I don't have episodes, Nyx," I say, and move to the back and head upstairs. "I'll be okay. Promise. See ya in the morning," I call down.

"Bye," she returns, but I'm already in my room changing.

In nothing but my bra and panties, I stand before the floor-length mirror and start fitting the blade sheaths to my waist, thighs, ankles. In the next second, and so fast that I didn't even see him enter the room, Eli stands next to me, my shoulder harness in hand. He helps me into it, adjusts the straps, and secures it in the front. One by one, he fills the sheaths with pure silver blades. His eyes are on mine the entire time.

The fact that he's so close to them makes me pause. "I can do that," I say, but Eli continues anyway. I let him. When the last blade is secure, he pulls my face to his and kisses me. For a moment, I lose myself in his possessive seduction. His tongue on mine. Teeth grazing and tugging my lips. Strong hands drag across my abdomen, my hips. Then, he envelops me in his embrace. My blades press tightly against my skin at his weight. Everything he does, I realize, proves his love for me. Proves his possessiveness for me. And I can't even return the verbal sentiment? Worse yet, his overprotectiveness is starting to really grate on my nerves. God, I'm such a bitch. A messed up one at that. Damaged goods to the nth degree.

"You'll run with me tonight," he whispers against my temple. "Until I'm sure you're okay, the only thing you'll do alone is pee."

I laugh, because Eli knows how I love my bathroom privacy. "I'll run with whomever I want to, and you bet your ass I'll pee alone. Goddamn, Eli, give me a freaking break, will ya? I'm fine. I can handle myself. Your own parents have taught me how. So, seriously. Step off a bit. Okay?"

Eli pulls back, holds my face in his hands, and studies me for several long moments. His eyes search mine. "I won't lose you, *chère*," he says, his French accent thicker. Demeanor determined. "I won't. But you can have your space. As long as everything goes smoothly."

I'm not that kind of girl who enjoys being the victim. I don't need the stereotypical knight in armor to rescue me. I am a strong, independent woman who has no problem handling her own goddamn self. But, I admit—this feels . . . nice. Eli is the epitome of strength, and I trust him completely. I revel in his embrace for a few more moments because somehow, I have another feeling, boring deep into the pit of my stomach, that this won't last.

Or at the very least, I won't remember it.

My annoyance dissipates momentarily, and I thread my hands through Eli's crazy, sexy hair, pull his mouth down to mine and kiss him thoroughly. He sighs against me, a deep groan inside his chest letting me know precisely what the gesture does to him. I end the kiss, smile, and move to my closet to get dressed. Eli watches in silence as I pull on a pair of low-waist khaki cargo pants, a snug black long-sleeved spandex shirt, and my worn Vans. Strapping on my holsters around my thigh, hips, and shoulder, I slide the sharp silver blades into place. The night will hide my weapons, so no need to wear a coat over them. I redo my ponytail, pulling the band snug, and I'm ready to go. When I get downstairs, Luc is just coming inside with Chaz. Nyx is sitting in the foyer, staring at me.

"I thought you were headed home," I say. I can tell by Nyx's expression that I've hurt her feelings.

"She's going to stay with Mama and Papa," Luc says. "I don't trust Valerian not to seek her out again, despite the Gullah charms protecting her place."

I simply nod. "Good idea."

Nyx jumps up and faces me. "Be careful tonight, okay?" she says, and pulls me into a hug. I hug her in return, but only briefly. I fear what happened earlier might repeat itself. I sense my lucidity is slipping. I really hate that.

I look at my best friend and smile. "I will. And I love ya for caring so much."

Nyx beams. "Love you too."

I hate that my confidence and assuredness seem so

fake and put-on to me, but right now, it does. I know this other thing exists inside of me, and it grows stronger. I fear losing my loved ones. I fear losing myself.

I have no choice but to fight it.

Fight it, and fucking win.

Nyx and Luc take off on Luc's bike. Eli and I take the Jeep. Within minutes we hit Monterey Square. I pull into the Duprés' drive and park. Zetty and Riggs get out of Zetty's truck. The Tibetan one-time bouncer for the Panic Room club had nearly become a newling but was also cleansed by Preacher, along with me, Seth, and Riggs. Now he's a human with wicked tendencies. We exchange greetings and head inside.

Zetty's eyes are on me the whole time. He's hard not to stare at, with his unique Shiva patterns tattooed across his forehead. At the advice of Gilles, Zetty had decided to wear less attention-grabbing clothes. Out with the traditional Tibetan wear, in with pretty much all black attire. Blend in with the shadows, so to speak. His long single braid down his back still gives him that unique and exotic look. Zetty is a badass. With or without tendencies. With them, though, he's a lethal badass. I'm glad he's on our side.

We don't speak. Simply bump fists as we enter the Dupré house.

I catch Riggs's eye as I pass. He smiles. I'm surprised the prepubescent little perv doesn't slap my ass.

He chuckles behind me. If I didn't know any better I would swear Riggs could read my mind.

Philippe Moreau, the Duprés' butler and all around trusted man, meets me at the door. His gaze lights over me and he gives a slight nod. "Ms. Poe. Ever so nice to see you."

"Phil, same to ya," I say, and it draws the slightest of grins on his usually serious mouth.

Inside, I follow the others upstairs. It's become sort of our meeting room, along with our training room. Gilles, dressed casually in pressed khaki trousers and a white button-up shirt, stands next to Elise, in classic she-loafers, black dress pants, and a plum silk blouse that accentuates her flawless pale skin. Both bespeak old Southern charm.

"Riley, sweetheart," Elise says, and grasps my shoulder with her petite hand. "How are you feeling?"

I shoot a look at Eli. He must've told her. With a sigh, I nod. "Much better, thanks."

While Elise Dupré looks sweet and demure, trust me—it's totally deceptive. She can kick serious, serious ass.

Elise's brow pinches together. "Something's wrong."

I shrug, because I know she's trying to read my mind and is unable. "It's a new development I guess."

"Here, love," Gilles says, and moves closer to me. "Let me try."

I almost laugh as Gilles concentrates, staring into my eyes. The only thing he doesn't do is the hypnotic hand wiggle thing Dracula does. After a few seconds, he huffs. "I cannot believe it, *ma chère*," he says. "I'm positive I don't like it."

"Neither do I," mumbles Eli.

I say nothing but I keep my gaze locked with Gilles's.

"Very well," he finally says, and addresses us all. "Ned tells me several rogues have moved into the area, unrelated to the Arcoses. A body was found this morning. Ravaged, with no control whatsoever. The work of a mindless newling."

My heart leaps, thinking of Bhing. But I'd seen her earlier, so it had to be another innocent. Or had any of it even happened? God, it hurt my head to think of it. Bhing hadn't acted any different toward me. Maybe it's all in my mind.

"I suggest we split up into threes," says Phin, perched on the windowsill. "Eli, Riley, and Riggs. Me, Seth, and Josie. Luc and Zetty, you're on your own."

They both nod.

"Let's split the city up," Eli says. "And meet back at the historic district and take that section together." He glances around. "Preferences?"

"We'll take Tybee Island, Skidaway Island, and Isle of Hope," says Phin.

Luc nods. "We got the South side up to Victory Drive, east and west."

Eli nods. "All right, we'll take Garden City and work our way through the industrial area and meet up at Forsyth Park. You know the routine. Clubs. Businesses. Dimly lit areas. Hangouts. These newlings aren't breaking into homes. Too much work for them. And they're looking for more youths."

"What about Noah?" Luc asks.

Noah Miles is a vampire, also bound by Gullah pact to protect Savannah's sister city, Charleston. He's probably one of the most beautiful beings I've ever laid eyes on, with his unique dreadlocks and flawless pale skin and mercury-colored eyes. He knows it, too. When we'd fought against Valerian's newling army in Charleston, Noah had been right there with Eli. Only Noah eggs me on. He wants to see me fight and trusts me to handle myself. Unlike Eli.

"They have their hands full right now," Eli says. "There are just as many newlings running in Charleston and surrounding areas as there are here." He glances at his father. "To break this, we have to break Valerian Arcos."

"And that seems impossible since he can shift bodies," Phin says.

And if what Vic says is true, Valerian can't be killed anyway.

"Okay, let's get going," Eli says. "Mama, Papa"—he heads to the door—"be good."

"Always," Gilles answers.

At the door, I stop Seth. "Hey," I begin. "I'm sorry, okay?"

My brother looks at me with those big, expressive green eyes, and right now they're filled with hurt. He hugs me. My heart melts, and I hug him back. I want to keep him in my arms forever. Safe. Alive. Sweet. "I'm just not myself, Seth. I don't know what's happening." I pull back and look at him. "My DNA, I suppose. It's acting all crazy and I can't control it. I'm having wicked dreams that seem so realistic, and I guess it's putting me in a terrible mood." I shake my head and knock Seth on the jaw lightly with my knuckles.

Seth studies me for several seconds, and he pulls me into one last embrace. He kisses the top of my head. "I love you, Sis," he mumbles, sounding like the much more grown-up sibling. "Be careful."

"I will, and love you, too," I say. "And *you* be careful."

Riggs is leaning against my Jeep when I walk out. Ankles crossed, arms over chest, looking way too cocky for his own good. "What say I ride up front with you, babe?" he drawls and glances at Eli. "You won't mind, will ya bro?"

Eli smacks him on the back of the head as he gives him a shove. "In the back, Squirt."

Riggs shrugs and gives me a sympathetic look. "Sorry sweetheart. Maybe next time."

I can do nothing more than roll my eyes and shake my head. What a goober Riggs is. "Maybe so," I respond. He smiles. I climb in the front seat, and Eli drives. We take off for Garden City.

Even though the October night air is cool, we keep the Jeep's top off for easy access in and out of it. Besides, Riggs and I both handle temperatures a lot differently now, so it has to be really cold for us to be bothered, or really hot. This night, my long-sleeved shirt is all I need. The temp is about sixty-two degrees.

Eli downshifts as we hit the squares, the night air cool as it brushes my cheeks. I close my eyes against the wind and inhale the brine of the salt marsh. Unfortunately, the closer we get to Garden City, which is just outside of Savannah, the brine turns into a stinky sulfur smell. Paper mill. It's enough to make you gag sometimes. Thankfully this night, it's not too bad.

Eli's hand slips over my thigh and rests there as we drive, and the sounds of the night, the wind, lure me into a calm rest. I'm not asleep; I still hear Riggs's iPod blasting in his ear. But I'm lulled. Yeah, that's what I am.

A flash of light illuminates a face hidden in a dark

hoodie. Jaw unhinged. Fangs dropped. Eyes white, pupil pinpoint red. He lunges at me—but the face isn't a newling. It's *me*. I scream—

"Riley?" Eli says, his hand wrapped around my arm, shaking me. "Wake up, we're here."

My eyes flutter open, and the moment they focus on Eli, he shifts, *his* jaw unhinges, *his* fangs drop, and *he* lunges for *me*.

Part Three

***

MALEVOLENCE

This is all new to me. I mean, I know it's not old shoe to Ri and Seth, but they've been involved a lot longer than I have. They've had time to adjust. They have powers. Almost like . . . they're not all the way human anymore. I am. One hundred percent. Which means vulnerability to the nth degree, and it scares me. I'm scared of losing Ri and Seth, and I'm scared of . . . monsters. Of what they'll do to me. Luc promises to keep me safe, and I believe him. But who's going to keep Riley safe? She's not herself lately. Not at all. She's . . . mean-spirited. And there's a look in her eye that seems, I don't know, predatory to me. I don't understand what's going on with her, but I hope to God this is all over with soon. I know our lives will never return to normal, but as close to normal as possible is okay by me.

—Nyxinnia Foster

"**R**iley?"

I blink, and Eli's face returns to normal. "Yeah?"

He studies me longer. Scrutinizing. "We're here."

The night air surrounds us, a blanket of darkness void of streetlights. I blink. We're at the Amtrak station just off of 516. These hallucinations are beginning to be a pain in my friggin' ass. "Okay, let's do it." I unbuckle and swing out of the Jeep. Riggs is already standing at the hood.

He draws a deep breath, then jumps *onto* the hood. He glances first at Eli, then me. "I can smell 'em."

"Well let's go then," I say with way more enthusiasm than I really feel. I'm getting used to hiding my true feelings again now that Eli can't read my thoughts. Dangerous. Seriously dangerous.

I don't know what you're thinking anymore, but I can certainly interject my thoughts into your mind. Just as you can. So if you need me, Riley, for God's sake, call me.

Startled by his sudden mind infiltration, I look at Eli over my shoulder. Is it a coincidence, my thinking of his inability to read my mind and his weird interjections? "I will."

I mean it.

So do I.

"Better," Eli says. "Now come on."

The three of us head out into the night. It's about nine p.m. With the Jeep stashed down an unused maintenance lane, we cover the mass of metal as we search the yard, old train cars, unused track, toolsheds. In the distance, the main Amtrak station depot has a faint glow as the lights burn. I can hear the people inside, what few there seemed to be. Some wait to catch a train. Some to pick up a passenger. All going about their ordinary lives.

None privy to the extraordinary creatures that slip through the night.

The train yard is full of shadows, and Eli leads us to a row of empty cars. In unison, we swing and bound up the side of the car closest to us until we land on top. The wind blows and I catch a whiff of something dead. A rabbit maybe? It's been dead a while, I can tell that. The stench is nauseating. I almost gag.

Eli stands, a silhouette. He turns his head, inclines it, and without words, Riggs and I follow as the eldest Dupré begins to leap the train cars. Eli's eyesight is nocturnal—he can see just about anything, at any distance. His hearing is acute, but not as severely as mine. Nor is his scenting as specific as mine.

I sense them. They're here. Three of them. I sniff the air. They've just fed.

Across the yard to the left, behind the maintenance sheds.

Eli doesn't question me; he doesn't even look at me or acknowledge the words I slipped into his mind. Instead he leaps off the train car and moves in the direction I say, then cuts left behind the sheds. I head right. Riggs is two steps behind me. We silently bound over stacks of railroad ties, steel beams, cargo trailers. In seconds we're in a maze of metal and wood. In the distance, the nine-thirty overnight train to Chicago blows its whistle. No, I can't tell the destination by the whistle. I Googled the train schedule on my iPhone.

Ahead of us, between two cargo trailers, are the newlings. On the ground, a motionless heap that had no doubt been a live heap not too long ago. The scent wafting off the dead human sickens me, and I suddenly realize it isn't rotting flesh or decay. The trace of remaining blood is stale. Stagnant. Dead. It all but chokes me.

I wonder how I can even detect it. Or worse—why it bothers me so much.

All at once, Eli, Riggs, and I surround the newlings. The first one notices us and instantly morphs. He lunges straight for Eli. I take my eyes off of them and find the other two. Behind me, I hear the newling gurgle as Eli twists off his head. I've learned that sound and know it anywhere. Both remaining newlings have turned, fangs dropped, and they bound for Riggs and me. Briefly, I keep my eye on Riggs. I forget how talented the little prick is. He sweeps a leg out and knocks one newling to the ground and is on him immediately, plunging a silver dirk into his heart. I turn and almost get coldcocked by the newling attacking me. He's big, out of control, and as rabid as a new vamp comes. I know he will not go down easily.

This newling is fast. *Fucking* fast. In the blink of an

eye he's on me, has me by my throat and is lifting me up. My hearing picks up Eli's voice. He's swearing. Now he's running. Unlike a newling, I have to have air to breathe, and this idiot is squeezing so hard I can barely draw in a breath. I can feel my larynx crushing under the weight of his fingers. But before Eli reaches me, I've got my legs wrapped around the newling's neck. He's strong as hell, but so am I. With one hand I reach for the silver sheathed at my waist, grab it, and jack it upward. It plunges into the newling's eye and, as I thought, he turns me loose. I yank out the blade and bury it in his chest. He stands there, stunned, and begins to convulse. I deliver a single kick. Down he goes. Standing there in the train yard, surrounded by shadows, I bend over at the waist and breathe.

"Nicely done if I do say so myself, Poe," says Riggs. He casually leans an elbow against my shoulder. "Couldn't have done a better job. That blade in the eye thing—" He produced an exaggerated shudder. "Sick, Poe. Truly sick."

I slide a glance sideways. "Glad to amuse," I say, and am at least glad he's stopped calling me babe. Then I shoot a quick look beside me. Eli stands, wordlessly. Scowling. I'm pretty sure that translates into *Are you okay* but he doesn't say it. Instead, he inclines his head. "Let's get out of here." I know Eli battles within himself to keep from overprotecting me. It's a good move on his part. He shows his faith by allowing me to round the train cars alone. I'd probably just get pissed off if he nagged me, and he knows I'm getting fed up with the overprotection. Maybe he's chilling after all.

We comb the rest of the train yard and find nothing out of the ordinary. Of course, newlings aren't going to be traipsing around with their fangs out and pupils all red and freaky. They're hiding. Waiting. Watching from the shadows.

And in the dark corners of Savannah, there are plenty of pickings for the newlings.

Through the back streets of Garden City we run. Garden City, in all its stinky sulfur-from-the-paper-mill glory, is an industrial town just outside of Savannah. It's still in Chatham County, but honestly—it ain't purty. Okay, I take that back. The nature reserve just outside the city limits is pretty cool. Lots of alligators and low-country wildlife. I haven't been back there in a while, though. No telling what you might find now.

Even the gators might be in hiding.

The night air, salty with a tinge of sulfur, washes over my face as I run. My muscles stretch, my lungs expand, and for a split second I feel invigorated. Alive.

Then that nagging weird feeling comes over me and that split-second euphoria evaporates. I'm just running on instinct now, half-ass following Eli. Like a robot. A vampire-slaying robot.

Eli runs just ahead of me and he darts down an alley in a dark subdivision behind Piggly Wiggly. Kinda difficult to speak of something dangerous and hideous as a bloodsucking newling and say the words Piggly Wiggly at the same time. Oxymoron, almost. Still. It is what it is.

"Look there," Riggs says, and points over my shoulder. "At three in the morning it's never a good thing to see a group of kids huddled against a wall down a dead-end street."

I glance at him. He merely lifts his dark brows.

"You got anything, Riley?" Eli asks without looking at me. I know what he wants from me. His eyesight kicks ass, but my other senses are better.

Closing my eyes, I draw in a deep inhalation and let the particles settle against my tongue. I do it again. My eyes pop open and search the canopy of oaks lining the old street a few blocks ahead. "Up there."

"How many?" Riggs asks.

"Four," I respond. I can detect each separate scent of the newlings. I can even tell their sex. "Three males, one female." They're hunting the humans on the street below.

"Let's split," I say, and glance at Eli. I can immediately tell he hates that idea. Again. "Less chance of one of them slipping through and getting to the humans," I add. "You know it's the only way." I quickly check myself. I say humans as if I'm no longer part of the species. Weird.

Eli mutters something under his breath—in French—and gives a short nod. The thing about Eligius Dupré when searching for newlings? He's all business until the business is done. He knows what we have to do and will do it, even if he hates it. Like now.

"Riggs, you take the ledge," Eli says, and points to the rooftop adjacent to the huddled humans. "Riley, you get the house next door," he inclines his head, "and I'll take the rooftop behind them. Wait for my signal. We don't want to have to fight the humans and the newlings at once."

I wait no longer. I nod and slip into the shadows and in three effortless leaps am on top of the roof next to where the humans stand against the wall. I glance over and notice Riggs is already in place. I can't see Eli but I am sure he's exactly where he said he would be. The night is stony still. Not a single breeze blowing now and the heartbeats of five humans resonate in my ears. The humans' low, muttered mumbling sounds like a clan of monks chanting. The thumping begins to jumble in my head, run together, confuses me. I have to shut my eyes for a moment, breathe. Concentrate and push the sporadic beats aside and focus on what's in front of me. I'm having trouble, though. Almost as if something is already inside my head, taking up all the extra room I have. I shake my head to clear my thoughts, and try harder to focus again.

A moment later, Eli is bounding off his rooftop. Despite the confusion in my head, I keep my eyes on Eli. He's crouching now. He lunges. I follow. Out of the corner of my eye, I see Riggs do the same.

We are now all together in the canopy of live oaks. I never was a tree climber but damn if I'm one now. I'm closest to the female so I take her first. She has short spiky black hair with red tips. Her eyes narrow to slits when she sees me, the pinpoint red pupils all but glow.

"Look what's come to visit," the female says out loud. Through the darkness I see the other pairs of eyes staring at me. Good. They're so fixated on me that they don't see Eli and Riggs.

"Back off, Seline," one of the males says. "I'd like a little piece of that fine ass before you rip her heart out."

Seline hisses. I roll my eyes.

Take the female down and get out of here, Eli says inside my head. I don't hesitate—he and Riggs have my back. I simply wait my turn. It comes pretty damn fast.

The female's quick—and goddamn strong. She grabs my throat and pins me against the rough bark. I'm distracted by something. Sounds. A particular sound, and I hear it all around me.

It's blood rushing through veins.

"You look scared, bitch," the female said, close to my face. "I like that."

"Yeah, I bet you do," I say, my fingers wrapping around the hilt of my silver. Quickly, I bury the blade into her heart. Her eyes widen and she begins to convulse. Problem is, she still has me by the throat. She falls to the ground. I go down with her. After slamming against the spindly branches of the oak, the she-vamp's body hits the sidewalk. Mine hits right beside her. Unable to help it, I let out an *umph.*

Shit.

The low murmurings of the humans totally cease for several seconds, then picks back up, grows louder, frantic, and as I stand, I glance over. They've, of course, spotted us, although I'm pretty sure they have no clue what's actually going on. But since they're up to something illegal anyway, they take one look at the body shaking on the cracked pavement beside me and strut right on over. A string of swear words floats through the crisp, still air, accompanied by idiotic laughter and the heady scent of Mary Jane. They haul ass in different directions. Damn, if they only knew that their high, pot-smoking butts have just been spared. Freaking idiots.

A body is thrown to the ground not four feet away. A male, convulsing. My eyes fix on his face, contorted, his jaw unhinged, fangs jagged and long. Nothing elegant about these guys—at least not in the Hollywood sense. His limbs contract, his body pulls into itself and for a moment—a solid split second—he looks at me. Those red pupils fix on mine. Pleading, almost. I look away, sickened. By what, I'm not sure. By what he'd become? Or by what I do to *them* now? Eli appears behind me, and Riggs drops from the tree.

Eli grabs my arm. "You okay?" he asks, and doesn't wait for an answer. He checks me over, his eyes studying my body intensely.

"Yeah," I answer, pulling my arm back. "I'm fine, Eli. Seriously." I'm not, though, and it's anything but the few feet I fell from the tree. That's nothing. Didn't even hurt.

I'm distracted, though. Something's pulling me in all directions and I'm having a helluva time ignoring it. Part of it's the constant killing. Yeah, I know they're bloodsucking vamps. But they weren't always and it bothers me. Go figure. Riley Poe with a conscience. For some reason, I keep it all to myself. I don't want anyone knowing of my weaknesses, I guess. Besides, I can handle it. I can handle me.

Eli's glare tells me he knows I'm bullshitting him. But I know he can't dig in my mind anymore and I let him stew. "Let's go," I say, and begin to move up the sidewalk. "We still have to hit the industry park before we meet the others." I adjust my blades and continue on.

There's hesitancy, but Eli follows. Riggs falls in behind us.

The industrial park is tall concrete pillars and steel buildings. All is quiet; happy to report not a single drop of blood or vampire dust is shed. Riggs is a little miffed about it, and I'm starting to think he digs the slaying a little too much. It takes us all of eight minutes to split up and scour the park. I use my senses to lead me, and thankfully they lead me nowhere. As I slip through the shadows, I inhale. Listen. Still, nothing unusual.

It's close to four a.m. I'm making the last turn before I circle back to meet the others when the feeling hits me. Almost . . . a sensation, and one that begins to crawl up my spine and spread through my arms, fingers, and over my face. A muffled *thump-thump* resonates within me. It sounds far off, almost as if in a tunnel. I feel myself moving toward it. The sound pulls me, and the faster I move, the stronger the beat.

The *heart*beat.

Then, I see her.

I stop in my tracks and ease against a brick wall, pressing my back against its scratchy surface until I blend in with the shadows and overhanging moss. With each beat that resounds within me, another sensation stirs. A craving. A desire so strong it makes my jaws ache, my stomach ping, and my breathing slow way down. Through hooded eyes I watch her. With the streetlamp casting a glow against her skin I see her perfectly. She has a slight build and shoulder-length red hair, and wears glasses. She sits on a bench, alone, crying. I pause.

Go to her, Riley. She has what you desire. What you need. You can see she no longer wants life. She weeps because her heart's been shattered. You can comfort her. Do it . . .

I turn my head to the left, then right. No one there. The voice, I realize, is in my head. Urging me. I want it to stop so badly, I cup my ears with my hands. It doesn't work though. The voice continues.

Go to her. Do not hesitate or she'll get away. This is your chance, Riley Poe. Listen with not your ears but your being. Her life force rushing through her with each beat. You know you want it. Soon you'll realize you need it. It will satisfy that unquenchable thirst. You have it, don't you Riley? A thirst that no drink can quench. A hunger no food can satisfy. She can help you. It will tame the darkness growing inside of you. Do it now, Riley Poe . . .

"No," I whisper out loud, but it's a weak whisper. The girl's heartbeat becomes louder, my senses homing in on everything that creates it. With each *thump-thump* that echoes through my body, desperation builds within me until it reaches such a pitch, I brace myself against the wall to keep from sliding to the sidewalk.

I . . . want it. Need it. Something pulses inside of me, driving me forward.

Yes, that's right. You're weakening, aren't you, Riley Poe? Save yourself. Go to her . . .

My insides are on fire now—a burning that feels as though no amount of water will extinguish the flames. With my stare fixed on the girl, I move slowly forward and silently toward her. . . .

"There you are," Riggs says. "Been looking for you. Eli's on fire, so heads up."

My eyes focus on Riggs. "What do you mean?" I ask.

Riggs shrugs, and the light from a nearby post gleams off his dark hair. "He's run around the industrial park twice looking for you."

Shooting a quick glance left and right, I turn my gaze back to Riggs. Confusion muddles my brain. "I . . . was right here all along."

Riggs walks closer and peers at me with a questioning look. "You okay, babe?" he says, ducking his head and inspecting my face. "You look kinda funny."

I feel a little spacey, light-headed, but I don't confess it. "Yeah, you always look kinda funny. Where's Eli?"

"Where've you been?" Eli says, suddenly beside me.

I look up into his penetrating stare. In the darkness

his eyes all but glow. "Thought I saw something. I came right back here."

As if weighing my words, Eli studies me. Concern pinches his brows together and it's a look that happens more frequently now. "You didn't see anything then?" he asks.

"No." I don't know what I saw. Everything is a blur to me now.

Eli pulls me against him with one arm and presses his lips to my temple. "Let's go," he says quietly. "It'll be dawn soon." His cell vibrates, and he pulls it out of his pocket and lifts it to his ear. "Yeah. We were just leaving. Be there in fifteen."

With a quick glance at Riggs, then me, Eli takes off. We both fall in behind him. Crossing Highway 21 at the side exit of the industrial park, we slip behind an old run-down oil and lube and hit the woods behind it. We reach the train yard within minutes, find the Jeep and climb in. Eli drives. From my peripheral vision, I can see he silently watches me. I know he's worried—I am too. I feel like something's missing, as if I fell asleep and woke up hours later. As we pull onto the service road, I rest my head and stare at the scenery as it flashes by. Quickly, we make our way to Bay Street, then hit Whitaker and take the squares slowly. We see nothing out of the ordinary. When Eli pulls into a parking space next to Forsyth Park, the others are there, waiting. The sun is a thin golden crack, edging through the clouds overhead, and the light surrounding us is hazy. A slight mist hangs low to the ground. Riggs leaps from the back seat over the edge of the Jeep. I use the door.

Seth immediately comes to me. "You okay?" he asks, carefully watching me, inspecting my face, my eyes.

"I'm fine, bro," I lie. "Glad the night's over though. I'm exhausted."

He nods and drapes an arm over my shoulder. "I think I could eat fifty Krystals by myself."

I glance sideways at him. "That has nothing to do with your tendencies, Seth Poe. You could manage that before."

My brother grins at me, and just seeing his warm, smiling face settles me somewhat.

"Anything unusual?" Phin asks. He's talking to Eli, but looking at me.

"Just your average cocky newlings," Eli responds. "Mostly male, a few females. All youth."

"Same with us," Luc says, and moves to stand next to me. "Zetty nearly got his ass beaten by a female."

I glance at Zetty. He merely growls.

"There's a place down on the Vernon," Josie says, leaning against Phin's truck. She has her hair pulled back into a single braid. "Don't forget about that."

"That's right," Phin says. The hazy early-morning light blends with the porcelain smoothness of his perfect features, which stand in contrast to the darkened area on his jaw that would be a beard, if he let it grow out. "An old dock house. Pretty big. Looks like several have been staying there."

"I could smell them," Josie says, and squinches her nose. "Newlings stink." She regards me silently, her mouth tilts into a grin.

"You should've seen Riley," Riggs brags. "She pulls this wicked-sick leg lock around this newling's neck." He throws a proud smile at me. "Kick *ass*."

"Then you should watch it, worm," warns Luc, who gives me a wink.

Traffic begins to move more frequently past the park, and Eli walks over to me. "Ready to go?" he asks.

"Yeah," I say, and I mean it. "I'm tired."

"Later, guys," Eli says, and we get into the Jeep. Seth walks me around to my side.

"I'll see ya later, okay?" he says, and gives me a quick hug. "I'm not too tired and we're going to work on our project for a while." Seth inclines his head to Josie.

Josie shrugs. "My mother loves to give us school projects. You know, like for science. I think she has us making a volcano soon. And a constellation mobile. I've made too many to count in the past but she loves them, even if they sound a little young. I've even asked if we can do something cool, like dissect a cow's eyeball or something. No go. But we'll study several things with the microscope."

I nod. "Sounds good. Catch you guys later," I say.

We all part ways; Eli and I head back to Inksomnia.

As we drive through Savannah's squares, even the annoying sounds of traffic—horns blowing, people shouting, and somewhere close by, a jackhammer— none of it is able to keep my eyes open. My lids feel heavy, and they drift shut. The sounds around me, even the wind, extinguish. I vaguely recall my body being lifted and carried indoors. Next thing I know, the world around me is pitch black, and I'm dead to everything except the sound of my sluggish heartbeat.

It's nighttime, and darkness envelops me. Not just the physical lack of sun, but inside of me is dark, also. As I walk along the sidewalk, it consumes me. I'm like a cat, always on alert to catch something unsuspecting off guard. Play with it for a while. Sink my teeth into it. Kill it.

What? What the hell was that? I stop in midtracks and look around. The street is empty except for the Savannah Yellow Cab that is parked a few blocks away. The oaks loom overhead; the Spanish moss hangs like wispy gray hair, matted and knotty. Shadows surge from the corners of yards and aged brick homes. I like the darkness, and I like the shadows even more. Menace. That's what I feel. But why?

I begin to move again, slowly up the sidewalk toward the cab. I have no intentions at first; I'm just there, a form of life moving through shadows, trying to find my way . . . some-where. I guess I have no purpose. But the very instant my eyes lock on the red ember of a lit cigarette flame inside the cab, I know. I am fixated on it now. On what's inside the cab.

The regular thump of the heartbeat of the cab driver reso-nates in my ears. Thump-thump. Thump-thump.

I have purpose. I have intention.

A craving roars inside of me. It takes on a life of its own and I am powerless to stop it. Or, I simply don't want to. The lines are blurred now. I'm confused. This thing inside of me? It pulses. Breathes.

Possesses.

I move through the shadows now, closer to the parked cab. Closer to the heartbeat. As I sidle up to the passenger side door, I tap on the window with my index finger.

The window rolls down.

"I'm on a break," the cab driver says with the cigarette clenched in his lips.

I smile and lean down to look at him through the window. My hair falls over my shoulder. "For how long?"

The cab driver's eyes dart directly to my low-cut shirt, where his gaze lingers on the swell of my breasts. I allow it. Encourage it by taking a few exaggerated deep breaths. Then, he looks at me and grins. "Till now. Hop in."

I grasp the door handle to the backseat and climb in.

"Where to?" he asks, looking at me through his rearview mirror. A panel of plastic glass separates us.

I shrug casually, lean back against the seat, and lock my eyes with his through the mirror. "Tybee. North Beach."

Again, he grins. "You got it." Only now does he flick the cigarette out the window. Then he puts the cab in drive and pulls out onto the street. At Victory, we take a left. We're both silent until well onto the Island's Expressway, nearly to North Beach. Silent, but the cab driver's eyes continuously flicker to the rearview mirror to watch me. Although I've looked at him, I can't tell you what he looks like. I don't know the color of his eyes, or his skin. I don't know how old he is. I know only that despite his cigarette smoking, his heart is strong. Damn strong.

We are just cresting the last bridge. The roads are empty, the night moonless. The tide is high, and the pungent scent of brine lingers heavy in the air. I see a side street edging the marsh. "Take a right," I say.

The cab driver does as I ask. Along the narrow side street he creeps. The road winds around, hugging the marsh and salt water. We're now at the back of a few rental houses on stilts. They appear to be empty.

"Stop here," I say as we near one of the stilt houses overlooking the salt water.

"Nineteen sixty-five," he says, and half turns in his seat to stare at me. "Long drive from Victory." Again, his eyes drift to my breasts and linger.

"I've got it right here," I say, and then use the power of seduction. I scoot back against the seat, my chest heaving out

of my shirt and the cab driver's eyes glued to it as though he'd never laid eyes on boobs before. Slowly, I ease my fingers to the opening of my shirt, the cabbie all but slobbering on himself. So engrossed with my fingers fumbling so close to my breasts to retrieve what he thinks is cab fare that he doesn't see what's really coming. The panel of plastic glass that separates us shatters as I lift my leg and slam my heel against it. The cabbie stares at me in shock, mouth open. With one arm I grab him by his shirt collar and yank him over the seat, right through the remaining shards of plastic glass. In the backseat I straddle him, and for a split second, his eyes lock onto mine and smolder. His cock hardens beneath me, and I almost laugh. The fucker thinks he's gonna get laid.

That thing inside of me is free now. My eyes close, my body convulses, but only for a couple of seconds. When next I open my eyes, I see nothing, I feel nothing. I hear only the heartbeat. The sound of blood coursing through veins. It beckons me, unleashes my craving. In one fluid motion I tear away the thin layer of his shirt, and I lunge at his chest. My teeth break through skin, bone, muscle, until I feel a pop, and warm liquid settles against my tongue. I'm in a feeding frenzy now, and the man's high-pitched screams barely break through my focus.

Those screams are quickly extinguished.

My thirst is finally quenched.

Grabbing his discarded and shredded shirt, I wipe my

mouth, my face, and climb off of him. Easing out of the cab, I leave the door open and begin to jog up the winding street hugging the marsh. At the bridge, I break into a run. The briny air whips at my face and hair as my speed picks up to an inhuman pace. That suits me. I'm no longer human anyway, so why fuck with human qualities? I can run like the fucking wind. And I do.

As I grow close to Victory Drive, I slow to a boring human pace. My insides soar; a strength I never knew could exist trembles within me. I feel good! Alive! With a quick glance at the oncoming traffic—minimal at this hour but there is a small trail of cars—I hurry across the street and slow to a walk on the sidewalk. Just as I reach the next block, I'm grabbed. A hand encircles my upper arm and I'm yanked to a halt . . .

"Riley. Wake up." A hand on my upper arm shakes me.

The voice is muffled, and far, far away. I ignore it, shrug off the hand. Exhaustion tugs me under and away from the voice. Am I asleep or walking along a sidewalk? Either way, I want to stay where I am. Not . . . with this voice.

"Riley!" This time, the voice and hand speak and shake more violently.

"What?" I say grumpily, and crack my eyes open. It takes a few seconds for my vision and mind to clear. I focus on Eli's face. My eyes scan the room. My room.

At Inksomnia. Slowly, I push up onto my elbows, then I sit up.

Eli lowers himself onto the edge of the bed. With one hand, he pushes the hair from my face and presses his lips to my forehead. When he pulls back and stares at me, I see concern in his eyes.

"What's wrong?" I ask. I feel . . . dirty. Grungy-dirty, like I need a shower.

Eli's cerulean blue eyes search mine. "You can't know how much I hate not being able to read your thoughts," he says. "What were you just dreaming about? Can you remember?"

"How do you know I was dreaming?" I ask, and let my brain settle on before. While I was asleep.

"You were thrashing around, mumbling," he says, and laces his fingers with mine. "Your voice—it didn't even sound like yours, Ri."

I look at Eli, and we study each other for several seconds. I'm not sure I'll ever get over how beautiful Eli is. Dark wavy hair sweeps over his forehead, and those blue eyes lock with mine. A strong jaw dusted with dark shade against flawless skin. Perfect facial structure. Perfect *period*. I exhale, and lean my head back. "All I can remember is walking along a sidewalk. It was dark outside, and I was alone. Then"—I look at him again—"someone grabs me from the darkness, and I wake up. Here, with you. Grabbing me."

Eli's stare is intense and bores into me. His gaze drifts to the black angel wings at the corner of my cheek bone. Tracing it lightly with his fingertip, he watches his own movement. Involuntarily, I shiver at the intimacy. Then his eyes return to mine. "I'm worried about you."

Unable to break his stare, I nod. "Yeah. I know. But honestly, Eli. I'm fine. I can handle myself and you know it." I glance at my arms, and at the dragon scales inked there. "I"—pasting on a comforting smile, I glance up at him—"have the DNA of not one but two strigoi vampires, plus my own crazy blood. I'm good. Damaged though I might be, I can handle myself perfectly fine, Dupré, so stop worrying so much." I punch his arm. "You know, not to brag or anything, but I was a bad little ass before I met you. Before all of"—I wave my hand in the air—"this. So chill." I lean over and give him a quick peck on the lips. "I mean it." I move to leave.

Eli's fast, and his arm binds my body against him. His profound blue stare nearly makes my heart stop. He studies me, searches my eyes as if trying to see inside my head, my soul. Pulling me to him, he presses his lips against mine, urges them to part and kisses me. Thoroughly. I pull away first.

"Where do you think you're going, *chère*," Eli says, his French accent thick and heavy with lust.

"I need a shower in a bad, mean way," I reply, and indulge in a little more of Eli's kiss before escaping the bed. "Hold that thought," I whisper against his jaw. "Be back in a few."

As I leap from the bed, Eli playfully slaps my rump. I shoot him a saucy look and hurry into the shower. As the hot water steams the bathroom and runs down my back, over my face, soaks my hair, a small, teeny slice of normalcy washes over me. When I say small and teeny, I mean just that. Most of the time, I don't even feel like the same person I was two months ago. Only like now, when I can somehow force myself to forget all the *crap*, can I feel slightly normal. So, I indulge. I use extra liquid soap with moisturizers that fill the steamy bathroom with the scent of jasmine and honey. I stand beneath the rainfall and close my eyes. Moments pass; how many, I don't even know or care. My body relaxes, the tense muscles ease.

Join me, Riley Poe. Although I cannot see you, I can feel you within me. Just as I know you feel me within you. We are one, you and I. While you fight who you truly are . . . what you're becoming . . . I can show you how to embrace it instead. The feeding is only one aspect of our existence, you know. Everything is heightened thereafter. Our scent, our beauty, our lust. We have eternal life, Riley, and the world is at our fingertips. You no longer belong amongst the ordinary. You belong . . . with me. I know that now . . .

"Riley! Damn it, what are you doing?"

I'm cold—frigidly cold. Every bone and muscle in my body aches. I'm shaking, quivering, and it's unstoppable. That frantic familiar voice sounds far away, and although I feel someone lifting me, carrying me, it doesn't seem . . . real. I don't actually feel skin to skin. It's more of a numb pressure. Like I'm lacking nerve endings. I can't even open my eyes. I'm so freaking cold, I just want to sleep . . .

A sharp sting spreads across my cheek, and my body viciously shakes.

"Riley, goddamn it! Wake up!"

Another sting, more shaking.

Slowly, I crack my eyes open. Again, I focus on Eli's face.

"You're freezing, Riley," he says, and it's only then that I notice I'm wet and naked beneath the large bath towel he's wrapped me in. Vigorously, Eli rubs my arms and legs and abdomen. My teeth chatter.

Finally, after he all but rubs the first two layers of skin off, Eli tucks me beneath the covers. He's sitting beside me now, the weight of his body tipping me toward him. With one hand, he grasps my face and tilts it upward.

"Where were you?" he asks. "I'm not being overprotective. I'm not being nosy or obsessive. I'm genuinely worried about you, and something's not right, Riley. So, please—where did you go?"

It's a weird question. Even weirder that I don't have the answer. "I was here, with you," I respond.

"And then?" Eli continues.

I think a moment. "I went to take a shower."

Eli studies me. "You don't remember going outside?"

I concentrate. Hard. Then I look at Eli. "No."

"That's where I found you, Ri," he said, pushing my damp hair off my face. "In the alley between Inksomnia and Bhing's store. What were you doing?"

"Naked?" I ask.

"Yes, like you'd walked straight out of the shower and out the door. You were huddled against the wall. Mumbling. Eyes wide open."

Slowly, I shake my head. "That doesn't even make sense."

With both hands, Eli rubs my arms. "We'll talk about it later. Warming up?" he asks.

I look at him. "Yeah, I'm fine. Where," I say, and search his eyes, "were you?"

"I'd fallen asleep, Riley," he answers. "You were gone when I woke up." His eyes are grave. "Three hours, Ri."

I stare off across the room. How can that be? "How

can I lose that much time, Eli?" I say. Something has to give, and I mean now. What the freak is happening to me?

Eli leans over and kisses my forehead. Pulling back, his eyes search mine. "I don't know, but I'm going to figure it out, Ri." He strokes my hair. "Your behavior is different. Your demeanor. It's why I always seem to be so in-your-face. I'm worried. We'll go to my father. He'll know what to do. Meanwhile, you need some nutrients. Want something to eat?"

"Yeah," I say, and climb from the covers, pull on sweats and a black long-sleeved Inksomnia T-shirt and a pair of thick wooly socks, and walk to the living room. I'm really not all that hungry now. I'm losing chunks of time, and that scares the hell out of me. I hope Gilles can help. What if I'm killing innocents? Who's going to stop me? Vic said he could help. But can he? Or is he just trying to change me? Make me his forever. I wouldn't put it past him. What did I do all that time? Outside, naked. Freaking naked! Goddamn almighty. I start for the kitchen, and Eli stops me.

"*Non*," he says, slipping into French. "I got this. You chill on the sofa."

"Eli, really," I say. "I'm not a baby. Or an invalid. As a matter of fact I can almost kick your ass."

He says nothing. The look, though, speaks volumes.

I sigh. "Whatever." I move to the sofa, plop down,

and grab the remote. "Thank you," I say. I don't like to be pampered and he knows it.

Eli simply grins.

Flipping on the TV, I turn to the local channel to check out the news. It's noon and something should be on.

Then, suddenly, there is. The news.

". . . the driver's mutilated body was found in his cab along the marsh on North Beach, at Tybee. It appears to be unrelated to the string of burglaries in the area. Tybee police have no leads as of now," the news affiliate said.

My insides grow cold. Hadn't I dreamed that? Oh freaking hell, had I actually been there? It seems too familiar, too . . . close. I stand and walk to the window, move the drapes and look out over River Street. No way could I have attacked someone. *Mutilated* someone.

"Ri."

Eli is behind me. So quiet, I hadn't even heard him move. I should be used to it by now, but I'm not. Maybe I never will be.

His arms go around my waist and pull me against his body, and his mouth nuzzles my neck. Funny how that doesn't even remotely frighten me. "I know you're tired of it all," Eli says in a low, crooning French accent. "The killing. The death. Hopefully soon, it'll all be over. You can't let it get to you, though." He pulls me tightly against him. "You're strong, Riley. One of the strongest humans I've ever known. So"—he kissed my throat—"fight it."

I relax against Eli's strong embrace, but inside, I'm cold. Numb. And I almost take pride that I hide it so well now. Before, I couldn't hide a damn thing. Eli could read my every thought. Now? With the DNA of two strigoi mixed with my own? Eli's oblivious. He has no clue that it isn't the fighting of vampires and finding of dead bodies that torments me now.

It's the fact that I may be the one hunting them.

Stranger still, I find that *tormented* isn't exactly the right way to describe my feelings about possibly being a killer.

It's more like . . .

Aroused . . .

Part Four

UNHINGED

I'm starting to seriously dig this feeling I have inside of me. Makes me feel alive. Mysterious. Kick-ass. I crave something, and it's strong, powerful, and pulls at me with a force I never knew existed. I don't even know what the hell it is, but I want it. Bad. Don't forget—I've had these cravings before. I used to be an addict, and this feels the same. Sometimes I feel like my insides are turning outside, every nerve ending is on fire, and that if I don't get whatever it is I'm craving, I will go totally insane. But you know what's starting to piss me off? Everything. And everyone. Eli. Luc. Phin. Josie. Seth. Zetty. Preacher. Estelle. Nyx. Irritating as shit, every one of them. Constantly watching me—especially Eli. I can barely have any time to my freaking self. You know what I want? I want everyone to leave me the fuck alone.

—Riley Poe

Everything's changed. Me. Them. All that's around me. Complete chaos. And I don't even think they can see it. At least, they don't see what I see.

And that's fine by me.

They all look at me funny, and that's something I don't like. I'm trying not to make a big deal about it, but it's starting to grate on my last everfucking nerve. I don't know how much more I can stand. Always watching. Always talking. Planning shit behind my back. Someone's always with me. Acting like I don't have a fucking brain in my head to make decisions with.

And Eli's eyes are constantly locked on to me.

Sometimes I feel like I'm losing my goddamn mind.

I've gotten good at hiding it though, and trust me when I say that's a plus. If they all knew what really went on inside my head they'd lock me away. But I didn't make it through drug rehab and vamp rehab to break down now. No, hell-sir no. I got it. I'm cool.

I'm blankly staring at images as I sift through the pile of sketches Nyx handed me an hour ago. Dragons. Japanese symbols. Japanese symbols with dragons. Japanese symbols with flowers. Skull with a Ranger's beret.

"Hey, Riley," Nyx says from her station.

I glance at her and she's smiling ear to ear. It irritates me. "Yeah?" I answer.

"Your ten-thirty appointment just called. They're running a few minutes late."

Damn. I hadn't even heard the phone ring. "Thanks," I say.

Just then the front door opens, and that raven above the jamb caws loudly. Swear to God, I'm going to yank that fucker off the wall and throw it in the river next time I get the chance.

"Riley? This guy wants to talk to you," Nyx says. She gives me another smile, all bright and cheery. Like nothing's wrong with the world.

I set the sketches aside and walk over to the man waiting for me. He's young, military, and gives me a nod and a wide smile. "Ma'am," he offers politely as a greeting. "I was told I could get inked by no one other than you."

Thump, thump.

The soldier's young, vibrant heartbeat echoed inside my head.

I smile up at him. "You got something in mind?"

It's warm enough inside the shop that I'm wearing a black Inksomnia tank, a pair of jeans and combat boots. The soldier checks out the dragons inked on my arms and smiles. "Sweet," he says, continuing to admire the work. Or me. "I was thinking of a snake wrapped around my arm," he says, "from here to here." He points at his shoulder and elbow. "With my infantry number in the body."

I nod. "I'm booked today, but check out the album over there"—I nod toward the image album on the coffee table—"and see if there's anything in there you like. I'll do a fast mock sketch and see what you think. Then we'll set you up with an appointment."

Soldier nods. "Cool." He turns, finds the album, and plants himself on the sofa and begins his search.

I return to my station and pick up the sketches. In the back, I notice Eli leaning against the wall. Watching.

I ignore him and continue on with my meaningless task. I can't believe I sit around and draw such stupid shit. God, the things people *think* they want inked forever into their skin. They are fucking clueless. Then, I'm interrupted.

Vic: It's getting worse for you, isn't it, love?

Me: Get out of my head, Victorian. I don't want to hear it.

Vic: A piece of me lives inside of you, Riley. You cannot fool me. I can sense the mayhem. What else is happening?

Me: Nothing I can't handle.

Silence.

Vic: Has my brother been contacting you?

Me: Maybe. Not really sure who it is. Or if they're real. Like I said, I can handle it. Doin' a fan-fucking-tastic time of it so far.

Vic: Riley.

Me: I'm losing chunks of time. They feel like dreams really, but then I physically realize I have lost time. Can't remember what I've done, yet some things seem familiar.

Silence.

Vic: Christ, Riley. Let me help you before it's too late. Please. I will take such good care of you. You'll want or desire

110

nothing, I vow it. I can give you such love, such pleasures, if you'll only allow me to take you away.

Me: (laughing) Vic, you know I can't allow that. No way am I leaving.

Vic: It's taking you over, love. It will overpower you and there will be nothing left of the Riley Poe you know. It's very close to succeeding even now. Please. Come with me. I am begging you.

Silence.

Me: Good-bye, Victorian. Leave me alone.

Vic: I will never leave you alone, Riley. Never. At least allow me a decent good-bye.

Me: What do you mean by that?

Vic: Meet me. Tonight. I won't ask for another thing from you. I vow it.

Me: You do realize your mind whammy doesn't work on me anymore, right?

Vic: Unfortunately, yes. I do realize. I only want to say good-bye.

Me: Yeah, right. Where do you want to meet?

Vic: I'm just across the river from you, love. At the Westin. Tower Suite.

Me: (laughing) Of course the tower suite. I'll be there.

Vic: What time?

Me: When I get there.

*   *   *

"Ma'am?"

My eyes focus on the young soldier who is now standing in front of me, grinning.

"Yeah?" I say.

His face falls slightly, but he clears his throat and continues. He holds open a page in the sketches album. "I found the one." Leaning closer, he shows me.

A winding serpent. I'd sketched it in under ten minutes. "You sure?" I say.

The soldier nods and answers without hesitation. "Yes, ma'am."

"Okay," I answer, get up and move to the computer up front. I click on the appointments screen and scroll down. "I can fit you in on Friday at five p.m."

The soldier smiles. "Sounds great. I'll be here."

I click in his appointment, calling him "soldier/ snake," and close the screen. Then without another glance or thought, I get up and walk to my station.

I'd forgotten Eli was even in the shop. But he was. Hadn't even moved from where I last saw him. I ignore him.

My clients come and go throughout the day. I don't make much conversation. I do the art, and get done quickly. The sound of heartbeats rush through my head with such vigor, I have to really concentrate to block them out. Which, in turn, blocks everything else out and that's fine by me, too. None of it's easy though. Along with the thumping of heartbeats comes a thrill I can't explain, and it shakes my whole body on the inside. I'm on edge, and I want to be alone. Vaguely do I recall inking a set of broken skeletal wings on the back of a very bony girl in her mid-twenties. That took a couple of hours. Staring at her back lined with drops of blood didn't do much for my mood. But some small slice of my pride must still exist because in the end, despite all of the frustrations and distractions, my work still kicks ass. Call it vanity. Call it whatever the fuck you want.

I am just finishing up a Japanese verse on the flank of a young guy when Preacher walks in through the front door, followed by Eli's brothers, sister, and Seth. My insides twinge; I haven't seen Preacher and Estelle in a week maybe? I've lost track. My surrogate grandfather, wearing his signature plaid button-up long-sleeved shirt and jeans, catches my glance and holds it. I feel cold all of a sudden, and the hairs rise on my arms. Preacher's eyes lock on to mine for several seconds, as if digging in my brain to find something. I feel like he's busting me for smoking weed. He turns, and I can tell something's up.

"Eligius?" Preacher calls.

Eli emerges from the back of the shop. "Yes, sir?" He

slides me a glance as he passes. His presence takes up the entire area. I forget he has that ability sometimes. Power. He reeks of it.

The old Gullah merely stares at Eli for several seconds; Eli returns the look. Without saying a word out loud, both leave Inksomnia, Luc and Phin following. Their expressions are unreadable.

I guess there's enough of the old pathetic me left to actually care to ask, "What's going on?"

Josie and Seth walk toward me. Josie watches me with depth. Precision. Weighs me. Large, cerulean blue eyes unblinking. But keeps silent.

Seth stops in front of me. His green eyes are solemn. "One of Capote's nieces was killed last night." Capote is an old Gullah, and Preacher's cousin. Plays a wicked saxophone, too.

"Killed?" I ask. "What do you mean?"

Seth and Josie simply stare at me. No words. No explanation. Then, I know. I realize it means only one thing.

Vampires.

I meet their stare for several seconds, then return to what I'd been doing in silence.

"Oh, gosh," Nyx says quietly. I glance at her. Now she's wringing her hands and pacing, her face pinched in worry. The beat of her heart increases. "How awful. Poor Capote." I think for a second Nyx is going to burst into tears.

Of course, Capote and Preacher are cousins, so the girl is related to Preacher as well.

A vampire killed a Gullah. This hasn't happened in centuries, save Eli's accident. The Duprés have always kept Savannah and Preacher's kin safe. Valerian's army is growing. Now, a young Gullah girl has been murdered.

What if I did it?

I continue cleaning my station until I feel a hand on my shoulder. When I glance up, it's Seth's eyes I'm staring into. "What?" I ask.

"Can we talk?" he replies. "Alone."

I shrug. "Fine by me. Let's go."

Seth's eyes lock on to mine for several seconds, then he turns and heads to the back of the shop. Nyx must be on a retro kick because she changes the tunes and The Monkees' "Daydream Believer" blasts through Inksomnia and follows me upstairs.

I walk straight to the fridge, open the door, and grab a beer. I've got half the bottle drained by the time Seth speaks.

"What's wrong with you?" he asks, and he doesn't ask it nicely.

I stare at him as I drain the rest of the bottle. "What do you mean?"

Seth rakes both hands through his hair and then

grasps his neck. For a moment, he closes his eyes. When he reopens them, his stare is hard. Hurtful. To him, not me.

"You're not the same, Ri," he begins. "You're . . . different. Hateful. Mean."

I laugh. "No shit, bro. I've got two fucking sets of strigoi DNA inside me." I shake my head. "What the hell?" I'm irritated now. He called me up here for this?

"I watched your face when I told you about Capote's niece," he says angrily. "Your expression didn't even flinch, Ri. It's like you don't care."

"You're still a kid, Seth. What do you know? Grow up and have some responsibilities and *then* tell me about my lack of care and expression, okay?" I answer.

Just then the door swings open and Eli walks in. His gaze sweeps over me and Seth. "Am I interrupting?" he asks.

Seth shakes his head and keeps his eyes on me. "No."

The silence inside the apartment is a live, palpable entity.

Eli walks to me and grasps my shoulders. "I have to go with Preacher and my brothers to Da Island," he says quietly, evenly. "I hate leaving you, but this is unavoidable. Did Seth tell you what happened?"

I simply nod.

Eli grasps my chin and tilts my face to look up into

his. "I hate leaving. I hate that Phin, Luc, and my father have to go, too, but we do. This is big. And it has to stop."

Again, I nod and remain silent.

"My mother and Josie will be here. Seth, Zetty, and Riggs, as well." He lowers his mouth to mine and kisses me. When he lifts his head, those cerulean blue eyes almost take my breath away with their intensity. They nearly pierce the anger subtly bubbling below the surface of my being. "For now, the night runs stop, and I mean that, Riley. It's too dangerous to go out alone. You're strong but not against a dozen newlings. Wait for us to return." He kisses me again. "They're waiting for me. I'll be back soon."

"Bye," I say, and with a final glance, he leaves. Fast. I follow him to the door but he's already gone.

"Listen to him, Ri," Seth says, and he's closer to me now. Like right behind me, crowding my space. "I don't know what's up with you lately, but please." He grabs my arm. "Listen for once."

I snatch my arm from Seth's grasp and glare at him. His sluggish heartbeat resonates in my head. "I don't need you telling me what to do, Seth. So chill the hell out and stop talking to me like I'm a kid."

Seth's face falls. Blanches, even. Suddenly, he's seven years old again and looking at me as I trip and fall up the steps to our apartment. Drunk. I vaguely remember those days. But I totally remember his expression. I'm not sure why it doesn't affect me, but it doesn't. I turn and head for my room.

"Where're you going?" Seth calls after me.

I don't look at him. "I need to work out," I say, step into my room, and shut the door.

Minutes later, I hear the apartment door open and close. Finally, alone.

Nervous energy simmers under my skin, and for a split second I feel as though I'm on fire. I claw and peel out of all my clothes except my bra and panties. Without bothering with a warm-up, I start kicking the bag suspended from the corner ceiling of my bedroom. I kick. I punch the bag, and I don't know how long I go at it, but it's a while. I don't even break a sweat. The exertion only helps a little. My thoughts are running ninety to nothing, my brain suddenly unable to filter out the constant rumbling of human noises outside the apartment. My head begins to throb. Mercilessly. Voices. Heartbeats. Crying. Traffic. The pain is so bad it sends shards of light shooting behind my eyelids. I gotta run. Gotta get out.

No, first watch this. Watch what you could be . . .

I jerk my head around and scan the room. I'm alone. The voice. It's familiar. Frightening. I sit on the floor and cradle my head in my hands, and only then does the vision appear behind my eyes. *It's dark. I'm running away. No, I'm chasing. Someone. Wait, not chasing. Stalk-ing. They're unaware of me. I slip through the shadows si-lently, yet I run. I want to get closer. I can already smell their scent. Hear their heartbeat. Almost feel the rush of their blood through their veins. I'm on Savannah's dark side, away from the tourists, away from the history, the moss, the charm. I'm where most people wouldn't dare go alone. Up ahead, the figure turns the corner. I'm right behind them. The moment I turn the corner I'm coldcocked by a heavy fist, and I land square on my ass. Warm liquid spills over my lip and onto my chin.*

"Damn, bitch," he says. "What the fuck's your problem? You a cop?"

I stare up at the guy in silence. I'm seething.

"Deke, man," another guy says as he steps out of the building's front door. "What's up?"

"This bitch was followin' me," he says. "I think she's a cop."

The other one lets the screen door slam and walks over to me. He studies me for a moment. Looks at my ink. "Naw, man," he says. "That bitch ain't nothin' but that. A bitch. She ain't no cop." *He shoves me with his foot.* "You ain't no coppy, are ya, bitch?"

He lifts his foot to shove me again. It never touches me. I grab it, midair, and with very little effort, send him flying backward into the shadows beside the duplex. I'm so fast that the other guy doesn't have time to react before I'm in the shadows with the first guy. In the darkness, I have his body pinned to the ground. I see only the whites of his eyes, the flare of fear in his nostrils. His mouth opens to shout for help, out of surprise, whatever. The words die on his tongue. Because he dies on my tongue.

My fangs sink deep into his throat. His body thrashes, then slows to erratic jerks as his nervous system detects failure.

"What the fuck!" his friend calls from behind me.

I leap upward, grab his shoulder, and swing onto his back, my legs wrapped around his waist, my arms tightening around his neck. His strength gives out and we tumble to the damp mossy ground. Before a single word escapes him, my fangs are buried in his heart. A deep, sadistic laugh reverberates off the trees and dingy buildings around me.

Just as fast as the vision appeared, it vanishes. I lose my breath for a second, and I choke. The sensation I'd had moments earlier seems so real. I blink, look around. I'm back in my room, in my apartment above Inksomnia. Why am I being tormented? Rising from the floor, I breathe. What was that? Was it real? I'm so confused, and the pounding inside my head returns. Quickly, I grab a pair of discarded jeans thrown across the back of a chair, a long-sleeved T-shirt, and boots and hurry out of my bedroom. I pass by Chaz, lying on his bed close to the hearth. He stares at me, lowers his head, and growls low in his throat.

I spare him the slightest of glares and leave the apartment. In seconds I am just another body slipping through the streets of Savannah.

The night air is chillier than it has been. I've been on the streets for hours, and I find myself in a half-packed parking lot of some random club. I don't recognize it, but that's nothing new. Clubs pop up all over Savannah, and they close just as fast. In some weird extraterrestrial font, the bar sign reads AREA 51.

The club is just a plain gray building with no windows, and from the smell of extreme marsh and brine hanging on the breeze, I guess it's close to the river. The scent is nauseating today, and I choke back a gag. I feel like I'm chewing on mucky saw grass. I make my way to the front door. Just as I reach it, a couple steps out. Chick. Dude. I don't see faces, features. Only silhouettes. I step inside.

Bodies. Heartbeats. Laughter. Some cosmic weird tunes echoing off the walls—almost like the sounds a supposed spaceship would make. Some dude pushes by me. His T-shirt says THEY ARE OUT THERE.

"Hey gorgeous," some guy says beside me. "You look lost. Want a drink?"

I glance at him wordlessly.

The guy chuckles, and his eyes divert to the ink on my cheek. His gaze travels down to my hands, where only the tail of my dragon wraps around my fingers, then back to my face. "Sweet tats." He glances at my shirt. "So what does Inksomnia mean?"

I lean in close, and his nostrils flare with male hormones. "It means fuck off," I say sweetly, blink, and move back. My gaze locks on to his. The thump of his fast-paced heart resonates inside my head. I can almost feel the blood rushing through his veins. My mouth waters. Maybe I shouldn't rush him away.

"Hey Aaron, come on," another guy says behind him, grabbing his arm. "We're late, man." The guy flashes me a shy smile. I think I scare him.

Aaron is transfixed. He can't move and his stare is locked on to mine in fascination. I lick my lips, and I watch his pupils dilate. Goddamn. I don't even have to say anything. Ole Aaron is ready to screw my brains out right here and now. It wouldn't take much, and this game is just too . . . invigorating. Powerful. I haven't even been in the club for fifteen friggin' minutes.

"Aaron, man," his friend urges, avoiding my glare. "Come on."

I lean in very close to Aaron, and my lips brush the shell of his ear. "Your loss," I whisper.

Aaron's eyes widen as his friend pulls him through the crowd and away from me.

My eyes immediately scan the crowd. Searching. Seeking . . . something.

"Is that what you're into?" a voice says close to me. "Geeks?"

I turn and look up. Brown hair. Brown eyes. Lean build. Sluggish heartbeat.

"Maybe," I answer, and lean closer. "I'm into a lot of things."

The stranger's pupils dilate, just a fraction.

Just then, a siren goes off overhead, followed by an announcement over a loudspeaker. When I search the room, I notice some guy wearing a THE TRUTH IS OUT THERE T-shirt and a big goofy-ass grin standing at the mic. "We've had another sighting! This one near Mobile, Alabama, and more than twelve people saw the lights!"

A huge roar went through the crowd as they cheer. I can't help but glance around at the people packed into the club.

"Are you fucking kidding me?" I mutter.

A large hand skims my hip. "You wanna leave?" the guy says against my ear. "With me?"

I brush his stomach with my fingertips. Not an ounce of fat. Nothing but rigid muscle. "Hell, yeah," I say in a low voice. "And don't make me beg."

The stranger stares at me for a moment, grins, then grasps my hand. I allow him to lead me through the crowd of *X-Files* dorks and to the front door. We push out into the night, and I only vaguely notice it's warmer than usual. Warm and muggy, as though rain is close, hanging in the air. Threatening.

I like threatening.

The swoosh of his blood through his veins echoes inside my head. I hear it. Feel it.

Taste it.

And goddamn, I want it.

We're walking beneath the shadows of the overhanging oaks now, and in midstride the stranger stops, turns, and slides his hands over my hips, pulling me against him. "What's your name?" he asks seductively. His fingers trail up my ribs. In the darkness, I can't see anything but his silhouette.

As I stare at him, a blank, hollow feeling washes over me. Forcing my brain to concentrate, I think. It's no use. I'm empty. Tapped out. In other words, I have no fucking clue who I am. Why can't I remember my own name? I look around me as if I expect my name to be written on something, like the trunk of a tree, the side of a building. I see nothing. I know even less.

"Hey," the guy says, leaning his head close to mine. I am still staring at him, but blankly. After a few moments, his features focus. "It's okay." He begins to walk backward, pulling me along. "Doesn't matter." He stops, turns, and backs me against a moss-covered brick wall. It's dark. No lights. A few sparse drops of rain fall through the canopy of oak. The scent of brine and wet vegetation permeates the air. The stranger lowers his head and kisses me.

I kiss him back.

Unfamiliar hands slide up my stomach and over my breasts, and I moan and push into him. We kiss, grope, touch until we're both breathless. He rests his forehead against mine. "Wanna go for a ride?"

I don't know who I am. I don't know what I'm doing. I want something. And it's something he's not going to want to freely give. I'll have to take it.

I will take it.

"Yeah," I say breathily. "Let's go."

I see a white flash in the darkness, and it's the stranger's smile. Without words, he pulls me away from the wall and leads me down the sidewalk, around the corner to a row of historic townhomes. On the street, a motorcycle is parked. He pulls me toward it and hands me the spare helmet strapped to the back.

As I pull the helmet onto my head, a vague familiarity washes over me. I've done this before. With this guy? Another? Whatever, I've done it enough that I don't even hesitate. The stranger eases onto the bike, I slide on behind him and wrap my arms around his waist. In moments we are on some street, heading in some direction or another. I don't really know or care.

In the end, what I want will be waiting there. Away from the crowd. In private.

I lean against the stranger's back as we ride, and I feel his heart beating against me. A craving gnaws at me, stirs some-

thing feral within me that is almost uncontrollable. I slowly lower my hands from his waist to his crotch, and the hard bulge I find lets me know he's ready for me.

Only, he's not. He's so fucking not.

His hand leaves one handlebar and covers mine, pressing mine hard against his cock. I can feel anticipation, smell his pheromones, and hear his heart rate increase.

I wait. We continue.

Down a winding two-lane road we travel, and I've no idea where we are. Huge mossy oaks drape the street, and we're hugging tight curves and the river as we go. The bike speeds up, dangerous, reckless, and I find myself liking the feeling.

After one more curve the bike slows and veers right; we pull into a long oyster-shell drive. A small, older concrete house on the river sits beneath several trees, and a long front porch lies open to air. All is dark, save the single yard light high on a power pole. It casts shadows that dance and play with the slight breeze rolling in off the marsh.

The sexual energy literally rolls off of the stranger. I have to wonder if he would be as turned on if he knew I could snap his head off like a dandelion bloom.

I dismount the bike, and he does the same. Immediately, he pulls me to him. Hungrily, his mouth takes mine, his hands move over my ass, up my spine, and the whole while he's touching me, kissing me, I notice—feel—one thing: his heart. I smell one thing: his blood.

The more frantic he becomes, the more ravenous I grow.

He's groping me now, through my jeans, pressing his hard cock against me. Somehow, we're on the porch, and the only sounds are the rush of air through the trees, his heartbeat, and his excited, breathless groans as I press my hand against his stiff ridge. It's all a game. To me, anyway. It's the only way I can get what I want. What I need.

But I can't take any more. Not one more fucking second. His blood rushes with each pump of his heart, and it's so intense it resonates literally inside my head. Taunting me. Begging me. My head begins to pound, my mouth waters. Shards of light intrude behind my eyes as the pain intensifies, and suddenly, I no longer feel his hands on me. I see him though, barely, and through my fog of delirium, I lunge. We struggle. He screams. All is silent.

A suffocating black shadow of agony swallows me whole.

"Damn it, Riley, wake up!"

Hands on me. Loud voices. I jerk my eyes open and stare, pissed off and confused. In one fluid motion I leap, shove the hands off me, and dart to the corner of the room. So fast is the movement that I barely feel my feet hit the floor. Only now, at the far end of the room, does my vision clear and I see the kid standing beside the bed.

A boy. Dark hair. Lean. Tall. Looks familiar. My brain strains, trying to remember.

My brother.

"Ri, what's wrong with you?" he asks. Worry laces each word.

Slowly, I take in the room. It's my bedroom. I'm in my apartment. Confusion webs my brain like a cocoon. Bits and pieces of memory filter in. "I, uh," I stutter. "Had a bad dream, bro. That's all. You scared the hell out of me." I want to be alone, want him to go away. But there he stands, looking at me. His brows pinch together in concern. I'm sick of him worrying about me so much. It's starting to get on my last fucking nerve.

Seth moves toward me. "You've been knocked out for almost twenty-four hours," he says.

I glance around the room. How did I lose that much time? "I must be coming down with something," I say. "Probably the flu. I feel like shit." I blink. "Is Eli still gone?"

Seth's eyes rake over me. Weighing me. Considering my words. "Yeah, they're still on Da Island with Preacher. Maybe you'd better see a doctor, sis. You're scaring me."

A cynical laugh escapes me. "Yeah, right. A doctor. That's what normal people do, Seth." I give him a hard look and push away from the wall. "We're not that anymore. Never will be, either. I'll just sleep it off." I throw myself back onto the bed.

"You've got clients waiting," he says.

"Later," I mumble into my pillow. "Tired."

A few seconds go by. I feel Seth's hand on my head, stroking my hair. "Come on, Ri. Get up. Please—"

In less than a half second, I turn over and shove him away. Hard. "Get away from me, Seth," I say angrily. "I fucking mean it. Leave me alone." My vision is fogging again, and I feel myself being pulled into blackness. I fight it, though, and keep my stare trained on my brother.

Hurt and anger crowd Seth's young features. "I'll never leave you alone," he says with ferocity, then does exactly that and storms out of my room. In seconds I hear the apartment door downstairs slam shut.

Without another thought I turn over and fall right back to sleep. Or, into the pit of darkness. What the fuck ever. Doesn't matter anymore. Shadows claim me, my thoughts, my memory. I'm aware of my own life force, the echo of my sluggish heart beating, but of nothing around me. Once more, I'm starkly oblivious. I like it like that.

I'm at a party. A ball? A charity? Everyone's in tuxes and evening gowns, me included. Must be something big. Can't imagine why I'm here. With a furtive glance, I check out my dress in the mirror I'm standing next to. Long, form fitting, garnet, thin jeweled straps and a plunging neckline. Backless. Slit from the floor to my thigh. Black peep-toe heels. The only jewelry I wear is a garnet velvet choker with a black stone inset. My hair is pulled up into a loose sort of sexy something, and someone curled my hair leaving long, spiraling hanks of midnight and fuchsia. The makeup is a little heavy, with my lips as garnet as my dress. I barely even look like me, except for the ink. My dual dragons running the length of my arms look wickedly out of place here. I like that.

A man appears beside me in the mirror, and I stare as he glides close to me. I've no idea who he is. Hell. I have no idea who I am.

"You came," he says excitedly.

"Not yet," I say, and I check him out from head to toe. A little young, but gorgeous all the same. Tall. Dark hair. Dark eyes. Perfectly structured face. "But that could change."

He blinks in surprise, then gives me a seductive smile and offers me his arm. "Let's dance." Inclining his head, his grin widens.

I shrug and accept. "Lead the way."

He does, and we make our way through a crowd of tuxes and gowns twirling around the dance floor to the music of a live orchestra. Once in the middle, he slows, turns, pulls me close, and immediately and with more grace than I credit him for, begins an unhurried, intimate dance. I let him lead, and I meet his gaze. His brown eyes sear into mine and he studies me with a burning, curious intensity.

"You don't know who I am, do you?" he inquires. The hand resting modestly against my back moves lower, urges me closer with the slightest of nudges. His fingers interlace *with mine. His whole presence exudes seduction. He's very male. Very determined. And very, very horny.*

"Not a clue," I finally answer. "But you seem to know who I am."

Brown eyes soften as he looks at me, and he smiles wide. "Let's pretend neither of us knows the other," he suggests. His accent is . . . I can't place it. But it's unusual, and sexy as hell. "To make it even. Yes?"

I give him a slight nod. "Why not."

The orchestra plays some old tune I don't recognize, and my dance partner lowers his head to my ear. Soft, firm lips brush the shell.

"Since we don't know one another," he whispers, "let's go for a walk and get some air." His lips brush the skin right below my ear. "Become acquainted."

"All right," I respond. "Let's go become . . . acquainted, then."

Wordlessly, he slips his hand to my lower back and leads me through the throng of partiers, to a set of French double doors near the back of the hall. Flanked by giant urns of green leafy ferns and marble statues, I can't for the life of me figure out where I am. Cotillions and soirees aren't exactly my thing. At least, I don't think they are. I make eye contact with very few, but it's because no one wants to look at my eyes. Instead they are fascinated by my dragons. I do notice that although the setting and music are both old-fashioned, most of the dancers are younger. Mid-twenties, maybe?

In the next breath we're outside. It's almost as though I somehow changed scenes in a movie. Literally. One second I'm standing inside. The next second, I'm beneath a canopy of moss and oaks, on a stone path through the garden. I glance up and around. The night is dark, starry, and moonless. A marble fountain spurts delicate sprays of water, pink from the lamp beneath the surface. A couple sits on a stone bench close by, their words whispered, muffled. My unknown date leads me past them, and as I glance down I see the woman's hand grope the man's crotch. His barely restrained moan reaches my ears. I notice he's looking dead at me. I also notice his eyes have a sort of . . . glow.

Soon, we leave the horny couple behind and I find myself completely alone with a total stranger. The slight strains from the orchestra carry along the breeze until it seems we're miles away from the ball. Shadows fall longer, the wood around the path grows denser.

"Are you afraid?" he asks. We stop. He rounds on me, facing me.

"Of what?" I return.

His hands ease to my hips, skim my bare back, and pull me close. I feel weird, as if I can't really help my reaction to him. Even when his head lowers, I'm unable to pull away.

"Of loving me more than you love him," he answers, his lips brushing close to mine, yet not touching them. "I think you are."

Of him? Who? I can't seem to help myself. I turn my

mouth to his, and immediately he groans and covers my lips with his. The kiss is slow, erotic, and he takes his time to explore my mouth thoroughly, as if this is the only chance he'll have. It feels like he's waited for this moment a long, long time. I find myself kissing him back, and my hands thread around his neck and hold him tightly. Again he groans, and his kiss heightens. His hands slide down my bare back, over my ass, until he finds the slit in the dress and grazes the exposed skin of my thigh.

Then, he stills. For a moment, we're both suspended there, in the dense wood, on a stone path. His hand leaves my thigh and cups my face. With a gentleness that surprises me, he strokes my lips with his thumb, then brushes a kiss there.

"You've no idea how long I've waited for this," he says, his accent thicker. He kisses me again, then moves his mouth to my ear. He says something in a language I don't understand. "Forever," he whispers. "And it's exactly how I imagined."

I'm looking at him, his face half cast in shadow, and I can't remember who he is. Familiar? Yes. Attractive? Totally. But there's something missing here. Something absolutely not right . . .

"Riley, didn't you hear what I said?"

I jerk, and again, my vision is blurry. Slowly, I focus. I'm confused. I'm pissed. And I don't like either.

Woman staring at me. Auburn hair pulled into high

pigtails. Bright red lipstick. Who the hell is she? Her eyes are wide and frightened as she stares hard at me. Her lips are moving but I don't know what the hell she's saying. There is no sound coming out.

All I can hear is her heart beating. Fast. Maybe I feel it more than hear it.

I turn to leave, to escape, and I then feel a hand close around my arm. I react. I turn and jack the woman up against the wall, holding her there by her throat. Although I'm staring dead at her face, I don't really see her. Her features are a fuzzy blur. Her body begins to jerk, and she's gasping for air, clawing at my hand with pale white fingers. Long legs clad in ridiculous-looking striped stockings kick the wall. I smile at her.

All at once I'm tackled and I hit the floor. Frantic voices, swearing, shouting surround me, and I start to struggle. A weight, almost unbearable, pins me down. Not for long, though, because I find my strength.

"Goddamn, Riley, hold still!" the voice warns, and straddles me in a way that I can't move my arms or legs. I don't recognize the voice, but it's deep, accented, and threatening. All I want to do is escape. Get away. But I can barely breathe, much less run away. Whoever is on top of me is one strong fuck.

"Nyx, call Mrs. Dupré," the same voice yells. "Now! And get Ms. Estelle over here, too."

I thrash some more. "Get the *fuck* off me!" I growl. I

buck, begin to pull one of my knees up under me. The body atop me grunts, mutters something in a foreign language, and holds me tighter.

"Hold her, Zetty," a female voice warns. "You've got to get a better grip on her legs or she'll kick right out from under you. I've seen her do it."

More weight, distributed over my legs and arms, and no matter how hard I pitch, I'm stuck. My face is pushed into the floor. I don't know who Zetty is, or Nyx, but they're both dead when I get free.

"Call, Nyx," the Zetty person says. "I can't hold her forever."

I hear the Nyx person speaking in an excited voice to someone, then she moves into my line of sight. Same stupid stockings. Must be the heartbeat I had by the throat. She comes closer, bends down, and looks at me. I'm so filled with rage I want to gnash out with my teeth and grab her.

"Riley, it's going to be okay," she says. Her eyes are wide and fearful, but there's pity in her voice. "I promise, it will be. And I'm so sorry."

I do nothing but stare at her and growl.

Her hand goes to her throat and she quickly backs away.

"Yeah, stay back, Nyx," the male says. "She's strong."

In the next instant, a small dark woman is suddenly there. She bends over at the waist and looks at me, the crinkles at the corners of her eyes deeply engrained into her skin. I try to lunge, but I'm trapped beneath the human. Her ebony face frowns at me, unafraid.

"Girl, we gonna git you right," she says, shakes a bony finger at me, then looks at the male. "You stay put on her dere, boy. She git loose an' we'll be in trouble."

"Yes, ma'am," the male says. He holds me tighter still.

I gather all of my strength, buck hard and scream.

The male, Zetty, has a tight enough hold that I barely move an inch.

The dark woman smiles and nods. "Good. I'll be back."

"Riley!" another male yells. "Zetty, what's happening?"

"No, Seth," another says, this time a small, petite woman. No, not a woman. She's pulseless. There are two without pulses in this room. With my vision cloudy, I seek them out. Short, compact, eyes aglow.

"Get away from me," I growl, squinting to make my vision clear. The younger male, human, edges closer.

"Riley, no," he says quietly. His face is pinched in pain, and I can't understand why.

"She doesn't recognize you, Seth," the young pulseless female says. "You'd better step back."

"No," he says, unbending. "She's my sister." This he says so soft only I can hear.

Not that I understand it.

The dark woman returns, and everything spins out of control at that point. I'm lost, suffocating, drowning, fighting. I feel like I'm dying, like I'm more thirsty than I've ever been in my entire life. No, not thirsty. It's hunger. Hunger and thirst combined. I need . . . something. A light-headed feeling comes over me, and now I'm dizzy. Something is forced down my throat, and although I thrash back and forth, I'm overpowered. Someone with very small but strong hands holds my head, and something disgusting is jammed past my lips. I cough, spit, but those same steely hands now grip my jaw closed. I have to swallow. I hear yells, cries, and what I can only assume is my own voice moaning in agony. My body goes limp. Feet shuffle around me. I hear the sounds, and the whispers, but nothing more. I can't understand any words. I can't see faces. I see only darkness, hear only whispers. They're frightening me now, the whispers, and I try to hide but my body won't move. They're after me. They want to kill me.

They want to eat me.

Soon, though, the voices, whispers, shuffling feet, all become muffled. Then, they disappear.

I am now in total silent darkness.

Part Five

✦━━◆━━ ✦ ━━◆━━✦

CARPATHIANS

I've never seen Riley like this. I was so little when she was messed up before, I remember almost nothing. I do remember my mom crying a lot, and Riley stumbling in at four in the morning, high as a kite. What I recall most is how she changed her life. Now? To see her like this again? It makes my stomach hurt to watch her. She's like a wild animal, and she recognizes none of us. And to know it's nothing as simple as crack or cocaine scares the hell out of me. She's turning. My big sister, who's always taken care of me, is in the throes of a dual-venomed quickening. I might not be so worried if Preacher and Mr. Dupré weren't so worried. But they are. So, I am. I can only pray what we're doing to her works. It's tortuous to watch—way worse than Da Isle and Gullah cleansing. I feel helpless. I . . . love my sister more than anything. I want her back. And I'll do anything to get that.

—Seth Poe

The voices. They're back. So I'm not dead after all. Or, maybe I am and this is what Hell is like at first. A load of weird scary shit to make you really think hard about what you did to land yourself a place here. That's the thing. I don't know.

I try to move; my arms and legs are tethered. I try to

crack open my eyes, but still I see nothing but darkness. Yet . . . I feel movement. Hear whispers. Air brushes my cheek and I feel a presence close.

"Riley," a deep, slightly accented voice says in my ear. "Can you hear me?"

I'm not sure if I'm who they think I am, but I try to respond. My mouth is frozen, lips won't move. I try to scream. Nothing comes out.

"Shhh, *chère*," the voice says, and I feel a lukewarm hand brush my forehead. "Be still. It won't be long. I'm right here and I'm not leaving."

The surrounding noises infiltrate my brain, and I detect a low, constant humming. Almost a whistle at times. I stop fighting, stop trying to see, and just fall back into the shadows.

I awaken to a jerking motion. This time, even for only a few seconds, I can see. I'm riding in something. A car? A train? Feels more like a train, and I can hear that constant clack-clack of the tracks. Where the hell am I? I stretch my eyes open farther, and I can barely see out of the window next to me. It's light outside. Foggy. And just as I look, we disappear into a tunnel bored straight into the mountain. Then, it's dark again, exhaustion overwhelms me, and I drift back to sleep with the clack-clack of the train as a lullaby.

*　　*　　*

When next I awaken, I know nothing except pain. Pain and starvation. Why won't someone feed me? I want to cry, and no tears will come. Fury overcomes me, and I gather what little energy I have to thrash against bonds still holding me prisoner. I don't know how long I fight, but it feels like a long damn time. Hands hold me down. Then, a scent washes over me. Exotic. Sensual. Seductive. I feel the fight leave me in hopes of replacing it with whatever accompanies the intoxicating scent. Eventually, though, I tire. I give up. The scent disappears as fast as it came upon me.

More whispers. One voice in particular whispers close to my ear in a language I don't understand. This one, whoever he is, is pulseless. And he never leaves my side. Always there, always touching. Then, as suddenly as I had awakened, I fall back into a deep, deep sleep.

"Jake, hold her steady," the accented voice commands.

"Damn me, but I am," someone responds. "She's like a rabid fecking dog."

"Eli, move over," another male voice says. "I got this."

"Hell no, Miles," the accented voice says. "You keep that shit to yourself."

Male laughter. "It's either me or Victorian. Which do you prefer, Eli?"

"Neither," he responds.

More male laughter.

"You boys mustn't horse around so," an elderly voice, also accented, commands. "That's the only bit of Preacher's herbs we have left."

"Well, she needed more than I thought she would, Papa," another replies.

"My father has called," yet another voice offers. "He wishes us to gather in the library."

"You don't have a padded room or something?" another adds. "She's going to go buck-fuck wild when we turn her loose."

"We'll see about that," another says. "She can't be all that strong."

More male laughter.

Energy courses through me now, and I'm angry. Pissed. Three males, all pulseless, surround me in some room I don't recognize. I've got to get out. Get away.

I lunge at the one closest to me and wrap my legs around his neck. We fall to the floor.

"Goddamn!" he mutters, and I twist around his body. In a half second I have him pinned, and just as I'm ready to strike, I'm knocked backward. I land on my feet, dazed for only a second. I lower, crouch, and eye my next target. He's closest to the window.

I'll go out of it if I have to.

"Eli, she's going for the window," one wisely notices.

I'm already moving. I fake left, bound off first a wooden bench, then the wall, use one male's chest as leverage and I push off, landing square on the sill in a crouch. I turn, glaring at my captors, daring them to come near me. The one I just pushed off of is just now picking himself up off the floor. I'm barely out of breath. One is moving toward me slowly.

"Noah," one says. "Watch your back. She's ready to pounce."

I seek him out. He grins. "I'm ready for it," he says. Cocky bastard.

Oh, hell no, he isn't. In one jerky motion I'm at him, legs wrapped around his waist, his neck in a choke hold.

"Fuck!" he yells, and tries to shake me off. I hold tighter. His arm reaches up to grab me, and I land two punches on his jaw. One more in his eye. All under three seconds. So fast he doesn't have time to react until I'm already finished. I pull my strength and use his body to push off of. I'm back on the window sill, glaring. *Daring*.

"Look at her eyes," another says. "Almost white."

"Bad juju right there," the grinning one says. "I mean *bad*. She's strong as shit." He's rubbing his jaw, smiling at me.

"She needs to be fed," one replies, and his gaze hasn't left mine the whole time. "Arcos? You taking care of that?"

"Already done," he answers. "Hurry."

I wait no longer. In the next breath I leap upward with all my strength, grasping one long rafter with my fingertips. It's enough. I pull myself up, then crouch and ease to the far corner of the room, high above all the others.

"Oh, shit," one says. "I told you this was a bad idea."

"How the hell are we going to get her down?" another asks.

"We wait," the one who constantly stares says. "She'll tire. She'll get hungry. She'll come down."

I peer at all of them from my corner rafter, high above the floor. I'm in the dark, swamped by shadows, but they all can see me perfectly clear. I grasp my beam and hold tight. I sit. I stare. I wait.

"Here. Sit up and drink this. You'll feel better."

My eyes crack open, and light pours in. Someone must have pulled me off the rafters. My body aches, and I feel beaten. I squint, blink rapidly, and allow the pulseless male to cradle my head. Something firm nudges my lips, the scent of nutrients stings my nostrils and I open my mouth like a baby bird awaiting a worm. Warm liquid drizzles down my throat. In seconds, I do feel better. No energy, but at least that roaring, fiery pain has disappeared. I drink for a while. Minutes. Finally finished, I drift. Again, I sleep.

"Wake her, Noah," an elderly accented voice commands.

"All right," he drawls. "Someone hold this for me."

"I hate this," a now familiar voice mutters.

I am awake. I'm just so drowsy I keep my eyes closed. I hear the voices around me. Suddenly, though, I get a whiff of . . . something. Then, it disappears. Then . . . an erotic feeling crashes over me and my eyes pop wide open. I stare into the painfully beautiful face of the same man whose ass I whipped the last time. Now, though, I don't want to fight. I grasp him around the neck, pull his mouth to mine, and kiss him. Hard. He kisses me back, but I barely notice because my fingers are searching for an edge of cloth—his clothes—to yank off. I can't get enough of him. I find skin. Stomach. Rigid muscles. I grope. He moans. I moan—

"Noah!" the familiar voice warns. I barely hear him, so engaged in disrobing whoever was driving me sexually insane. Just the feel of his tongue against mine nearly makes me orgasm.

"Bind her now," an elderly voice says. "Bring her to me."

With my mouth still latched on to my new obsession, my hands are pulled behind me and tethered. My feet are bound. I don't care. Only when the male I'm sucking on is pulled from me do I become alert. I blink several times, shake my head, and look around. I am put in a straight-backed chair. I watch closely.

I'm in a room. A strange, large, empty room. Windowless. And in it are six males. All pulseless. There's only one heartbeat within, and it's mine. So sluggish, it barely thumps five times per minute.

Two elderly males stand close, facing one another.

"Gilles Dupré," one says. "We've but one choice to right this matter."

The one called Gilles nods. "*Oui*, Julian. You are unfortunately correct." He glances at me. "There is no other way?"

The one called Julian shakes his head. He has long, straight silver hair pulled into a silver clip. "No. A force stronger than Valerian's must enter her, and the only force stronger than his venom is mine." His gaze passes over me, then over the others before returning to the one called Gilles. "In return for my aid, I require the return of my eldest son, Valerian." He looks at one of the males in particular. "Unharmed and intact."

"He needs to be punished for his actions," that one called Eli demands vehemently. "He cannot simply go free."

Julian nods. "Of course. And we shall see justice

served. Through our counsel, punishment will occur." He again looks at Gilles. "Agreed?"

Gilles glances at the others, then back to Julian. "No harm will come to this girl?"

Julian gives a slight nod. "I vow it."

Gilles nods. "Very well, then."

Julian meets the gaze of one of the males—dark, tall, young. "Victorian?"

"Yes, Father," he answers.

In my next breath I am leapt upon by the male Julian. His face is clear before me, contorted, gruesome, his eyes white, the pupils red and pinpoint. Long, jagged fangs drop from his top jaw, and immediately he sinks them into my throat. Cradling my head so I can't move, he sucks. Fire shoots through my arteries, travels my body and jumps track, then courses through my veins. I thrash against him, but it's useless. Inside, I'm on fire. Literally.

"Non!" the familiar accented voice belonging to the one called Eli shouts, and his voice is angered now, almost a growl. I see nothing. I hear commotion.

"Hold him," the one called Gilles orders. "Hold him tightly."

"Let her go!" Eli shouts. "I will kill you right here!"

Pain tears through me as needle-sharp fangs remain buried deep into my throat, suckling my life force. I'm hot, on fire, and my body begins to seize.

Then it's over. The fangs are withdrawn. My head is now free and falls forward as the one called Julian releases me. I am weakened now, and haven't the strength to raise my head. I gasp for air as intense agony courses through me. Tears spill over my lids and run down my cheeks. I watch them splatter onto the wood floor beneath me.

"Andorra, Miles," a growl says menacingly, evenly. It's the one called Eli again. "Let me go. *Now*."

"Jake, Noah, free him," another says.

Then, in less than a second, he's here, beside me. The familiar one. Holding my head up and cradling it in a much different way from the other one. I feel his body shaking as he holds me to him. I want to thrash out, fight him, but I can't. Part of me doesn't want to anyway, and I don't understand why. I'm motionless, with no energy. Helpless. That, I hate. *Loathe*.

"Shh," he whispers. Then, with his mouth to my ear, "*Soyez toujours. Ce sera pas mal, l'amour.*"

I've no idea what he's said to me, but it's soothing, and somehow it calms me.

Even if only for a moment.

The commotion that follows is too much for my comprehension. The familiar one moves, lightning-fast, and lunges toward the one that bit me. Before he reaches him, though, three others jump him. He struggles. Swears violently. Thrashes.

Then, he changes.

I'm beginning to blank out, my vision is blurry, but yet I can see him. He's as frightening as the old one, with long jagged fangs and a distorted face.

"Why, Arcos?" he yells at the old one. "Why!" He continues to push against the three holding him secure.

The old one shrugs. "'Twas faster," he says. "All is well and done. The only way she'll ever be able to maintain control of her indistinct DNA and to ward off my elder son's venom is to add mine. It is done. But," he continues, "you must all remain here, at Castle Arcos, until the time of the quickening passes for her. She will be in a most weakened and vulnerable state, followed by"—he chuckles—"let us just say she will be very difficult to handle while her DNA is changing."

"I can handle her," the familiar one named Eli says with ferocity.

Again, the old one laughs. "Oh, my fierce Dupré," he says. "I think not. Whilst she will not become vampiric, she will in fact have the venom of three powerful strigoi brethren circulating within her body. She'll be as close to being a vampire as a human can be. Yet, in the end, it will be her only rescue. She'll need it to ward off the cravings placed there by Valerian."

"There are other ways!" the familiar one shouts. He tries to lunge once more but is restrained. He is so enraged, his voice doesn't sound like his own.

"*Mon fils,*" the other elder says, his voice stern, calm. He lays a hand on his son's forearm. "Let us leave for now. Julian," he addresses the old one, "*merci beaucoup.*"

The old one gives a slight nod, accompanied by a chilling smile. He looks dead at me, wipes a drop of my blood from his lip, and licks it off. "My pleasure, Monsieur Dupré."

Then, another is beside me. This one familiar also, yet still, unknown. "I'm so sorry, Riley," he whispers. "Truly."

"Get away from her," the other, Eli, demands. The warning is clear, even to me as I begin to drift.

All at once, my body shudders, the angered familiar one is there, suddenly, holding me close, and I succumb to blessed darkness once more.

"Riley, Riley, shh . . ." a voice soothes, consoles. Is it that one called Eli? It sounds like him. Why is he so concerned about me? "I'm here," he says.

A cold, wet cloth mops my forehead, my cheeks, my throat. A fiery fever ravages my body from the inside out, and I can't stop the violent tremors. My skin is so hot, it burns like the worst case of sun poisoning. Baked, white skin on a cloudless, treeless, windless August dog day of summer in the South. Water. I want water.

No. I want something else.

"Here, here, *chère*," he croons, and places something to my lips. At first, just a drizzle slips down my throat. But the moment my taste buds register to my brain what it is, I guzzle. Gorge. With my arms, I'm reaching, clutching out to *him* and holding on while he feeds me. It's warm, thick, and it soothes my burn like some internal balm. I don't know what it is, but my body likes it, demands more of it.

But after a few minutes, he takes it away. I scramble and grab, but he's fast. I know his name is Eli, and his voice continues to feel familiar to me, but I don't know who he is. Yet I'm getting used to him. He may be the one keeping me restrained, but he's also the one who gives me what I need.

"More later. For now, rest," he says.

I rest. Until, the pain awakes me. Fire. Scalding lava instead of blood coursing my veins and arteries. It feels like my skin is peeling off, and I writhe in agony. My voice, screaming in anguish, sounds disembodied. I scratch, claw at what skin I can reach. My hands, my arms are bound, and I feel like my muscles are coming apart.

"Can't you do anything for her?" he yells. I feel his hands, a cold, wet cloth, on my body. "Papa? Please!"

"*Non*," an elder voice says calmly. "It must run its course, as you know. She is strong and will survive."

A wave of convulsions shakes me until blackness engulfs my mind.

I awaken, huddled in a darkened corner. I've no idea where I am, how much time has passed since that pulseless elder sank his fangs into my throat. I only know that this place surrounding me is cold, damp, and pitch black. There's a musty odor hanging in the air. I sense . . . beings close by. They're calling out *Riley! Riley!* That's not me. Riley is a human name. I'm . . . something different. I've got to escape. Get away. Run. Waiting for silence, it arrives. I slip from my hiding place, check the corridor to find it empty, and ease out.

It's a long hall. Wall sconces adorn the stone walls, and amber light falls over a narrow strip of carpeted walkway. I follow it to the end, where a winding iron staircase leads upward. I can mount the steps and take the twirling stairs two at a time. If I can make it outside, I'm gone. Almost there . . .

No sooner do my feet hit the first step than a body crashes into me, then pulls me back. We land on the corridor floor. Finding my footing, I'm up, turning, backing away, and my vision falls on another. Pulseless. Beautiful. And a wicked gleam lights up a mercury pair of eyes. His mouth tips up at the corner. Challenging.

Steeling myself, I lunge, slide, sweeping his legs out

from under him. He falls onto his back. Just as fast, he's up and springing at me. I leap and fall onto his back, my legs locked around his waist, my arm forcing his head into a choke hold. He backs and plows me against the stone wall. Back, back, he slams me, over and over, but I hold tightly. I'm trying to rip his head off. The goddamned thing won't budge.

"Riley, it's Noah. Get off me!" he yells.

Voices fill the corridor and I turn and glimpse three others running toward us. I turn Noah loose and land in a run, heading for the spiral steps. I'm up them in five seconds and onto the roof.

"She nearly took my fucking head," I hear one say.

"Goddamn, Noah," another exclaims. "Goddamn."

Outside, I'm free. There is a multitude of reddish steeples and turret roofs. This place . . . it's on a rocky hilltop, surrounded by thick forest. A soupy mist hangs over the estate, slips through the trees. That's where I have to go. The woods. There, I can escape. Disappear into the fog. I run along a narrow path with a short wall that barely comes to my waist. They're behind me. All of them.

Reaching the far corner, I don't hesitate. I clear the edge, slipping over and down the sun-bleached white stone and mortar. Digging my fingers into the surface, I find pigeonholes that keep me from falling. The last thirty feet or so, I drop, land in a crouch, scan my surroundings, then take off. Already, the mist envelops me. They'll not find me—

My body hurls through the air and lands with another atop me.

"Riley, 'tis Victorian," he says. "Stop fighting!" He holds me still, tries to pull my arms behind my back but I buck him off. I blindly leap and hit a rough, wooden base. A tree. I don't even look; I begin to climb.

"Riley, come down from there!" he calls after me.

I ignore. I don't look down until I'm far up. Clinging to a thick branch, I glance to the ground. Tall, beautiful, with long brown hair pulled back, the pulseless one stares up at me. Then, he shakes his head, mutters something unintelligible, and throws himself at the tree. He's climbing. Toward me. Fast.

I leap several trees before dropping to the ground at a dead-run. The mist is thicker now, and I can barely see my hand in front of me. The voices behind me are growing faint; I'm getting away. Free at last. I run faster, weaving through the dense wood. It's a blind run now as the fog is so soupy, I can only see the almost-black trunks of trees as I move. My insides are buzzing; adrenaline fires through my bloodstream and I'm almost hyper. The noises and sounds of the wood increase in pitch and all at once. It's so discombobulated, it makes me dizzy. I try to tune it out, but it doesn't work. Only gets louder—

A body slams into me and we both go down. He's strong, this pulseless one, and he holds his hand over my mouth. His entire body covers mine, holding me with his legs like a vise. "Be still if you want your freedom," he warns. "And do as I say."

I go dead-still. I don't trust him. I buck—hard. His body shifts and it's just enough for me to writhe out from beneath him. He's strong, but so am I.

Just as I escape, my ankle is grabbed and down I go. I scramble, arms and fingers clawing and digging into the bracken of the forest floor. I see nothing but white as the mist slips between us, and frantically I try to pry the hand grasping my ankle loose. I kick with my other foot. I'm released for about a half second, and again I scramble. Grabbed again and dragged across the damp leaves and dirt. My arms are yanked behind me and bound. As I'm forced to stand, I growl. My skin feels flushed with fire as I'm jerked around to face my captor.

It's him. The familiar one. The glare I give him almost hurts my face, it's so severe.

"You can give me da plat-eye later, Poe," he grumbles, then ducks, dumps me over his shoulder, and puts one arm across the back of my calves. The other is firmly holding my ass. "Let's go."

It's the voice of the one called Eli, but what's da plat-eye? He'd said it in a strange accent, not his own. What the hell is going on?

He runs with me. I struggle, but it's no use. Deeper into the misty wood we go, until the trees and fog blur together. Suddenly, I feel queasy, and it's then he stops running. We're at a building of sorts, and we enter through a door. Inside it's dark and old smelling. The door slams shut and is locked.

"You'll be safe here," he says, and sets me down. The moment my feet hit the floor, the pain starts. I crumple. Fire shoots through me, and my body seizes.

"Riley, shhh," he says in a low voice. "It will soon pass."

Nothing's passing. Pain rips through me, setting my insides writhing in agony. The scream I hear is mine, but I barely recognize it. Soon, blackness washes over me.

Even though my body is relaxed now, I'm not in control. I'm drained again, listless. I've no energy, not even to weep. I can barely open my eyes, even a fraction, but I force myself to. He's beside me. I'm sure he's never left. The room is hazy, cavernous, and cool. A soft, yellowish light falls over a hearth, a wardrobe, a single chair, a chest of sorts.

"Riley," he says softly.

He calls me that frequently. I'm not sure if that's just what he's named me, or if it really is my name. I can't remember. All I know is I can't even move my head to look at him.

His hands move over my body—my wrists, my ankles—and his fingers move over the skin where tethers once bound me. I want to lunge, escape, but I can't move. I'm barely breathing. Somehow, in my distorted thoughts, I find that better than the pain. Perhaps I'm slowly dying? Might be best.

He grows near, gathers my body to his. I feel his embrace encircle me, and for the first time I notice his scent. Intoxicating. It hurts to breathe in deeply, so I allow my shallow breath to take it in. I close my eyes.

In the next instant, his mouth is at my ear.

"Je suis désolé, mon amour." I don't understand the words, but his tone is . . . regretful. Saddened, perhaps. His breath fans over my throat, his lips caressing my skin. *"Mais il n'y a nulle autre voie. Il fera seulement mal un moment . . ."*

The sound of his voice, the tone of his unusual accent, comforts me. I relax, draw in a breath—then it catches in my throat as something razor sharp pierces my throat. My artery is punctured. I know this because I feel it pop. His mouth is against me there.

I'm paralyzed at first; my body stretches, arcs, then goes completely rigid. The pain is so intense, nausea again sweeps me, and then the uncontrollable shaking begins. I feel tethered once more, unable to move. My breathing is fast, shallow. Soon, I pass out.

"Riley?"

The feel of knuckles caressing my cheek, along with the voice, awakens me. My eyes flutter open, and I turn toward the one sitting beside me. At first, my vision is blurry. Blinking furiously, it clears. I see him.

"Eli?" I say. My voice is cracked, deep, and gravelly. "What happened? I feel like I've been hit by a truck."

With one hand, Eli smoothes the hair back from my face and caresses my cheek with his knuckles. Cerulean blue eyes fasten on to mine, and he smiles. *"Ma chère,"* he says softly. Somehow, it sounds different than usual. It has more . . . feeling.

With effort, I turn my head and glance around the room. The walls are stone. I'm in a large bed; a hearth sits on the far wall across from me. There is one window. Dark beamed rafters are overhead. "Where are we?" I say, then reaching up, I touch my neck. It feels stiff, as though I'd been craning, or straining. No, it hurts deeper than muscle. "Damn, my throat hurts."

Eli reaches, grasps my hand, and laces our fingers together. He leans closer. "Riley," he says, his expression grave. "What's the last thing you remember?"

I don't like his intensity. Not now. Something's up. "What?"

He shakes his head. "Don't try to analyze anything right now. Not this time, Riley. Just tell me," he says again, and squeezes my hand. His lukewarm skin comforts me. "The very last thing you remember."

Despite my irritation at Eli's odd demand, I search my brain, and I think really, really hard. What in hell *is* the last thing I remember? I stare at some random point on the wall across the room. "I remember feeling . . . angry," I say. "I don't know why, but I was. Angry at everyone." I turn my head to him. "Including you."

He stares at me. "What else?"

"Why does it matter?"

"What else, Riley?" he insists.

I take a deep breath and think some more. Then I remember. I push myself up by my elbows, fear gripping me. "Oh my God. Bhing, from next door." I look at Eli. "She was attacked by a vampire, I'm pretty sure. I . . . fought it. She ran off."

Eli's eyes watch me closely. He doesn't blink. He doesn't move. "Riley," he says slowly. "That happened weeks ago."

Ice grips my insides. I look at him like he's lost his mind. "That's impossible."

"You know it's not."

My mind rushes in furious circles as I try my best to recall something. I squeeze my eyes tightly shut. Nothing comes. Only that of Bhing in the alley.

"You've been experiencing a quickening. You've been"—his gaze doesn't waver—"changing."

Even opening my eyes and looking into Eli's doesn't soothe me. I don't even have to ask *what into*. I immediately know.

"My quickening. Was it worse than my cleansing at Da Island?" I ask. That had been pretty intense. I remember most of it, and it included Preacher's root doctor herb and potions, being tied down, night sweats, and a lot of pain.

"Yes."

I lie back down and stare at the ceiling. "What the hell?" I ask out loud.

"The strigoi venom—Valerian's in particular—was taking over you," Eli explains. "It began . . . morphing. Changing. I didn't realize how severe."

I turn my gaze to him. "How severe?" It now dawns on me, and my insides freeze. "Oh, Christ—did I kill someone? How's Seth? Nyxinnia? Preacher and Estelle?"

"They're all fine, Riley."

I don't like the unanswered tone in his voice. "Who isn't fine, Eli?"

He only stares at me.

"Eli!" I yell. "Please!"

"We're unsure," he answers, just as calm as I am anxious. "A young Gullah girl was killed. But we'll worry

162

about that later. We knew we couldn't risk any more time."

As his words settle uncomfortably into my brain, my gaze scans the room. Where am I? Old. Stone. Not Inksomnia, not Preacher's, and not the House of Dupré. I look at him. "What did you do, Eli?"

His hard stare fixes to mine. "The only thing I could do, Riley." He goes through the motion of taking a deep breath. "We brought you to Castle Arcos. We're in Kudszir, Romania, Riley, with Victorian's father, Julian. You've been here almost three weeks. My father, myself, Noah, Jake Andorra, and Victorian have been here as well."

Jake Andorra? Why would he be here? I've never even met the guy. I only stayed at his house in Charleston when we fought Valerian's vampire fight clubs a little while back. I lay my palm against my forehead. "This can't be happening."

"There's more."

With my hand still fused to my head, I look at him. A bad feeling pits my stomach. "What? What else can there be? Where's my brother?"

Eli edges closer. "Seth is safe. He's at home with my mother and sister. Listen, Riley. Look at me." I do. "In order to balance the strigoi DNA in your system, Julian had to inject his venom. It was the only way to give you control over Valerian's urges."

I blink. "How did Julian . . . inject his venom?"

Rising from the bed, Eli walks to the fireless hearth. He runs his hand over the back of his neck. "The same way I did."

The moment the words are out of his mouth, I freeze. My insides grow numb, and mindlessly, my hand reaches for my throat. No freaking wonder it's so sore. "You *bit* me, Eli?" I ask. Shock beats through me. Confusion makes my head spin.

In the next breath, he stands beside me, and he lifts my chin, forcing me to look at him. His gaze, harsh and desperate at the same time, may have at one time scared me. "It was the only way," he says, his voice low, unsteady, as though he were about to totally lose it. "I couldn't stand the thought of all those Arcoses binding with your DNA." He drops his hands from my face, squeezes his eyes shut, lowers his head, and gathers his control. When he lifts his head, and those blue eyes stare into mine, I can plainly see he has gained it again. "I wanted you to have *my* DNA, Riley. *Dupré*. Not just Arcos." His French accent thickens with his last words.

A mixture of emotions crowd me at once, and I slowly stand. Part of me—a big part—understands Eli's actions. He didn't want three powerful and deadly strigois' DNA binding with mine. *I get it.* But the other part of me is pissed *off*. I know I was incapacitated, unable to make rational decisions. I know that. But still. Somehow, I feel . . . violated. Like I am nothing more than a beat-up doll thrown into the midst of four vampires who all take turns at me. Each trying to claim me. Well, I'm not anyone's bitch. I'm not available to *be* claimed. "What part of me left is actually *me*, Eli?" I ask, and I look at him. "Any of it?" I thump my chest. "Is there anything left of Riley Poe inside? Or am I just some fucked-up mutated human with vampire tendencies?" Anxiety and irritation claw at me. I pace. The need to run takes over. Eli senses it.

"Riley," he says, stilling me with one hand against my shoulder. "Stop."

"No!" I reply. I'm angry. Hurt. Confused. "I need to talk to Seth. To Nyx. I . . . gotta be alone for a while, Eli. Think things through."

"*Non.*"

I meet his look with silence. "Don't follow me. You know I will outrun you."

Eli's eyes are hard, face determined. His grip tightens around my forearm. "Don't do this, Riley. You're not in Savannah."

I give Eli one last look that hopefully conveys the message that I need to be alone. After several seconds, his hand drops from me. I turn, search the floor for shoes that look like mine, find a pair of worn brown hikers and pull them onto my bare feet. I head for the door in a house unfamiliar to me, and run.

Far into the wood I go, beneath a misty canopy of tall aged trees and atop thick bracken. Twice I look over my shoulder. Eli hasn't followed. Finally, I slow to a trot, then, I walk.

For the first time, I notice what I'm wearing: jeans, a tank covered by a long-sleeved button-up shirt. I'm hardly ever cold anymore, but Romania seems a little different from home. I notice a biting cold wind whipping through the trees. It rustles an array of various colors above me. Some fall to the ground. Is it October? November? I don't even know anymore. So consumed am I with the new knowledge of just what I have become, I barely notice my unique surroundings. The cold. The leaves. I don't care.

"You're deep in the Carpathians, love," Victorian's voice pushes through my mind. *"My home."*

I quickly look around, my gaze darting through the brush, along the beaten path through the bracken. No sign of Vic. *"Yeah, I can see that,"* I say. *"Did you help bring me here?"*

He sighs. *"Yes. 'Twas for your own good, I'm afraid. Like I said in Atlanta—my father is the only one strong enough to overpower Valerian's forces growing inside of you. Had he not intervened, you would have surely turned. Already you were experiencing a fierce quickening, Riley Poe. You nearly ripped the jet apart. Dupré had a difficult time containing you.*"

"*I hope so,*" I answer, and continue to walk. Past a large boulder, with several scattered rocks beside it, I meander along a path well worn by others before me. "*Where are you?*"

"Here."

Startled, I jerk my head behind me. Victorian Arcos steps from behind an aged fir tree. I don't know why, but for some reason, the sight of him comforts me. Yeah, it bothers me that I feel that way—that I ran from Eli, but am comforted by the sight of Victorian. I can't explain, so I won't even try. Not even to myself. Not now.

"Hey," I say, and move toward him.

He gives a slight nod. "It's good to see you . . . sane." He smiles.

I give a slight chuckle. "Not so sure about that, Vic." I look at him. "You following me?"

His smile lingers. "Of course." He cocks his head and studies me. "How are you feeling?"

Turning, I shrug and begin to wander down the path. Something, and I don't know what, warned me not to tell Victorian about the newly added Dupré ingredient to my DNA. "How would you feel?" I respond.

With a long stare, he finally nods. "So right, so right. My father . . . he can be quite, well, abrupt."

"Hmm," I say, and continue on. "I can hardly wait to meet him."

In the next natural blink of my eyes, Victorian closes the distance between us and rounds on me. His hand on my shoulder stills me. "I would have never let him harm you," he says, determination tightening his words. "Never."

As I look into his unusual chocolate eyes, I see it. "I know that."

With a single nod, he turns me loose. We continue on in silence.

After a while, the dense wood thins, and a small, ancient-looking village lies ahead in the mist.

"The belfry at the citadel has the most stunning view of all Transylvania over the village and back up to Castle Arcos. Would you like to see?"

Sliding Victorian a gaze, I smile. Then I laugh. "Are you freaking kidding me?"

Victorian stares, confusion making his eyes question.

"We're in Transylvania. A family of vampires?" I encourage.

Victorian grins.

"And you're my tour guide now?" I say.

If a vampire could blush, it'd be Victorian Arcos who could pull it off. He smiles. "Of course. And, of course."

Now that I take a closer look at everything around me—the ancient medieval village, the cobbled streets, the colorful buildings, the old-as-dirt-church and the castle? It totally reminds me of a scene out of *Van Helsing*. Any minute I expect Drac's brides to come flying over the belfry to swoop down and nab some dinner from a hapless villager.

"We never feed from our own villagers," Victorian offers.

I snap my head toward him. "I thought you couldn't hear my thoughts."

He blinks, stares at me, and smiles. "Well, I just heard you clear as a bell. It must be your new metabolic changes that have given me the communication back. Sweet."

"Sweet?" I ask at his use of modern slang. Then I chuckle. Vic makes me laugh.

Just then, the bell in the church tower tolls. It sounds positively spooky.

As we descend from the forest and onto the path leading into the village, I notice my surroundings. Breathtaking hardly describes them.

"It's true," Victorian offers. "Our land is second to no other." With an elegant sweep of his arm, he describes the view. "We're surrounded on three sides by the Carpathians," he says in his unique accent, and as I look, I see it's true. Rigid pikes, most with snowcaps, form an almost complete circle in the distance. "Reminds me a little of the Rockies," I answer. When I notice Victorian looking at me, I explain. "Big ink conference in Denver."

"Well, very much like your Rockies, there are large animals in the wood," he says. "You need to take caution, Riley, when taking off alone."

"What kind of animals?" I ask.

"Bear. Lynx"—he meets my gaze—"wolf."

"Warning heeded," I respond. Suddenly, my brother crosses my mind. Then I look at him. "I need a pay phone."

Victorian immediately withdraws a mobile phone from his pocket. As we walk toward the church, he punches in a few numbers, then hands me the cell and guides me to sit on a little stone bench facing the cobbled streets. "Just dial your area code and number. I'll be right back."

I don't even think. I grab the phone and dial Seth's cell. It rings three times before my brother answers.

"Hello?" Seth says.

A whoosh of relief rushes through me at hearing his voice. "Hey, bro. It's Ri."

After a moment of silence, he answers. "Riley?"

I smile. "Yeah. How ya doin', squirt?"

"Riley!" he says excitedly. "I miss you! How—what's going on? Are you okay?"

I laugh at the excitement in my brother's voice. I feel like I'm smiling on the inside. "God, I miss you, little brother. Yes, I'm okay. A little weird, but okay."

"Weirder than before?" he jokes.

"A lot more," I answer. "How's Nyx—"

"What do you mean, a lot more?" he asks. Worry now laces his words.

"It's nothing, Seth," I say, not wanting to stress out my fifteen-year-old worrywart brother. "Nothing I can't handle. Seriously."

"I miss you, Ri," he says, and for a second, sounds like my old baby brother. Before vampires. "When ya comin' home?"

"I'm not sure, but soon," I say. "Nyx?"

"She's fine," he answers. "Luc pretty much stays at the shop with her during the day."

"Good. What else is going on?" I ask.

"It's . . . been busy," he answers. "A lot of activity between here and Charleston. Valerian's gang has been on the move. We've managed to intercept several kills. They're random and unorganized, almost as if some of the newlings have split from Valerian. Noah's guys have been here twice. We've been there three times and headed back tonight."

If Noah's little clan of humans with tendencies have been helping Seth and the others, then Valerian must be out of control.

"How's Preach and Estelle?" I ask.

"Well," he sighs, then continues. "Ever since the Gullah killing, things have been tense. I repapered the entire upstairs of Preacher and Estelle's apartment, and just started on the kitchen. Fresh coat of haint blue on the door and ceiling. And Estelle's been making some stuff that stinks like crazy."

Haint blue paint is a Gullah belief; they use it on doors and ceilings to keep the bad spirits out. Estelle is a superb brewer of root potions, but they stink like hell. And work like hell, too.

I close my eyes briefly. "The killing. Tell me."

"Eli didn't tell you?"

I sigh. "I didn't give him a chance. I ran out as soon as I woke up."

"Woke up from what?" he pushes.

I give up. My baby brother deserved to know. "I had two quickenings to get through. They're all done now, so no worries. Got it?"

"Two?" he asks.

"Yeah. Another Arcos. And a Dupré. I'll explain that one later, so don't ask."

"Did they hurt you, Ri?" he says solemnly.

"No, Seth. I'm fine. Honest." I see Victorian heading

toward me with something in his hand. "About the killing?"

"It's been kept quiet, but I overheard Mrs. D. talking to Mr. D. on the phone about it. We didn't know her, but she was one of the nieces. Seventeen years old. Preacher knows it wasn't the Duprés. Feels sure it wasn't you either, Riley. The attacks haven't stopped though. Seems like someone turns up dead every day, no matter that we run the streets each night. It's almost like the ones we've saved haven't mattered."

"They've mattered, bro. Every single one matters. And Seth, you guys have to check on Bhing," I say. "I think she was attacked. She could be in the quickening."

"Okay. I'll see about it."

Victorian hands me something wrapped in a thick brown paper. "I've gotta go, bro. I love you. Be home soon. And stay safe, okay?"

"I will, and I love you, Ri," he answers. "Be careful. And don't fully put your trust in Victorian. I know he's there, and that he has helped you. But, I don't know. Something about him. I'm not sure I like it."

I smile. "Okay, okay. Got it. Watch your back. And I love you."

"Love you, too."

The click on the line lets me know my little brother has ended the call. I give Vic back his cell.

"Is all well there?" he asks, then sits beside me.

I shrug and peek inside the paper. A fried dough pie of sorts, and it smells like pot roast inside. "Well, my brother's okay." I lift the pie to my nose and sniff, then look at Vic. "But there's a lot of shit going on. Your brother is on a rampage and doesn't seem to have his army under control." My teeth sink into the meat pie, and the moment the spicy flavors hit my tongue, my stomach growls in answer. I had no idea how long it'd been since I'd eaten anything. Normal people food, that is.

Victorian's chocolate brown eyes stay locked on me. "Yes, it's a bad situation there. My brother"—he looks away—"is out of control." He stares off, toward the jagged mountains. "Despite my father's crassness, he is still very much a believer in following the codes of vampires." He looks at me then, eyes hardened. "If caught, Valerian will suffer in ways you can't fathom."

I continue eating, almost to the point of cramming larger bites into my mouth to feed my starving stomach.

"Good, yes?" Vic asks. He nods in the direction he walked from. "Best baker within a hundred miles."

I nod in agreement, thinking he has to be right, and continue devouring. As I chew, I glance out over the small village, and the people moving about the cobbled streets. An old woman—red scarf tied over her hair, a brown dress and brightly colored apron tied over the front, and a woolen sweater, with sturdy, shin-high black boots—hustles across the street with surprising agility. As she passes us, she glances first at me, then at Victorian, and then mumbles under her breath.

"May God walk with me through this dark place, to my house of prayer," she says, quietly but audible. Then she moves fast into the little church and disappears behind a thick wooden door that looks as though it has been around since King Arthur.

"Do many people here speak English?" I ask, and finish my pie.

"She wasn't speaking English."

I swallow and wipe my mouth. "What was she speaking then?"

Victorian grins. "Romanian. Seems like you've picked up a little trait from my father."

"Great," I answer. "Can't wait to see what else pops up." I stand and look around. "All right, Vic. I'm gonna head out." I give him a quick look. "I need a little time alone."

"Wait," Victorian says, and leans close. He lays a hand against my shoulder. "There's something else I should warn you about."

I give him a skeptical look. "What else could there be? That I now have three powerful strigoi bloodlines converging with my own? Yes, I know. Yes, I'll be careful—"

"You may experience things," Victorian says, ignoring my rant. "Out-of-body type of things. You will see more than just through another's eyes," he says seriously. "You'll actually be there. Or so it will seem."

My mind doesn't grasp this at once. "You mean . . . like becoming two people? Me and someone else?"

He shakes his head. "No. Almost like . . . converging with another's soul. You'll be inside of them, hearing, seeing, feeling everything that they do. Only they won't know you're there."

I rub first my eyes, then my forehead. "That's . . . sick. Any way I can avoid it?"

A small smile tips the corner of Victorian's mouth. "Hardly. But you can learn, over time, how to control it. You'll have to. Because although the soul and body you're visiting can't hear or see you, they feel your emotions. Whatever you experience, they experience." He shrugs. "If you're frightened, they're frightened. Heart rate speeds up, breathlessness, adrenaline."

I shake my head. "Why?"

Again, he smiles, and it's more of a regretful type of smile than anything else. "Because it's what the strongest of the strigoi are capable of. They do it on purpose to gain control of their victims."

I think on that for a moment, and then look at Victorian. "Thanks for the heads-up."

He nods. "I will see you later, love. Be careful. And watch for the bears and wolves."

The feeling that I need to heed way more than Romanian carnivores strikes me full force as I take off at a slight jog along the path out of the village.

I run toward the ridgeline of the Carpathians in a hurry.

To what end? I have no freaking idea.

Part Six

NEWBLOOD

I thought Miles was bullshitting me when he told me about Riley Poe. Damn if he wasn't right. I'm not sure I've ever met as strong a woman— human or otherwise—like her. Good thing, too, since most experienced humans with tendencies would have a hard fucking time handling three strigoi bloodlines. Bad thing, though, is she has no idea what's coming. Eli says she can handle it. Noah Miles swears I'll enjoy watching her handle it. Little does Riley Poe know that she's about to merge more into my world than she ever dreamed. I'd be a liar if I said I wasn't looking forward to it.

—Jake Andorra

The one thing that I severely notice as I run is that my heart *maybe* beats about ten times per minute. I'm pretty sure any cardiologist would love to see that in action. I guess I'm lucky the damn thing beats at all.

As I slip into the forest on another worn path leading up and through the dense wood, Victorian's words echo in my head. "*. . . although the soul and body you're visiting can't hear or see you, they feel your emotions. Whatever you experience, they experience.*" I've sort of had that already. Valerian's thoughts and actions were ones I could see, and feel, right after he was released from his tomb and started preying on innocents. I could feel what they felt, see what they saw, but I was me. I tried to warn them, to run, but they couldn't hear anything. I couldn't control them, either. I was an invisible bystander, but I couldn't stay out of the situation. Hopefully, with this, I'll learn. I can't imagine just . . . falling into someone's body. Into their psyche. That's utterly weird.

The dark bracken crackles beneath my booted feet as I run through the wood. I pick up speed—which seems to grow faster than ever with each step. I mean, ridiculously fast. So much that the trees and bushes and rocks blur. My reflexes are lightning fast, and I impress myself by not slamming into even one low-lying limb. I bound off trees and rock, and leap over anything within my path. I feel strong. I feel good. *Fucking good.*

I don't know how long I run, but it's a damn long time. What little light filters through the trees begins to fade; the mist grows thicker. I slow my pace. I'm completely lost and I don't even care because somehow, I'm fearless, even here. I can find my way back. I glance upward, through the canopy of leaves, and watch a crescent moon begin its ascent.

I feel his presence before I see him, so I slow, then stop.

Eli emerges from behind the trunk of an aged fir tree

and I feel the adrenaline surge through me. Just seeing him does that to me, and I can't explain it other than that he makes me *feel*. It seems so long since we've been together, and to myself, I admit: I miss him. Miss the hell out of him, actually. I know that what he did, he did for me. For my benefit alone, not for him or anyone else. No way could I ever stay angry at that, and I'm not so sure why I was so pissed to begin with. No, that's a fat lie. I do know why. Because he freaking bit me. I do understand why, though. I know he did it because he loves me. Deeply. I get that.

As Eli stands, he says nothing. Only stares. And waits. The wood surrounding us is wildly alive, yet acutely silent. Suddenly, his presence overwhelms me. It almost . . . crowds me.

His eyes say everything.

Instinctively, I go to him. As if I'm just laying eyes on him for the very first time, I'm drawn to his scent, his eyes, the shape of his jaw, the fall of his hair. He mesmerizes me, and yet now, I *know* him. I know his behavior. I know what's in the heart he swears he doesn't even have. I know his soul that he swears is hell bound. He's wrong about that. Never have I met a more caring soul. I crave him even more than before.

The moon, rising higher, bathes Eli in a silvery hue, making him look like the surreal, mystical, cryptic vampire he is.

Every bit the fierce and loyal vampire he truly is.

Magnificent.

It makes my heart race.

A biting wind whips through the air, stirring the canopy above, and carrying with it anticipation, excitement, as though the wild Carpathians knew what was up, what was about to occur, and waved their encouragement.

An ancient feel accompanies that wind, and it makes a tingle cross my spine, wrap around each vertebra, and nip. I've gone too long without Eli, without feeling like myself, and although I don't even know who myself is anymore, there is one constant now that feels right. Him. I shiver, and Eli grasps my fingers as though he knows, without words, without being able to read my mind, what I feel. He probably does. Silently, we walk. I'm not sure how long we walk like that, fingers laced, shoulders brushing, but it's a while. How Eli knows where he's going is a mystery to me. I simply trust him and soon, a small stone lodge appears. Smoke trails from a single chimney. It's not the same place he'd taken me to before. Without a word, he leads me up the walk and through the front door. Inside, all is dark except the embers burning red in the hearth.

He retrieves a large quilt thrown over the back of a sofa, and he lays it on the floor in front of the fire. Kneeling there, he grabs a poker and stokes the embers, adds a log until the flame grows. I stand silently, watching the play of light lick his face, his jaw, and throw his eyes in shadow. To me he is the most breathtaking soul I've ever laid eyes on. Then Eli rises and turns. His eyes lock on to mine. We say nothing. Only stare.

Everything freezes in that moment as Eli stands, staring, the light from the fire glinting off his hungry eyes. Ancient eyes that know secrets, have powers, have seen so many things. He could have anything and anyone in the world that he wanted. A rich, high society, untarnished young woman, maybe.

Yet, he chooses to be here, with me. With me and all of my tarnishes.

My pulse quickens, as fast as it will anyway, and blood rushes on powerful thrusts in my veins as I lock eyes with his. Eli's muscular chest rises and falls in a rapid, irregular rhythm, his jaw flexing, making the shadows jump on his face.

"Take off your boots and socks."

I blink. Before, my first reaction to the blatant, male command would have been *go fuck yourself*. Only Eli all but quivers with forced restraint, and he doesn't command me as a domineering barbarian or a mind-controlling vampire, but as a wild, hungry Alpha who's just found a delectable morsel he wishes to savor, make last, instead of gobbling it up.

Without a word, I toe off my boots. Since I have no

socks, I now stand with bare feet on the smooth wood floor.

"Your jeans."

Heat pools in my lower stomach as I unclasp each button, keeping my eyes on Eli's. So erotic a feeling, him watching my fingers work the buttons loose, that when my thumb brushes my panties, just inside the fly, it makes me shudder. I stifle a gasp, and wish it was Eli's hand there instead. Now. Not later.

Eli's nostrils flare.

The last button undone, I ease the material over my hips, the feel of soft worn denim scraping my permanently smooth legs, giving me goose bumps. I drop the jeans to the floor, then step out of them.

"Kick them aside."

I kick them.

"Take off your shirt. Slowly."

With a ragged breath, I unsnap my long-sleeved shirt, pull my arms out, and drop it. Grasping the hem of my tank top I lift it, one inch at a time, over my stomach, ribs, then over my head. I drop it atop my pile of clothes.

For a moment, Eli simply stares. He licks those full, sensual lips, catches the bottom one between his teeth, then swallows.

"Your bra. Don't take it all the way off. Just unclasp it."

I glance down and reach for the clasp.

"Look at me."

Lifting my head, I keep my gaze on Eli's as I finger the small metal clasp between my breasts. My breathing becomes more rapid, watching him stare at me like a ravaged animal, his sexy French accent deepening to a primal, barely controlled tone each time he speaks a command.

Wetness dampens my panties, so turned on am I by Eli's blatant display of desire and control. I throb with need, just below the very thin surface of the silk material covering me. I wait, watch, anticipate. I *want*.

Eli steps closer, then slowly circles me, the air stirring from his body's movement the only part of him touching me. His alluring scent envelops me, drugs me, and I fight to keep my eyes from rolling back in my head with desire. God, I want him *yesterday*.

He leans close and smells me, but keeps moving in a slow, predatory ring, almost as though he was staking his claim, marking his territory, stalking his prey. Then, in a deep, purred whisper, tinged with French, he brushes my ear with his lips.

"Are you wet for me, Riley?"

"Yes," I answer, my breath ragged.

He keeps moving, his boyish fall of dark hair brushing my bare shoulder as he leans close, making me shiver. "It's been a long time, Ri. This time, no interruptions." He stops behind me, his head close to my ear, his whisper a deep purr. Yet we're still not touching, and it sends vibrations of pleasure across my skin. "I'm going to bury myself deep inside of your tight wetness, feel your muscles grip my hard length as you take all of me in," he whispers erotically and licks my lobe, his breath caressing my cheek. "Make me come. But first," he says, his raspy words vibrating against my throat, making me shiver with excitement, "I'm going to make you lose control right where you stand."

Never have I been so worked up, so turned on. Every nerve ending hums with power, ready to un-leash the energy simmering in my veins. So erotic are his words, his voice, his promise, that sexy accent, I have to clench my female muscles to keep from coming right then. I reach for him.

"Don't touch me, Riley. Just *feel*."

He moves behind me, still fully clothed, and brushes my hair to the side. His mouth hovers over my skin, his breath coming in light puffs, and then the wet velvet of his tongue strokes me where his breath has just been. He trails my spine with his lips, his teeth, his tongue making small circles against each vertebra, and I clench my fists, aching to touch him, but I manage con-trol and keep them by my side. Fiery liquid pools be-tween my legs, making me pulsate with desire. "Eli, please . . ."

Finally, he touches me. His hands skim my calves, up my outer thighs, over my hips, inches up my ribs. *Not* the place I want to be touched. I'm nearing the breaking point, and at any second am going to use whatever powers I have to throw his ass on the floor.

"Christ, you're beautiful," he whispers close to my ear, sending another wave of shivers through my taut body. His hands move to my shoulders and push my bra straps down, the soft silk cups catching on my breasts. Slowly, he slides them over the tightened peaks.

His sharp intake of air is a small victory.

I don't know how much more I can take.

I want it to go on forever.

Eli's large hands close over my breasts as his mouth claims that portion where my neck meets my shoulder. His thumbs brush the hardened, sensitive tips, and my head drops back to rest against his chest. A moan escapes me.

He moves his leg between mine. "Settle back against me, Riley."

I'm out of my mind with need right now, and I do exactly what he asks, and the full erection pressing into the small of my back makes me moan again.

His lips scrape my jaw, the rough scruff of his stubbled cheek grazing my skin; then he moves his mouth to my ear. "I want to see how ready you are for me. Can you stand it?"

Between breaths, I shiver and whisper, "Can you?"

A low growl rumbles deep in Eli's throat. "Be still."

Keeping one hand possessively cupped over my breast, Eli slides his other hand over the flat of my stomach, over one hip, then slips under the low waist of my silk panties.

The moment he touches me, an uncontrolled growl of desire tears from my throat.

"Christ, Riley," he says, holding his hand still against my wetness. His whisper turns hoarse. *"Now."* He dips inside of me with one finger, holding me tight against him, and his lips press and suckle against my throat. I suck in a raw breath and hold it, squeeze my eyes shut, and struggle not to explode against Eli's hand.

It doesn't work.

A gradual climax, one pulse at a time, increases with each beat, with each movement of his hand against me, until I turn and press my face against his shoulder as the orgasm claims me. Slowly, it subsides.

Without another word, Eli lifts me and lays me on the quilt before the fire.

Damn it, I didn't want to lose control. I couldn't help it. I wanted the moment to go on forever.

The erotic fire quickly rekindles as I watch Eli strip his clothes away.

He doesn't tease, doesn't do it slow, doesn't put on a show. Centuries-old vampire or not, he's still one hundred percent male, and he yanks his shirt over his head, toes off his boots and socks, unbuttons his jeans, and kicks them off. He's totally bare under the worn denim. My heart leaps.

Bathed in the amber glow of the fire, Eli stands tall, thick, muscular and powerful, worthy of his ancient heritage, of what Fate led him to be, and volts of energy shimmer off his body in sizzling waves. His hair hangs loose and disheveled, making him seem wild, untamed, and I easily drum up a vision of him two hundred years ago, in a white linen shirt with laces at the throat, tight breeches, and high black boots. The beauty of the vision sucks the air from my lungs.

Eli eases down beside me, pulls me close.

"Come here, *chère*."

I inch closer, eyes locked, something more than lust propelling me. Inexplicable. I push it to the far corners of my brain and just accept Eli, the man.

"Look at me."

I do.

"I can't offer you normalcy, Riley Poe." He brushes my cheek with his knuckle. "Things will never be normal for us. But I can offer you whatever soul I have left in me. It's yours. Forever."

I watch the firelight flicker in the depths of his blue eyes. "I know," I answer, and I did know. There was nothing else that could be said. Somehow, we understand each other, and that's all that matters. Now, anyway.

With the pad of his thumb, he traces my lips, hooking the corner, then lowering his mouth to mine, urging it open. Our tongues meet, slow, exploring at first, and then he breaks the kiss, angles my head, and moves his mouth over my throat. Sensations ripple through me. The lack of fear that a vampire hovers over my artery doesn't faze me. Eli's unique taste settles on my tongue, making me crave more.

Eli gives it. He rolls over me, bracing his weight on his elbows. His eyes sear into mine.

"Hold on to me, Riley. Lock your legs around my waist."

As I slide my legs around his waist, he eases into my slick wetness with one swift push, burying himself all the way inside. I gasp, moaning as my feminine muscles stretch and accommodate. I almost come again.

"Put your arms around my neck," he whispers.

When I do, his mouth claims mine, devours me, his tongue tasting every corner. He moves his hips, pulling himself almost all the way out, then thrusting back deep inside. His motions mimic his tongue, both making love, and I hook my ankles around his waist and move with him.

He thrusts faster, once, twice, a third time and I close my eyes as darts of heat flash my skin, and behind my eyes light erupts. Waves of powerful orgasm break over me, my muscles contract, pulse, and squeeze in an unstoppable rush. A moan rips from my throat on a ragged breath.

Eli's body jerks as his own climax convulses him, the muscles in his stomach flexing with each thrust, the vein in his neck thick and protruding. His movements finally slowly ease, and he wraps his arms around me tightly. He kisses my mouth in a slow, erotic movement of possession. He kisses my throat, makes my head tilt back, and he gently licks the small hollow where my pulse beats.

With one hand, Eli palms the back of my head, bringing our mouths a whisper apart. He stares, the firelight licking his skin, and he kisses me deeply, then brushes whispered words against my ear from a language I don't know, words I had no understanding of. I didn't dare ask their meaning.

Suddenly, they register.

I will love you forever.

Slowly, I wrap my arms around Eli and press my body as close to his as I can. I feel every inch of him against me, and there's not an ounce of flesh not claimed by him. Grasping his jaw with my fingers, I pull his head close, my lips to his ear.

"I'll love you forever, too," I whisper back.

When Eli pulls away and looks at me, surprise first

fills his cerulean blue eyes. It's quickly followed by more love than I'd ever hoped to find. One corner of his mouth lifts in the sexiest grin I've ever seen.

Then, he kisses me. I feel every ounce of love in that kiss.

If nothing else stays with me for all of my days, I hope this moment in time does. This kiss. The look in Eli's eyes. God almighty, I pray it does.

For the first time in . . . Jesus, I can't even remember, I fall asleep in Eli's arms.

There is blood. A lot of it. There are screams filled with terror. I feel him, I know who it is without even looking, or without seeing his face. And I know it's me he wants. Somehow, he knows what's inside of me now. Not just his DNA, or his brother's, but . . . more. His desire for me feels sexual, but I know it's way more than that. He not only wants my sex, he wants my soul. Wants my blood. Wants my life.

I remain . . . wherever this place is, and I can feel the pain and terror of those around me. Valerian is torturing them to torture me. He won't stop. He'll never stop.

Unless I stop him.

"Are you awake, *chère*?"

My eyes flutter open. I feel the adrenaline pushing through my veins and the deathly slow beat of my heart.

Then, Eli's face, hovering above mine. Safety. Contentment. Desire. "Yeah, I'm awake." Lifting a hand, I stroke his dark stubble-dusted jaw with my knuckle. "Why? You want something, Dupré?" I smile.

Settling his lips over mine, Eli nudges my mouth with his and kisses me slowly. "Hell yeah, I want something. But so does Julian Arcos." He kisses my nose. "And my father."

"I know why," I say, and move from the quilt. The embers from the night's fire smolder in the hearth. "Valerian. He knows about me. We need to get back home."

"Then let's go," Eli says, and pulls his jeans on.

We hurry, dress, Eli smothers the embers in the fireplace, and we leave the cottage.

"Dupré, Poe," Noah Miles says with his cocky grin and strange mercury eyes. "Nice you could make it."

Eli ignores his friend and moves by him. As I follow to do the same, Noah's eyes lock with mine. The corner of his mouth lifts. "Miss me?" he says.

I jam my elbow in his ribs. "Hardly."

Noah laughs and puts a hand over his heart. "You wound me, Poe."

I shake my head and follow Eli into the foyer. Suddenly he turns, stops, and slips my hand into his. "I forget you were out of it most of the time you were here," he says, glancing down at me. "Stay with me. Closely. And try not to start any fights."

I just stare at him, and he grins and leads me into what is hands down the epitome of what Hollywood would consider Dracula's castle. Dark. Gothic. Ominous. Brass sconces embedded into the stone walls hiss and flicker as we pass, and large tapestries stretch from floor to ceiling. Long beam wooden rafters crisscross overhead, and ornate chandeliers cast a low amber light over the massive room. The fireplace, large enough for three people to stand upright in, takes up one whole wall. A group of people stand there, four men and two women, none of whom I've ever met. We move toward them.

As we near, a big man who seems to be addressing the group turns and faces us. He wears his nearly waist-long black hair straight and pulled into a ponytail. Green eyes meet mine and fasten. I can tell he's weighing me. Probably trying his damnedest to read my freaking mind. Good luck with that, Tonto.

"You've missed a button," he says to me, and inclines his head toward my shirt. I ignore him and meet his stare wordlessly.

He smiles, and I'll admit right here and now: the man is ridiculously sexy.

"Riley, this is Jake Andorra," Eli introduces. "Jake, stop being an ass."

Jake inclines his head. "My apologies," he says without breaking his stare, and I notice he has an odd accent. Not Romanian. Not French. Something else. Something old.

"Pict," he whispers close to my ear. "And Tonto would've never made it out of here alive."

I lift a brow. "Nice. Now stay out of my head."

Chuckles break the silence of the others.

"Jake runs WUP—Worldwide Unexplained Phenomena," Eli explains. "He's not used to being one-upped."

"I'm not yet still," Jake corrects. "Nice to finally meet you, Riley Poe."

"You've got a great house," I say, remembering the beautiful manor home on Charleston's battery. "So what do you want with me?" I ask bluntly. With all the hell going on in Savannah, the last thing I want to do is linger in Drac's castle when I could be on a plane heading home.

"'Tis I who want to meet you," another man with a similar accent says. He approaches and without warning, grasps my hand in a shake. Unlike Eli's lukewarm skin, this man's is warm. "My name is Darius."

And the moment his hand envelops mine, I experience firsthand the powers given to me by Julian Arcos.

My equilibrium tilts, my body goes rigid, and everyone around me fades into shadows . . .

When my vision clears, I'm not alone. I'm not at Castle Arcos. I'm not even me . . .

*   *   *

"Darius? What have we done?"

Gasping for air, Darius fixed his stare on the bloodstained earth he knelt upon. Resting his forearm against the hilt of his sword, he wiped his sweating brow and glanced about. Eleven Celtae druids lay dead, their bodies entangled within their black robes.

"What we had to do," Darius answered. He rose and met the questioning eyes of the younger Druthan. "The dark magick within the Dubh Seiagh is unimaginable. The Celtae used it, Ronan. To allow them to live would mean destruction for us all."

Ronan nodded and wiped a streak of blood from his cheek.

Just then, a sharp gust of wind swept over the moor, stirring the robes of the dead, and a blanket of mist settled over the browned and bloodstained heather. The twilight's dim glow made the desolate moor hazy, and thunder crackled in the distance. Darius glanced up. "We havena much time."

As the wind grew fiercer, the other Druthan warriors gathered, making their way through the fallen Celtae to stand at Darius's side.

Darius met each of his brethren's gazes. "You know what must be done. Four of our future kinsmen will become the immortal Arbitrators. I sacrifice my own bloodline. Who else?"

Three more Druthans raised their hands without hesitation.

"Well done," Darius said.

"What of the Archivist? Whose bloodline will he come from?" asked Ronan.

"None of ours."

The wind screamed then, and Darius quickly muttered the ancient Pict verse that would name the Arbitrators twelve hundred years into the future. And, the Archivist, centuries beyond. By that time, the language of the Dubh Seiagh would be dead and forgotten. Only the Archivist would have the ability to read it. Thus, destroy it. Until then, it would stay forever hidden.

When the last word was spoken, a deathly silence fell over the moor.

It was done.

As the Drutha glanced around, gasps filled the still night air. Darius hurried to the first Celtae body and knelt down.

'Twas as though every ounce of bone and muscle and matter had been sucked out of the Celtae's skin, leaving it a flat and empty sack of cauterized flesh.

Just then a scream, high-pitched and chilling to the bone, ripped over the moor, followed by another, and another, over and over. The wind picked up once again and roared through the air with gale force.

"Darius!" Ronan yelled. "What is this?"

Darius closed his eyes.

They'd killed the Celtae.

But their souls had escaped . . .

Quickly, he mouthed another verse, unrehearsed, un-planned. Desperate.

And prayed with fervor that it worked.

As fast as it occurs, it stops. Only now do I realize the scene lasted only a few seconds—as long as it takes Darius to shake my hand. The second he releases me, the vision disappears. My head is spinning as vertigo grabs me. A small wave of nausea washes over me, and for a minute I think I'm going to barf all over the guy. Surprisingly, after a few deep breaths, it subsides.

I look at him wordlessly. He's tall, muscular, with dark auburn hair pulled back much like Jake's, and disturbing, ancient amber eyes. The vision I'd witnessed was from a long time ago. I'd been nothing more than a fly on the wall, watching.

"What did you see?" he asks quietly.

I look at him. "Everything. You, others, on a windy moor, blood," I say. "You killed the others. You instructed them."

"No, you don't understand." A woman I hadn't noticed before moves closer to me. "There's more to it," she insists.

"Ms. Maspeth," another big guy warns.

"I'm Sydney," she says, looking at me with an almost desperate look. She's blond, pretty, yet . . . harsh at the same time. Sort of like me, I guess. "Please."

Then, she places her hand on my shoulder.

And the whole goddamn thing starts over again.

This time, though, it's different.

I feel myself waver, as though I'm going to fall, but instead of falling straight onto the floor, I just keep falling, falling, until I suddenly stop. A faint light, starting as a pinpoint in the distance and growing larger as it moves toward me, makes my vision go from blurry to clear. When I blink, I'm still me. But I'm somewhere else. I feel . . . enclosed. Trapped. And I'm looking through eyes not my own . . .

Niddry's in Old Town, Edinburgh, has always felt safe to me. Small, dark, and nondescript, it's a pub very few tourists ever venture into. Low-lit alcoves line the ancient stone walls of the building, and Victorian-era lamps, emitting a soft glow, perch on tabletops. It allows me to blend in with the local working class of the city, drink a few pints, to feel somewhat normal for a short period of time.

It allows me, even for just a few moments, to forget.

The glass feels cool against my palms as I lift it to my mouth, and the dark lager slips smoothly down my throat. Draining the glass, I set it down on the chipped mahogany table and glance at the other Niddry's patrons from my alcove. Most I recognize, like the three off-duty cops—two of them brothers— the owner of the chip shop just up the street, and a handful of students from the university. A cab driver—

this one I recognize because I've used his service before—sits at the bar nursing his third whiskey. Two women who work at the Safeway up the street sit together at a table close to the bar, giggling and sharing some inside joke. Normal, everyday folk living their normal, everyday lives.

I stare down at my empty glass, at the impression my lips leave on the rim, and then out the window to the rain-dampened sidewalk. A streetlamp blinks and then turns on. It will be dark soon. The gray will become black.

And these people have no fucking clue what's really out there . . .

"Another pint, miss?"

The bartender, Seth, stands there with a white cloth thrown over his shoulder, smiling. His grin is welcoming, friendly, the dimple in his left cheek giving him a boyish look. He wags his reddish brown brows and widens his smile.

I smile back. "One more, thanks."

He gives a nod, makes his way back to the bar, retrieves another lager, and brings it back. "Here then, lass."

As he makes his way back to his station behind the long, polished mahogany bar, I find myself thinking how lucky the guy is, how lucky they all are, to be so oblivious to what lies beyond the doors of the pub.

Sometimes, I wish I were oblivious, too.

Taking a long pull on the lager, I continue to stare through the window. Despite the cold October rain, passersby scurry up and down the sidewalk, their overcoats swishing around their legs, on their way home from work, probably, or headed to their favorite meeting place with friends to have a few drinks.

I remember similar carefree evenings, when I would meet with friends, or go to my parents' house with my fiancé for dinner, or simply stop by the mall to shop for a new outfit. I never even thought for a second how my life could change so drastically. How I would never see my family again, rely on my mother's comforting hug, fall into my fiancé's easy embrace.

But that sounds selfish, doesn't it? Selfish and childish. Me, me, me.

Strangely enough, I'm really not so bitter anymore. But in the beginning? When everything first happened? Jesus, I was a hateful bitch. I didn't want to accept what had happened to me, or what I was to become.

What I am now.

With my fingertip, I wipe a streak through the moisture gathered on the glass, then I lift it up to drink. Over the rim I see one of the cops looking at me. He gives a smile and a brief nod. He's cute, and there once was a time when I would have indulged in an innocent flirtation. Not anymore. So I meet his gaze for a moment, then look away, back to the outside. The constant drizzle is falling harder now. I think it rains every damn day here.

It's been nearly a year since I came to Edinburgh. God, when I think of who I was before, such a short time ago, it nearly makes me laugh. I am so different now. Before, I was innocent, naïve. Sweet. Fun-loving. Carefree. I baked cakes, for Christ's sake. I don't bake anymore.

Not even a shadow of who I used to be is present now.

I drain my glass and wipe my mouth. It's funny—I can sit here all night and drink as much as I want, and never get drunk. I can smoke two packs of cigarettes a day and I'll never get cancer. I don't gain weight, nor do I lose it. I don't get wrinkles. My hair doesn't grow. I can't catch a cold, the flu, tuberculosis, Ebola—I'm immune to all of it.

Thanks to my destiny, I'm immune to death.

My fate is unchangeable. But mankind's is—and it's up to me to make it happen. So when I have moments of self-pity, like the one I'm having now, I slip over to Niddry's and steal a few moments alone, before Gabriel, my mentor, seeks me out. I . . . reflect. I give myself a scant few moments to mourn my old life, to miss my mom and dad, my sisters, my granny and grandpa. It helps somewhat. Time, Gabriel says, will ease the pain.

I finally stopped crying over my fiancé. For some reason, his love was easier to let go of than it should have been. We were only two months shy of marriage, yet . . . I mourned him very little. I suppose that's a good thing for me. I try not to dwell on that too much, though. I've come to realize that dwelling on the past serves absolutely no useful purpose anyway. I do what I have to do now so that my loved ones can survive. So everyone can survive. It's up to me. Only me.

Well, me and the other four Druthans.

My vision blurs as I stare at the lamppost outside, and at the torrent of rain pouring down. A few more minutes and then I'll go. Until then, I'll catch you up to speed on things, to where my life is now. Maybe, you'll understand.

I'll spare you a long, boring history of me before Scotland. Suffice it to say I was your average American girl. I was born twenty-five years ago to James and Lucinda Maspeth. They named me Sydney Jane, after my mom's grandparents. I grew up on the Outer Banks of North Carolina. I went to UNC, graduated with a B.S. in education, and started teaching first grade in Kitty Hawk. I frequented the spa. I got my nails done every other week.

All that changed one May afternoon when Gabriel—an imposing wall of sheer muscle clothed in head-to-toe black—walked easily into my empty classroom, right up to the desk where I sat grading papers, pulled me out of my chair, looked me dead in the eye, and with a sincere apology, slipped a silver blade into my heart.

I died in his arms.

I awakened sometime later—weeks later, actually—in his bed. He sat in a dark alcove, watching me with those silvery eyes. I'll never forget that first brooding, profound stare. To me it sums up his entire character. Silent power barely checked.

In a matter-of-fact tone, and with a mesmerizing accent, he told me my old life was gone, and that I was now immor-

tal, like him. He told me to rest, that I was still going through the transformation and was very weak. Then he stood, tossed a newspaper on the bed beside me, and left the room without another word.

One thing I learned pretty fast about Gabriel—he speaks very little, but when he does, it's potent.

The newspaper proved to be one from back home in Kitty Hawk. It was the Obituary page, and as I thumbed through it I found my own smiling face staring back at me.

Fishing a few pounds from the pocket above my knee, I put down a tip, nod to Seth who smiles in return, and make my way through the small crowd. The rain is only a drizzle now, and Gabriel is probably waiting for me. At the doorway, I slip my arms into my black trench coat, button it up, and put on a black skully and scarf. Funny. I go from sandals, French manicures, and flowery sundresses to black fatigues, boots, and a trench coat. I look like goddamn Mission: Impossible. My sisters would die laughing.

My granny would wash my mouth out with soap.

I'd give anything to let her.

I step out into the cool night air and start down the sidewalk, and before I can walk ten feet, someone behind me grabs my arm.

"Just a minute, miss."

I turn to find the cute cop. He's medium height and build, with dark, close-clipped hair and wide blue eyes. He gives me a crooked grin. "Sorry. I, uh, well, was wonderin' if you, ya know?" He glances at his feet and mutters, "Shite." He looks me in the eye and smiles again. "I tried to get your attention back there." He inclines his head toward Niddry's. "I'm Sean. I, eh, don't mean to sound so forward, but I noticed"—he gathered courage and met my gaze fully—"well you looked nice to talk to, is all."

I meet his wide blue eyes with my own stare. I never can quite get over how charming the Scottish accent is. Even now, it sucks me right in. Sean's is a bit thicker than the Edinburgh burr. Glasgow, maybe? Nice.

In another life, I would be grinning like a fool and batting my eyelashes. Sean's a good-looking guy, confident, charming. And blessedly ordinary. But I'm no ordinary girl.

Sean can't handle me.

But instead of blowing him off, I stick out my hand. I can't date him, but a friendly face every now and then in Niddry's can't hurt. I smile. "Sydney, and it's nice to meet you."

He smiles and shakes my hand. "Och, an American." He nods toward Niddry's. "Do you care to step back in? I would have come up to you earlier, but I'm a wee bit shy—"

Powerful fingers close around my arm and I immediately know who is there. Sean's gaze rises above my head, directly behind me.

"She's with me," Gabriel's deep voice vibrates above me.

Sean glances at me, almost as if looking for an approval of the possessive grasp the newcomer has on me. I give him a slight smile, he shrugs, and returns the smile. Defeat dims his blue gaze. "Right. See ya then, Sydney." He turns and walks back to Niddry's.

Gabriel turns me around, pulls me close and lowers his mouth to my ear. "You're late." The words brush against my ear and I shiver. He has that ability—to unhinge me—but I'll never let him know it.

With deft fingers he opens my trench coat and eases my blade from his to my hip. Those mercury eyes never leave mine as he fastens the small scabbard holding the Druthan silver to the loops on my pants and closes my coat. "Let's go."

He turns and heads up the sidewalk, and I'm right behind him. Gabriel's posture is guarded, although no one notices but me. I've spent nearly an entire year in his daily company. I know his gestures, his habits, and I know when he is on high alert, when his body is on edge. Like now.

We wind our way through the streets of Old Town. The castle is lit and stands formidable on the rock it was built on. During my training, when I was learning every street, every close, every pub, club, business, and landmark, the castle stood as a focal point, a guide, a beacon. It still does.

And I now know the streets of Edinburgh like the back of my hand.

The Druthan blade brushes against my thigh with each step, and I button just the top of my coat, leaving the last two undone. If I need to withdraw my weapon, it has to be fast. I have to be ready. Always ready . . .

We're on the outskirts of Old Town now, and Gabriel takes a turn left and eases down a set of cracked stone steps, between the tight-knit quarters of Pippin's Close. It's cold, gray, and deserted. Not derelict, just empty. No one lives here now.

No one, except the dead.

I fight a smile as I walk behind Gabriel's big self. He takes up every inch of the close, and has to turn slightly sideways to fit properly. I know that irritates him, too. It makes him feel vulnerable, as if he can't protect me fully, if the need arises. But only I know that.

I hug the wall and continue to follow, through the narrow close and down one more set of steps before coming to a lone door. The thump of a nearby nightclub vibrates on the air, and laughter rings out. But that's coming from several streets over. No one knows I'm here except Gabriel. And no one knows what is about to happen except us. Briefly, I think of Sean, that cute cop from Niddry's. I can't help but wonder what he'd think if he knew.

Gabriel stops just before the door and looks down at me with that ever-present profound stare. His long hair, nearly black, is pulled back at the nape of his neck and damp from rain. A long strand is caught on his cheek, but he ignores it. The light from a streetlamp finds an opening through the close and falls on part of his face, casting the other part in shadow. He is magnificent and immortal, lethal, and so sexually charged that the air hums with it.

No, I'm not used to it yet. Even after a year, I have to check myself. But those are the mannerisms of a Druthan warrior, and it has nothing to do with him being a man and me a woman. He cares for me only because of what I am. He is from a secret sect of ancient Pict druids. There are only three others besides Gabriel.

And they're nearly five hundred years old.

So when I say Gabriel is looking at me with an ancient gleam in his eyes, I really mean it.

His dark brows pull together into a frown. "Finished?"

I shrug. Yeah, he can read thoughts. He doesn't stay in my head twenty-four/seven, but when he thinks I'm straying from task, he'll do it in a heartbeat. Anything to keep me safe. I suppose I should appreciate that. "Yes. Let's go."

I don't even have to ask what's going on. Standing here, beneath the eave of Pippin's Close and by the door of an empty flat, with rain spitting and sputtering against my already damp cheeks, and the cold October air freezing my skin, I know. And if I hadn't known, the nauseating stench from behind the door would be all the warning I'd need.

One of them is in there. And it's feeding.

I slide in front of Gabriel and press my back to his front, and his body goes rigid, still, with just the smallest movement of lung expansion as he breathes. Goddamn, it's hard to concentrate in such an intimate position—

"Steady, lass," he whispers against my ear.

As if that helps the situation.

"*I willna be far behind. Now go,*" he commands.

I take a deep breath, withdraw my sword, and I go.

The door is slightly ajar, so I place my fingertips to the wood and push a space big enough for Gabriel and me to fit through, and I slip inside the dark interior. A tinge of must mingles with the foul smell and nearly makes me gag, but I swallow several times to fight off the urge.

Reaching into my thigh pocket, I withdraw a small torch. I can hear the familiar gurgling noise, coming from another room near the back, so I feel pretty sure nothing is right before me. My heart slams against my ribs as I sweep the beam of light across the bare floor.

It falls across a woman's shoe.

Jesus Christ.

As I move toward the back, I feel somewhat comforted that Gabriel is right behind me. Knowing he is there won't erase from memory what I'm about to witness. That vivid scene, along with the odor, will stay forever emblazoned in my mind.

My fingers tighten around the sword hilt, and my body tenses as I prepare. I ease toward what I'm pretty sure is the kitchen. The chewing and gurgling sounds grow louder, more intense.

And then, it stops. Silence.

It knows I'm here.

I wait, because I have to have it in full view before I make a move. One wrong step and it's my shoe on the floor.

In the next breath, it leaps, landing just a few feet away. It doesn't see me yet, but I'm pretty sure it can smell me. I can definitely smell it. Vile. There's no other word for it.

With the torch off, the room is once again cast into darkness. I can judge where it is, though, and I can hear it, allowing to my vision almost a full outline of its body. Amazing, the senses that have heightened since my death—

A cold, wet hand closes over my throat, pinching off my air. Its body is close to me now, too close to poke my blade into, too close to punch. So I pull back my leg and shove my knee into its groin, I do it once more, and it finally howls, turns my throat loose, and stumbles back.

A powerful swoosh slices through the air, followed by a heavy thump. Something bumps the toe of my boot.

"Torch on, Ms. Maspeth," Gabriel says directly over my shoulder. "Now."

Immediately, I flip on my torch and point it down.

The head of a Jodis lies at my feet, a nasty, white ooze spilling from its neck cavity.

Gabriel pushes past me and steps over the Jodis's body, which is still twitching. He stops at the kitchen, looks in, and crosses himself, and in ancient Pict, gives what once was an innocent woman her last rites.

I know the verse by heart now. I've heard it scores of times over the last year.

With God, find peace hereafter.

I can do little but breathe. I feel my knees weaken and I stumble back, rest my head against the wall and swear.

Gabriel holds my chin and lifts it up. I squeeze my eyes shut, out of embarrassment and to hold in the goddamn tears. Even after a year of training, the monster beats me.

"Open your eyes, Ms. Maspeth," he says quietly. "We have bodies to dispose of."

"Riley? Wake up."

I feel a tight grasp around my shoulder. I'm being shaken. I toss my head a few times, blink, and glance around. I'm back in Castle Arcos. Everyone is staring at me. Sydney Maspeth is standing a foot away. All eyes are on me.

"What the hell is this?" I say, and back away from them. "Don't fucking touch me again. Any of you." I sling my arms as though shaking off water. "Damn it!" I try to clear my head. All I see is Edinburgh, Scotland. That apartment. Sydney. That . . . thing.

"I'm sorry," Sydney says. "I honestly didn't think . . . I didn't believe it could happen."

I shake my head. "Well it did. But don't worry about it," I say, feeling like someone who has just told a kid there's no Santa Claus. "No problem. Just . . . warn me next time."

"So 'tis true," the third big guy of the group, whom

213

I recognize as Gabriel, says. "Your blood survived three strigoi?"

"I don't have normal blood to begin with," I offer. "And if you touch me I will throw your ass through that window," I say, and incline my head.

Gabriel's smile isn't very noticeable, but it's there. He simply nods. "Another time, mayhap."

"I don't think so," I answer.

I slip a quick glance at Eli. "What's going on?"

"My name's Ginger Slater," the other young woman says. She maintains her distance, which I sincerely appreciate. I'm in no mood to slip into anyone else's body just right now. "We"—she glances at the man beside her—"we need your help."

"All of us," Sydney adds.

I exhale and glance at Eli. "Again. What's going on?"

Eli inclines his head to the sofa near the hearth. "Sit."

With a quick glance at the small group gathered, I concede. I sit.

And wait.

Part Seven

REJUVENATION

There is something incredibly different about Ginger Slater and Sydney Maspeth. I'm still so busy trying to let my brain wrap around the fact that Victorian was right—one little touch put me directly into Sydney's body. I saw what she saw. But she felt what I felt. Weird.

Ginger I'll keep at arm's length. Haven't touched her. I can tell, though, that she is dying to get her little fingers on me. I'm ready for it. I still have processing to do.

Darius is definitely a different story. He's old as dirt,

although he looks around thirty, and has some sort of magical powers. That much I can tell. Not a vampire. Neither is Gabriel or the one who has done nothing but stare at me. Lucian. There's something—I don't know—*feral* about him. Unpredictable. Frightening, even. Unlike a vampire. This whole thing is strange. And I'm ready to get the hell out of Romania.

"These are two of WUP's most crucial cases right now," Jake Andorra says. "Ginger just lost her partner." Jake flashes a warning look at Lucian. "And inadvertently gained another."

I shake my head. "Lost her partner?" I ask.

"I'm a field agent, presently stationed near the village of Dunmorag in the northwest Highlands," Ginger offers. "Relatively new to WUP, but I've been studying shifters ever since high school. We've"—she inclines her head toward Lucian—"chased our unsub to the Carpathians."

"Shifters? Unsub?" I ask.

Ginger grins. "Shape-shifters. Those who can morph from one being to another. Say, from a man into a wolf." She slides a glance at Lucian. "And unsub—that's the term we give the bad guys."

I simply nod.

"Sydney and Gabriel are knee-deep in shit over in Edinburgh," Jake adds.

"So I see," I answer. I slide a glance to Sydney and

Gabriel. She looks like she can handle her own. I admire that.

Jake chuckles. "Ah, so you have. They have their hands full of the Jodís in Edinburgh. Along with a mortal group who call themselves the Gemini. There seems to be a band of Black Fallens taking over the city."

"Black Fallens?" I dare ask.

Jake nods. "Fallen angels. Bad ones."

"All threatened by nine malevolent spirits Darius there tried to take care of centuries ago," Sydney adds. "They were a little smarter than he anticipated."

Darius remains silent.

Rising from my place on the sofa, I pinch the bridge of my nose, shake my head, then meet Jake Andorra's gaze. "Fascinating. Really. All of it." I step closer, tilt my head, and look up at him. "But what's any of this got to do with me?"

Out of the corner of my eye, I see Eli lean closer to me.

"Well," Jake continues, and his green eyes all but glow as they stare down at me. "I was hoping to offer you employment once all of your present matters are handled."

I gape. I glance at Eli, who shrugs. Then I move my gaze back to Jake. "I'm a tattoo artist. I own an ink shop. I'm raising my little brother. That's what I do."

Jake merely smiles. "You've too many . . .

capabilities, Riley. Way too many to waste. You'd be the perfect addition to our team."

I open my mouth to retort, but Jake holds up his hand. "Just . . . think about it."

"I've thought about it. No." I move away from him, because, really, I don't trust him.

"Wait," Ginger says, and steps toward me. "Seriously, Riley, think about it."

Then goddamn it all, she does it. She grasps my arm before I can snatch it back. The room spins, my eyes cross, and everything goes blurry once again. . . .

"So, you think you can handle this one, huh, newbie?"

I'd glanced at Paxton Tarragon, the arrogant senior field agent I'd been training with for the past three months. He had been in his mid-thirties, had worn white, spiked hair, and had looked like Billy Idol. I'd narrowed my gaze, sick to death of being called newbie. The only thing I'd hated worse than that was being called blondie. Typical straight blond hair and blue eyes had been roadblocks in my career. No guy took a blonde seriously. Then add in the name Ginger? I'd always had to prove myself. Bastards. "Hell yeah."

My conversation with Pax replayed in my head more times than I could count. Why had he had to have been so damn cocky? That seemed like a long time ago now.

Over the course of the next week, Lucian slowly introduced me to my new world, my new body, my new senses. I would not be able to master them all for some time; my hearing was exaggerated and sometimes hurt my ears and insides. My sense of smell was so intense, it overwhelmed me, and I couldn't determine one smell from another—except for Lucian's scent. His was unique and solely Lucian's, and I could detect it a mile away. My strength and speed were immature but growing fast—almost too fast. I tripped, I fell, I hurled myself to speeds which my old body couldn't handle yet. I busted my ass more times than I could count. But Lucian was right there to help me up.

Each night, we made intense love and fell asleep wrapped in each other's arms. Each night, I dreamed. Pax pursued me in his human form, always in a heavy mist, always through a dense wood. The white fog slipped through the trees and brush like long, reaching fingers, and I ran hard, stumbling and not in control of my new speed and strength. Pax, for some reason, was. His white spiked hair appeared behind every tree, every rock, as though he was toying with me. And every time, he'd catch me, back me against the base of a tree. "This is your fault, newbie. I'm here, trapped as an abomination, all because of you. I don't know whether to thank you or rip your throat out." I'd awaken, shaking violently, breathless, just before Pax shifted into his wolf form and lunged at me, teeth bared. I kept the dreams from Lucian. I thought I could handle them, or that they'd just go away. I was so very wrong.

My arrival in Dunmora, and the events that had followed, haunted me.

"So you have a couple of years behind you, and what?" He cocked his head and stared at me. "Think you're ready?" He'd shaken his head and had popped the hatch. "I've been at this for ten years, newbie, and trust me—you're never ready."

I'd met Pax's stare for a few seconds, had told him to eff-off in my head, had grabbed my pack and shouldered it. Then I'd really taken a good look around at the secluded Highland village. "Desolate" was the first word that had come to mind. A half dozen gray stone and whitewashed buildings hugged the pebbled crescent shore of a small lake—or, rather, a loch. Beyond the village, the Rannoch Moors were even more desolate than Dunmorag. Tufts of dead grass, brown heather, and rock stretched for miles. Far in the distance, dark, craggy mountains threw long shadows and loomed ominously. The skies were gray. The moors were gray. Even the water in the loch was gray. Well, black.

"Foreboding." That was the second word that had come to mind.

"You gonna stand here all day and take in the scenery or what?" Pax had asked.

I'd given him a hard look, which he'd ignored, instead inclining his head to the pub behind us. "I'm ready," I'd said. I had shifted my pack, had snugged my leather jacket's collar closer to my neck, and together we'd crossed the small car park. The wind bit straight through my clothes, and I'd shivered as I'd stepped onto the single paved walk that ran in *front of the stores. I'd glanced down the row of buildings. A baker. A fishmonger. The Royal Post. A grocer. An inn and a pub. And absolutely no people around. Weird. Very, very weird. Good thing weird had been our specialty.*

A black sign with a sliver of a red moon painted on it had swung above the pub on rusted hinges, and the creaking noise had echoed off the building. In silver letters, the sign read THE BLOOD MOON. *Pax had pushed in through the red double doors—quite befitting, the red—and I'd followed. Inside, it had taken my eyes several seconds to adjust to the dimmer light. A hush fell over the handful of people gathered in the single-room dwelling. "Guess we found the villagers," I'd whispered to Pax. They had stopped what they were doing or saying to stare at us. No one had uttered a word.*

I'd glanced at Pax, then all around, until my eyes had lighted on the man behind the bar. He had dark, expressionless eyes that reminded me of a shark's eyes, and they'd bored straight into me. His head, shaved bald, had shined beneath the pub's overhead light. He'd said nothing. I had walked up to him and had met his gaze. "We're looking for Lucian MacLoud," I'd said. "Know where we can find him?"

It was weird, mine and Lucian's relationship. I felt completely at ease with Lucian, as though we'd known each other forever. He'd had nearly three weeks to come to terms with the fact that I was his marked mate; I'd had about twenty-four hours. Still, I accepted it readily and willingly. It felt . . . natural, as though my life was to turn out no other way than to be here, in the Highlands of Scotland, with an ancient Pict warrior-wolf. It felt even more natural to become a wolf, too. I can't explain it without sounding like a lunatic, but there you go.

Lucian and I left the bothy the last day of my transition and traveled north and west to the MacLeod stronghold. Situated on a sea loch, the massive gray stone fortress, complete with four imposing towers, dominated the seascape. It literally stole my breath.

"You live here?" I asked incredulously. I glanced at him.

Lucian laughed, and reached over and grasped my hand. "Nay. We live here."

My heart swelled at his words. We'd not exchanged the L-word yet; somehow, it just didn't seem right. But we'd both claimed each other, and the word "mine" sounded nearly as powerful as, if not more than, the word "love." There would be an adjustment period for both of us. But one thing of which I was absolutely positive: We were meant to be together.

Lucian pulled onto a single-track gravel lane that led to the massive front doors of the castle, and before we had the Rover in park, five big guys emptied the entrance and made their way toward us. All had dark hair in various lengths and bodies that looked like they swung axes and swords and kicked ass for a living.

Lucian glanced at me and laughed. "They won't bite."

I looked at him and raised a brow. "Doubt that."

I climbed out of the Rover, slammed the door, and faced the MacLeods.

"Gin, my brothers. Arron, Raife, Christopher, Jacob, and Sean."

Arron walked up and embraced me; the others followed. "Welcome," Arron said, his eyes flashing quicksilver.

"About time we had a lass around the place," Jacob said, and the others laughed.

The MacLeods welcomed me, and as it was with Lucian, the same held true with his brothers. It felt like I'd known them my entire life.

The MacLeod fortress entailed no less than two hundred acres and the shoreline, and inside the castle was a modernized habitat befitting an ancient wolf clan of Pict warriors. Primeval mixed perfectly with contemporary. It was mind-numbing to think how long ago Lucian and his brothers were born, how long they'd lived.

They prepared me for my transition that night; in all honesty, there wasn't much they could do except stand by and wait, help out if needed. Lucian warned me the first time would be painful, and he apologized more times than I could count. He held me in his arms, kissed me, smoothed my hair from my face, and promised to not leave my side until it was over.

By nightfall, as the moon began to rise, Lucian and his brothers walked me to the shoreline, encircled me, and waited. I immediately knew it had begun when my skin began to itch.

I felt as though I wanted to crawl right out of it, and I clawed and scratched at my arms, my neck, my abdomen. My temperature rose, higher and higher until I thought I would self-combust. My skin was on fire, and I began to pull at my clothes. No matter that it was October in the Highlands; I was hot. I didn't have time to yank them off, either. I felt my skeleton give way, the popping and rubbing sounds reverberating inside my head. I cried out in pain, and in my peripheral vision I saw movement and knew it was Lucian. He stopped abruptly, and didn't advance farther.

My heels and long bones shifted, elongated, contorted, and just when I thought I couldn't take the pain and heat a second longer, I fell to the ground, let out a low, long bay, and it was over. I leaped up, shook my body, and met the silver gazes of six other wolves, their shaggy dark coats glistening in the moonlight.

We ran that night, my new brothers, my mate, and I. We ran from the west coast of Scotland clear to the east, along the shores of the North Sea, and it was invigorating, mind-freeing. My new body rocked with sensations, and I wanted to keep running. I saw everything through my new eyes, and it was as though I was seeing the world for the very first time. Lucian ran beside me, his silvery blue gaze watching me closely. We spoke to each other in our minds. He never left my side. At some point, exhaustion overtook me. We made it home, and I fell hard asleep.

When next I woke, I was in my human form, tucked

closely against Lucian's body. The sun had not yet risen, and I felt invigorated. I wanted to explore the shore, so I slipped from our bed, quickly dressed, and headed outside. No one else stirred. I was the only one awake.

The brisk Highland air greeted me, along with a healthy dose of mist. I found it strange not to be cold, but my core stayed over one hundred degrees, so there was no need for a jacket. I breathed in the air, sweet with clover and something else I couldn't name, and took in my surroundings. On the left side of the gravel lane, a meadow, and at its edge, a dense copse of wood filled with towering pines and oaks.

Then I saw it. Through the slender ribbons of mist I saw something white move into view. I stared, my newly sharpened vision trained on the spot. Before my brain registered what my eyes saw, I knew. Pax. He waited for me. Without thought, I took off toward him at a jog, and by the time I reached the wood line, I was at a full run. Pax had disappeared.

I eased through the trees, the canopy above keeping out any light that may have filtered in, and searched for Pax. Deeper into the wood I moved, determined to settle things with my old partner. Surely, no matter his fate or mine, we could come to terms. We'd been partners. We'd sort of been friends. He'd watched out for me. I knew, despite the awful dreams, he wouldn't hurt me.

In the next instant something heavy slammed into my body, and I was knocked hard against the base of an aged oak.

I was turned abruptly, and when I looked, the man who pinned me against the tree was not Pax. I frowned, shoved, and cursed. "Get the hell off of me," I growled and shoved my knee into his balls. "Now!"

He sucked in a breath but quickly recovered. "Oh, no, love," he said, his accent thick, his tone full of hatred. He pushed me hard against the tree. "We've been waiting for the chance to get at Lucian MacLeod and his brothers, and you're it." Without warning, he punched me—caught me right in the jaw, and my head snapped back and slammed into the hard wood of the tree.

I glared at him. "He'll kill you," I said, my pitch lowering. The man laughed. "Right. We'll see about that."

Four other men emerged from the wood. One of them was Pax. He ambled up to me, his eyes laced with disgust. He pushed the guy away from me and leaned close to my ear. "You did this to me, newbie," he said, just like in my dream. "I can never go home now. I'll never see my wife again, thanks to you." His breath brushed my neck. "I've half a mind to just rip your throat out now instead of letting these assholes use you to bait your mate."

I met Pax's hard glare. "Do it," I said. "Stop talking about it and do it."

A low growl escaped Pax's throat, and in the next second he shifted into his wolf form. His fangs, dripping with saliva, hovered close to my ear, my throat. In my head, I imagined myself in my wolf form; nothing happened.

In the next second, in a flurry of fur and fangs, a pack of nearly black wolves entered the wood at full speed. The men with Pax shifted, and the fight began. I was knocked into a tree, where I fell, crouched to the ground, and watched.

I couldn't make myself change. I was helpless.

The melee was horrific. Bones crunched. Blood. Cries of pain. No human words met my ears, but I heard them in my head.

Then, a large wolf with a band of white on his chest charged me. It was Pax. I knew it. And I was no match for him. I rose, my back against the tree, and kept my eyes trained on my old partner.

Just before he lunged, a large black wolf leaped from out of nowhere and slammed Pax to the ground. They fought; fangs gnashed, massive claws raked, bodies smashed into each other. The black wolf was Lucian—about that I had no doubt. With a final agonizing cry, Pax's neck was broken, and Lucian— God, it was awful—tore into his throat.

Then it was over.

Lucian moved toward me, shifted, and stood naked before me. He was covered in Pax's blood. Anger radiated off him. Anger and relief.

"Let's go," he said, and grasped my hand, threading his fingers through mine. "This is over," he said, and squeezed my hand. "For now."

Together, we walked back to the hall, and Lucian bathed and got dressed. Lucian's brothers cleaned up the aftermath, and Lucian explained to me what was to come. I can't say that I was shocked.

"I'm verra sorry about your partner," he said, folding me into his embrace. He rubbed my back, a rhythmic motion that calmed me instantly. "He was no longer himself—you understand that?"

I nodded against his chest. "Yes."

He looked at me for a moment, searching my eyes. "There are others. From all over the world, no' just Scotia. As you worked for WUP, your talents will be trifold as a MacLeod warrior. We go where we're needed. We fight to protect innocents. And you are one of us now, Gin. Your skills will grow and you'll become as fast, as strong as I." He kissed me then, long, erotic, slow. When he pulled back, his gaze all but worshipped me. "But you're not there yet, and I'll no' take any more chances with your life. You're mine," he whispered against my mouth, then brushed his lips across mine. "And I'll no' leave your side until you have full control over all of your new powers." He rested his forehead against mine. "I canna lose you, Gin. You're mine forever."

Suddenly I'm Riley again, and I fall back as Scotland and wolves and blood and bone-crunching fade away, and the interior of Castle Arcos emerges once again. I stumble, shake my head, and press my fingers into my eye sockets to try and stop the vertigo from sending me sprawling. "Damn it," I mutter, and then feel two strong hands steady me.

Surprisingly, they aren't Eli's.

"Please, lass," a deep, heavily accented voice says quietly in my ear. "Please."

I turn and meet the intense gaze of Lucian MacLeod.

A fast flash of his body morphing painfully into a wolf scrapes behind my eyes. I see it. I feel it. It's like . . . I'm him. For only a brief second. Then he steadies me and turns me loose.

Lucian is a werewolf.

And so is Ginger.

The sincerity in Lucian's gaze nails me. Paralyzes me. His words sink deep into my psyche, and never have I known myself to fall so hard for a plea as I was falling right this very minute.

"I'll think about it," I say to Lucian.

His gaze lingers, and I can only conclude that he's trying to see if I mean what I say. Finally, he gives a slight nod and moves away.

"But," I say, looking directly at Jake Andorra, "I want to know more about . . . your organization. As in, everything. As in, what would be expected of me."

He smiles. "I shall tell you everything, indeed."

"Ah, there you are," a voice calls out. Smooth. Flawless. Powerful.

Immediately, I know it's *him*.

He moves so fast, I don't see him until he's standing right beside me. Eli protectively pushes between us.

"Back down, boy," Julian Arcos says. Gilles and Victorian have entered with him, and both stand a ways back. "I will hold counsel with Riley Poe. Alone." His voice is cold, his gaze icy as he inspects me from head to toe. "Now."

"*Non*," Eli says, his fingers lacing through mine. His voice is harsh, determined, deadly. "Not without me."

Julian Arcos passes a long, cold gaze over first me, then Eli. "Alone."

Not only does Eli stiffen, but Noah, Jake, Gabriel and Lucian all take a step closer.

The male adrenaline in the room pulses.

"It's okay, Eli," I say, and move forward. I throw a glance behind me. "Guys, it's all right. I'll go." *He's not going to do anything to me, Eli. With you, Gilles, and the others here? No way. So chill out. I got this.*

Eli's glare slides over me, and I know he's on fire. Not only does he hate losing control to Julian, but his protectiveness over me has all but consumed him. I can tell. So I put a hand on his forearm, squeeze, and move in front of him.

Julian's long silvery hair gleams beneath the lamplight as a chilling smile touches his mouth. "Come," he says to me, and grasps my hand, tucks it into the crook of his arm, and without another word, leads me from the others.

I'd be lying if I said I wasn't a little intimidated. He's an ancient, powerful strigoi vampire with more control than even I can fathom. He's evaded a vampire's death for centuries. He's badass and knows it.

I know it.

" 'Tis true, my dear," Julian says quietly, bending his head slightly toward mine.

I don't even look back as we leave the great hall.

Julian guides me through the manse, down long corridors and up stairs. By the time we enter the room, I know I've lost my way. No doubt he's done it on purpose.

The moment we enter the room, Julian moves away. Here one second, gone the next, and I'm pretty sure he's doing it to freak me out. He continues to shift as he speaks. *Shit head.*

"Riley Poe. I've heard much about you over the years," he says, appearing next to the wall of books across the room. He slides one out, examines it with long, elegant fingers as though completely uninterested in my presence. " 'Tis all Victorian has talked about since his return home." He slips me a glance and a smile. "Riley, Riley, Riley." He sighs and replaces the book and looks at me. "I can now see why my son is so obsessed with you."

I blink, and he's gone. Turning my head, I search the massive room for his silver head of hair. He's nowhere.

Then he's everywhere.

"The power you have over him intrigues me," Julian says in my ear. I snap my head to look at him and he's gone again.

"How he's controlled himself around you intrigues me just as much," he continues. A long finger traces the black inked wing at my cheek. "What is it about you, Riley Poe, that completely drains my youngest son of all decent vampire capabilities? Do you know the power he exerted in order to keep from killing you once he'd tasted your blood?" His lips brush my cheek. "Myself as well?"

I try to move but nothing happens. I'm paralyzed, frozen in place. Only my mind races. I try to speak—even that doesn't work. Senior Arcos has me under his power, and it's damn strong. My eyes, though, work perfectly, and I keep them trained on Julian as he moves in front of me. I decide to speak to him in my mind. *So you brought me in here, deep into the belly of your moldy old castle, far away from the others, just to suck the life out of me? Where I come from, that type of person is called a pussy, Jules. I'm just saying.*

Julian stares at me, then laughs. "Of course not, dear. I merely wanted you to understand my position." He inclines his head. "And to make you an offer."

I stare at him, waiting.

He smiles. "If ever you tire of living the life you lead, Riley Poe, Castell Arcos could surely use a queen."

What the hell? Julian Arcos is coming on to me? I continue to stare. Dumbfounded. Is it my strength? My powers? Our blood bond? Whatever it is, uh . . . no way.

Julian shrugs as he hears my thoughts. "For Victorian, one day." He strokes my cheek. "Or for me. And the answer is yes to all of your own questions. We'd be . . . invincible together."

Thanks for the offer, Jules, but I've got a life already and I'll keep it, if it's all the same to you.

Julian's icy gaze moves over me, slowly. "As I said. If ever you tire of the life you lead." His gaze lingers on my mouth. "And I fear, my dear girl, with all of the powers inside of you, one day, you will."

Our gazes clash and lock.

"In the meantime, make sure my eldest is returned to me, unharmed," he says. "And one more thing. Valerian will not be an easy foe to capture. Mention his mother and you may have a slight advantage, even if momentarily."

I blink, and Julian Arcos disappears.

My body relaxes, and I'm in control once more.

And Julian Arcos has just given me a tip on how to catch his son.

Easing from the library, I slip out into the ominous hallways of Castell Arcos.

"Don't mind Father," Victorian says from an adjacent alcove. "He likes you."

"Yeah, I got that," I say, and look at him in the low light of the sconces. "You've been out here the whole time?"

Victorian shrugs. "Of course. I wasn't about to let Julian Arcos take you into the bowels of the castle alone." He grins. "Not that he would've harmed you. But he may have frightened you."

For a long moment, I stare at Victorian Arcos. Not in a million years, especially after that first night in Bonaventure, when the Arcos brothers both took my blood, would I have ever dreamed he was anything other than a filthy bloodsucker. He seems kind, loyal, and loving. So very different from his brother. So very different from your typical vampire, actually.

"I am different," he says, his smile wistful. "Yet it's not enough."

I'm guessing that, since my latest DNA donors, my mind is an open target for most, if not all, vampires. I'll have to investigate that. Possibly see what I can do to change it, as it annoys the hell out of me.

"Enough for what?" I ask.

He takes a step closer. "To win your love."

The play of light in the brown depths of his eyes as

he watches me almost paralyzes me. "I feel something for you, Vic. I just don't know what that something is. It baffles me, but there is a connection there. But of one thing, I'm absolutely positive," I say. "I'm in love with Eli. My loyalty lies with him alone."

A slow, wistful smile lifts the corner of his perfectly shaped mouth. He lifts a hand, pushes a stray strand of hair from my face. "Your bald honesty is only one of the things that fascinate me about you, Riley Poe," he says, his elegant fingers lingering on my jaw. He leans in, his eyes searching mine. "Allow me just this one private good-bye," he requests. "I've waited . . . forever."

With his other hand, Victorian cups my face, lowers his mouth to mine, and gently presses his lips against mine. The kiss doesn't last long, but I feel every ounce of Victorian's emotion in the kiss. He breaks it, momentarily rests his forehead against mine, then presses his lips to my temple. *"Te iubesc,"* he whispers. *"Mersi."*

I love you. And, *thank you.*

Victorian pulls back, looks at me, then blushes furiously. Damn, his cheeks literally turn fire pink. "I forgot you can now understand Romanian," he says quietly, the *r* rolling with his accent. "Forgive me." He meets my gaze. "But I cannot help it."

I shake my head and study him. Such an anomaly. What I once thought was a monster proves to be a sweet, romantic, blushing, young, and beautiful man. Who just so happens to have to live off human blood. I link my arm through his and tug him toward the end of the hall. "I think in another place, another time, Vic"—I look at him—"who knows? But for now, I love you . . . as a friend. And one I feel a strong connection to."

He smiles at me, and I'm positive it's a smile that has brought many a young maid straight to her knees. "And I accept that, Riley Poe," he says. "As long as you realize"—he looks down at me—"that I will wait for you. For however long it takes." His eyes glow. "Forever."

I smile back. "I'd expect nothing less from you, Mr. Arcos." We hit the steps and make our way back to the great hall. "You're coming back with us, right?" I ask.

Victorian nods. "Much to your lover's disdain, yes. I have to ensure my brother's safety."

I nod. "Good. We can use your help."

"Go to your man," Victorian whispers, and hangs back. "The lucky bastard awaits you with the others. I think they are arranging a formal meeting for you."

With a final smile at Vic, I walk ahead and join Eli and the others. Gilles has joined the group. All heads turn my way as I approach.

Eli, pacing, stops and walks directly to me. He grasps my shoulders. "Well?" he asks. "Are you okay?"

Giving him an assuring smile, I lean up and kiss him. *"Oui, Monsieur Dupré."* I blink. The French rolls off my tongue as though it's my first language. Intrigued, I decide to give it another try. *"Est-ce-que vous avez été examiner pour la rage récemment?"* I wait expectantly for praise.

A moment of silence hangs in the air before laughter breaks out in the Arcos great hall.

Eli's lips purse tightly together, and he covers his mouth with his hand before shaking his head.

"What'd I say?" I ask. I look at Gilles. He's still chuckling.

"Damn, girl," Noah says, wiping his eyes. "You just asked Eli if he'd been checked for rabies recently."

"Oops," I say. "Guess I need to work on that, huh?"

Eli pulls me into a hug. *"Non,"* he whispers against my ear. "I like you just the way you are."

I fall easily into his embrace. How simple it is for me to take comfort there. Much easier now that I've admitted to myself, and to Eli, how much I truly love him.

From the corner of my eye, I notice Victorian hanging back somewhat from the group. And for a moment, my heart aches.

He smiles at me. *No, love. Do not ache for me. As I said, I will wait for you. And I shall also enter your thoughts routinely. You'll grow weary of hearing me, no doubt.*

I do nothing more than smile back at him.

"We must prepare for departure," Gilles announces, drawing everyone's attention. "Luc has called several times. The situation is growing, and it's no longer safe to leave the entire city and our loved ones solely in the hands of my children and wife." He faces Eli. "Valerian has been in hiding, commanding his newlings. They've converged now. A large clan descends upon Savannah. We must leave at once."

Jake Andorra moves to Eli. "My team and I will accompany you."

Eli nods and grasps his shoulder. "*Merci*. We can use all the help we can get. *Merci*."

"I will help as well," Victorian adds, standing tall, erect, and meeting Eli's hard gaze without flinching. "'Tis my duty to bring my brother home."

Eli looks first at me, then back to Victorian. "Only because Riley trusts you so much will I allow this."

Victorian simply nods and leaves the hall.

"Well," Noah says, clapping his hands together and rubbing them vigorously. His smile is lethal, predatory. "Time to make like a tree and get the fuck out of here."

I shake my head. Noah's mercury gaze lights on me and I can't help but grin at him. Sick fool.

Within an hour, we'd packed up and, thanks to Julian Arcos, boarded two helicopters bound for Bucharest.

Apparently I'd been so out of it on the journey that I'd missed the flight to Castell Arcos. But even I have to admit that the sight of the massive, ancient castle rising out of the misty rocks of the Carpathians is one I'll not soon forget. Turrets and towers—foreboding, all of it. Yet . . . enticing. I guess that's the whole vampire lure. To me, though, it is sheer beauty.

At the airport, we board the Arcoses' private jet—a Gulfstream, no less, manufactured directly in my hometown of sultry Savannah, Georgia. The jet is immaculately decorated and lavishly furnished; I admit that it is pretty kick-ass to roll in so much luxury. Not sure I'd ever buy one myself, but it damn sure beats sitting all cramped in coach, with someone kicking the back of your seat or, worse, falling asleep on you. Had that happen to me once. Some weird dude who looked like Satan, complete with pointed goatee and all, fell right over on me. Tried to snuggle. No, thank you.

As we take off from Bucharest, the sun is setting, and the sky we fly into is various shades of orange, red, yellow, and purple. The Carpathians rise in the distance, and for a solid second, I feel sad that I'm leaving. It's weird—I've never had the first little desire to go to Romania, yet I have some sort of connection to it. I now have the urge to return. Someday.

It's not weird, love. The connection to my home is inside of you now, just as my blood, my brother's, and my father's circulate with each pump of your heart. It's natural to feel this. Mayhap one day you'll come back?

My eyes shoot over to Victorian's, and he's of course watching me. I smile and shrug, then turn back to the window and watch Bucharest fade away. Maybe I will. One day.

I settle down next to Eli and take notice of my traveling companions. Five vampires, two werewolves, two ancient Pict Druthan warriors, and one mortal-turned-very-important-immortal. And me.

I have to wonder what exactly the pilot is.

"Well," Jake Andorra says, addressing everyone. "Since we had to hurry and leave in such haste I suggest we take this time to acquaint Ms. Poe with WUP"—he slides me a glance—"and what would be expected of her." His gaze lights on everyone. "Agreed?"

The plane fills with various forms of agreement: ayes and yeses and *ouis*.

Jake nods. "Good." He's sitting in the seat across from me, so he leans forward, clasps his hands together, and meets my gaze. "As you can see, my WUP team is made up of . . . rather unique beings." He nods to the various occupants of the plane. "Werewolves. Vampires. Immortals." He smiles. "And you, Riley Poe."

"What am I?" I ask.

Jake shrugs. "That, I haven't figured out yet, but trust me when I say, you'll fit right in with the rest of the team. You see, we take on cases too dangerous and powerful for mere mortals to handle. This case is probably our most dangerous thus far."

I keep my gaze trained on Jake.

"You see, there's really only one thing more lethal than a vampire," he says. "A Black Fallen."

"What's that again?" I ask, not sure I got the full scoop earlier.

"'Tis a fallen angel, engulfed in the blackest of magic. And three of the Fallen have descended upon Edinburgh, Scotland, with a vengeance."

"Why?" I ask.

Jake glances at another. "Gabriel?"

The big guy, Gabriel, meets my eyes. "The Black Fallen seek two things: one, a soul. No' just any old soul. A pure one."

"And the second?" I ask.

"'Tis an aged tome—the Seiagh—a dark, ancient book of the most potent spells, stolen from the Fallen's possession centuries before." His unusual eyes bore into mine. "They'll stop at nothing to get both."

"Aye, and it'll take all of our powers combined to stop *them*," Jake says.

"Ms. Maspeth," Gabriel continues, "was chosen at birth to be the only one capable of reading the ancient script of the Seiagh." He nods at Sydney. "The Fallen want her as badly as they want the bloody book."

Across several rows, my eyes meet Sydney's. Neither of us says a word. We don't have to. I've been inside her body, linked to her soul. I've seen what happens in Edinburgh with the Fallen. I've been witness to the . . . things the Fallen have created to help seek out a pure soul to steal. They're vicious, horrible creatures that are hideously gross when killed. What a frickin' mess. And Sydney has kicked some major monster ass.

I move my gaze back to Jake. "And what about Ginger and Lucien's deal?"

"It's . . . complicated," Jake begins. "But it's a war brewing between two werewolf clans. Major treaties are being broken, and innocents are getting killed."

I glance at Ginger. No lie, innocents are getting killed. I saw that while in her body, too.

I think for a moment, and raise my gaze to meet Eli's. We look wordlessly at each other. For several long seconds. Then I glance at Jake.

"I'll consider joining the team, Andorra," I say. "If you consider taking my brother on, as well. I'm not leaving him behind, and he's a damn good fighter."

Jake grins and nods. "I know that to be true. Done, Riley."

"I said I'd consider it," I repeat. "I haven't signed a contract yet."

Jake merely grins again. "Ah, but you will. And I'll

be ever so grateful for it. Besides, you owe me a new jet. You all but tore the other one to shreds."

"Sorry 'bout that," I answer, and Jake continues grinning at me. Prick.

Ginger, her head against Lucien's shoulder, looks at me. "Your powers, your energy, they're fantastic," she says. "So many innocents can benefit from them, Riley. Join us, please?"

My gaze moves to Sydney, who echoes Ginger. "Please?"

I simply shake my head and sigh. "I will . . . heavily consider it."

"You won't regret it," Ginger says.

Glancing out the plane's window, I stare at the weightless, empty air. I'm in an airplane with two werewolves, several vampires, a couple of immortals, and whatever you want to call me.

How life has certainly changed.

When I think back on me as a kid, doing such stupid, stupid things like drugs, drinking, and quitting school, and then when I think of my life now? It's impossible to even fathom. Absently, my fingers move to the black wings inked at the corner of my left eye. Damn, I've done some idiotic things in my life. I hate worse than anything that my mom had to suffer through them. She didn't deserve all that I gave her. And she damn sure didn't deserve to die the way she did.

I can't help but wonder what she'd be like now. What she'd think of Seth and me now. Would any of this even have happened? To be perfectly honest I'm surprised I didn't die young. All the shit I got into as a preteen? How it must've killed her inside, to see her baby become such a . . . loser. I know that I might not be who I am now had it not been for those poor choices, but it's hard not to hate myself for putting my mom through it all. My heart still hurts, still longs for her. Sometimes I can even feel her close to me. Sometimes, I swear to God, I can smell her. I get a whiff of someone wearing some perfume that reminds me of her and— *whack!* Heartbreak all over again. I really miss her. At times, I wish she could see, just for a second, that I didn't stay a loser.

Eli's hand finds mine, and he laces his fingers through mine. He looks at me with those enigmatic eyes, and I immediately feel calm. He smiles, and it almost makes my heart seize.

I lay my head against Eli's shoulder. My eyes grow heavy, and I close them. After tucking a pillow under my head, since Eli's bicep isn't the softest of things, I drift off to sleep.

"Riley, wake up," Eli's voice whispers against the shell of my ear. "We're home."

My eyes flutter open, and the moment my brain registers my whereabouts, I sense newlings. I look at Eli. "We've got to hurry."

The urgency in his face makes me know my words ring more than true.

We race from the airport in three cars, through Industrial Park and up Bay Street. I'd slept so hard on the flight home, I don't even remember landing twice for fuel. Well, I'm full of energy and ready to fight. I'm sick and tired of our lives being disrupted. It has to end. Now.

We drive straight to Monterey Square and to the House of Dupré. It's now four p.m. Seth meets me at the door and grabs me into a fierce hug. My feet literally leave the ground.

"Ri!" he says into my hair, hugging me so tight I can't breathe. His arms are like bands of steel around me. He looks at me, those green eyes revealing every single emotion he possesses. "I was going crazy here, worrying about you," he says. "Are you okay?"

"Yeah, of course, squirt," I reply, having to almost look up to answer him. I smile at him. "You've grown."

Seth blushes. "Yeah, a little." He kisses my cheek. "I'm glad you're home, Ri. This time for good, right?"

I drape an arm over his shoulder. "Damn right."

We walk in together.

The crowd behind me files in, and the moment Elise spies Gilles, she hurries to her husband and flings herself into his arms. They embrace for a long time.

"Riley!"

In the next second, Nyxinnia Foster throws herself at me, almost impales my eye with a pigtail, and hugs me tightly. "I've missed you!" she says. "Luc wanted me to stay here. Things are bad, Riley. I'm glad you're home."

"Yeah, looks like you brought the whole country back with you," Luc says, walking up and pulling me against him. "Nice of you to come back mostly normal, Ri."

"She's never been normal," Phin says, and he, too, pulls me into a hug.

"Whatever," I answer. "And Nyx must be rubbing off on you guys. All this hugging."

Phin says something to Luc in French. *She might not be normal, but she's still hot as hell.*

"Yeah, I'm hot as hell all right," I say. Then smile.

"Damn," Luc says. "What happened?"

"All right," Gilles says, and walks to the center of the room. "We've guests and introductions." He looks around the room and his gaze lands on me. "Then we've business to discuss."

"Where's Preacher and Estelle?" I ask Phin.

"On Da Island," he answers. "They're there with Josie, Zetty, and Riggs."

Gilles makes fast introductions, then inclines his head. "Philippe will show you to your chambers," he says. "You may settle in and meet in my study in thirty minutes. There is much to discuss."

Eli now stands on one side of me, Seth on the other, and Phin and Luc fill in the spaces. "You brought back a pair of wolves, bro?" Luc asks. "Sick." He glances around. "Arcos is staying here, too?"

"Yes," I answer. "And don't be an ass, Luc. He's here to help."

Luc glares at me.

"I want to hear more about what's happening in Edinburgh," Phin says. "How old is Darius, anyway?"

I shrug as I watch the ancient Pict climb the Dupré staircase behind Gabriel and Sydney. "Old as dirt, I think," I answer. "Pretty cool guys, though."

"And they're here to help, too," Eli adds. "So be nice."

Luc shrugs. "Cool by me." He leans toward me. "That whole vampire versus wolf thing? It's all Hollywood. No bad blood between us."

"Good thing," I say. "Because Ginger looks like she can kick your ass."

Luc rubs his chin. "You're probably right."

"All right," Eli says. "Let's get ready. We've got to get a plan together. Tonight."

Thirty minutes later we all meet in Gilles's study. Philippe passes me as he brings in a loaded tray of food. One gray eyebrow lifts, as does the corner of his mouth. "Mademoiselle," he says. "So nice of you to return . . . as yourself. Mostly."

"Oh, I'm anything but myself, Phil," I say. His other eyebrow lifts and he continues on. Damn, no telling what I did before Romania. It must've been pretty bad, though.

Gilles is front and center, and the others line the walls in chairs. "I've spoken to Preacher," he says. "And to Garr in Carolina. The newlings are being led. They're merging. And they're coming here."

"Led by Valerian," I say.

"*Oui,*" Gilles answers. "And it's you, Riley, that he wants."

I sigh. "Figured as much," I mumble. "So what now?"

Eli's hand grasps mine.

"We lure him out," Gilles says.

"You mean Riley lures him out?" Eli answers. "No, Papa."

I roll my eyes. "Okay, Eligius," I say, and turn to him. "Seriously. After all this, after all we've been through, after all I've endured, you've seen what I'm capable of. Now's not the time to be overprotective."

That little speech wins me a frown from Eli.

"It won't be as easy as you think," Victorian adds. "My brother is cunning. He suspects something is up."

"Have you told him anything?" Luc says.

"No," Victorian answers, and looks at me. "I wouldn't."

250

Gilles nods in satisfaction. "There is an old woman. Gullah. She's been . . . in hiding for many years. Preacher says she's back and knows something that will help us." He looks toward me and Eli. "I want you two to go and speak with her."

Eli nods. "Done. When?"

"Tonight."

"You others will span the city," Gilles continues. "Nyx, love, you will stay here, with me and Elise."

"Okay," Nyx says.

"Garr believes the research facility off the coast has been taken over by Valerian and his clan," Gilles says. "Drummond Research. The Gullah have watched them for years, but to my knowledge, they've been one hundred percent scientific in their research."

"We'll check it out," Eli says. "After our visit."

"*Bon*," Gilles says. "Her name is Darling. You'll find her in LaFayette Square after nine p.m., so says Preacher."

"I want no less than four visiting the research island," Gilles said. "If Valerian has taken over, it will not be easy to maneuver."

"Will do," Eli says.

Gilles glances around, then nods. "Eat. Rest. And be careful."

"You better hit the platters of food before the wolves do," Luc whispers in my ear. He grins.

I shake my head and head for the spread. He may be right about that.

By eight forty-five p.m., we are all ready to head out. I've showered and changed into a pair of green cargos, a black tank, and a black, long-sleeved tee over the tank. Plus my Vans. Every holster I own sits against my body, filled with silver blades.

I'm ready.

We all exit the Dupré House at the same time. We all head in different directions. Wolves. Vamps. Immortals. Humans with Tendencies.

As I step out into the chilly October air, a new scent invades my senses. It surrounds me, invades me, and I draw it in and taste it on my tongue.

It's a fight. A big fight.

And it's close. . . .

Part Eight

—◆—◆—

FERAL

Damn, it's almost funny to watch Eli with Riley these days. She has changed, yet . . . not. It's almost like she was born to belong to Eli, born to become what she is now. Like it was her destiny or something. She was sick before. Now? It's hard not to stare when she does . . . anything. It blows my mind to think there's anything human left in her, but there is. And that's why Eli won't budge from her side. I don't blame him. If she belonged to me, I'd do the same. And yeah—she hates when we say she belongs to him. Cracks my ass up, though. The one thing I don't understand about her is her liking for Victorian Arcos. It's fucking bizarre. I guess she has so much of his DNA inside of her? Who knows. What I do know is, you don't fuck with Victorian. Not that he can't handle himself. For such a pretty boy, he is tough as shit. But he has it bad for Riley, and if he doesn't watch himself Eli will be all over him. Damn, that would be a fight worth taking bets on.

—Luc Dupré

Eli can't help but stare, and to me, it's pretty funny to watch. I'd never met the woman, and I have to admit even I've never encountered such a soul before. From what we can see, Darling is beyond bizarre in all her dark, glorious three-hundred-plus pounds of splendor. She wears colorful beads woven in her hair by the dozens, and . . . plants? Eli bends his head to my ear as we cross the square. "She wears nothing but weeds?"

I elbow him in the ribs. "No, Dupré, not weeds. Palmetto fans. She's woven them together for a dress. And don't forget—she's not just eccentric. She's paranoid schizophrenic. Don't antagonize her. And the dress? Come on, you've seen that before. You've lived here for centuries. And it's the only thing she ever wears." I lean in. "The only thing, might I repeat."

Eli shudders. "I thought I'd banished it from my memory."

I silently chuckle. Surrounded by no fewer than a dozen filled, handheld plastic bags, Darling claims the bench in LaFayette Square, talking to herself.

Or, maybe to the Marquis himself.

As we approach, I pull Eli back. "Let me go ahead. She might start yelling at you. No need for a scene."

"*Non.*"

I narrow my eyes. "*Oui.*"

Eli stares hard. "I'm right behind you."

With reluctance, Eli lets me walk ahead. I repeat. *Lets me.*

"Darling?" I say, stopping a few steps from the bench.

Darling jerks her head up, surprised by my appearance. She squints. "Who dat?"

"Preacher's goddaughter. Riley Poe."

"Preacher?" Darling said, laughing. "You all white, girl. Preacher Man, dat old cod is black as da night. You ain't his kin. Go on."

"I'm his goddaughter, Darling. Preacher and Estelle raised me and my brother after my mom was killed." My voice lowers. "I slay vampires."

"Hot damn, girl!" she exclaims. "Yeah, I remember you." Black as coal, appearing to be in her mid-fifties, with cataracts clouding both eyes, Darling stares hard at me. Recognition sets in to match her words.

"Don't say dat out loud, girl," Darling says in a hushed whisper. "Damn. People tink you crazy." She erupts into a cackled laugh.

Eli stands silent behind me. I'm surprised Darling hasn't mentioned him yet. She probably doesn't even see him.

"Darling, listen. I need your help." I go down on one knee, closer to the woman, but nonthreatening. I hope, anyway. "Have you seen or heard anything about the bloodsuckers lately? Or about me?"

Grabbing one of the bags next to her, Darling begins rifling through it, searching for . . . something. Then, she stops and turns her head, away from me, as though someone sits down beside her. "What dat? No. I don't like dat. No!"

I sit still. Eli doesn't move a muscle.

Darling scrunches her features, looks in the direction of whomever she was speaking to in her mind. Finally, she sighs. "Fine. I do it." She waves to me. "Tell dat big boy behind you to come here."

I turn, meet Eli's gaze, and incline my head. He eases up beside Darling.

Darling peers up at him through white, foggy eyes. "What you doin' here, boy? You one of dem, ain't ya?" She shakes her head, beads clacking together. "One of dem bloodsuckers. But you different, dat's right." She waves her hand at him. "Don't matta. You here to watch over Preacher's baby girl, don't forget dat." She reaches into her bag and tosses something at me. I catch it. It's cool and flat, like a piece of metal.

The Gullah woman lowers her voice. "Girl, dere's an evil place 'round here. People get took dere, but dey don't want to go. You don't want to go, either. It's out in da water, and it's a bad place." She leans over, close. "Dere's monsters dere. And bloodsuckers. Some dead. Some not dead. Some wish dey was dead."

My insides chill at her words.

"Darling, how—"

"Shush! Watch your mouth, girl. I ain't done." She cocks her head at Eli. "You listenin' too, boy?"

"*Oui.*"

Darling bursts into laughter. "*Oui?* What da hell does dat mean? You crazy, boy?"

She turns her head again, to the unknown soul whom she speaks to. "Oh," she says to the air beside her. "Dat means yeah. Okay den."

I share a puzzled look with Eli, then I shrug and turn my attention back to Darling.

The old Gullah continues. "Dey all hidin' from you. Been hidin' from you for a while now. Maybe 'cause dey busy workin' in da graveyard? Don't know why. But soon dey gonna stop hidin' and git you. You don't wanna go wit dem. Dat one who was locked away in da ground for all dem years wit his brodder? He's out. And he's bad. The brodder ain't so bad for a blood-sucker." She points at Eli. "You watch dis hardheaded ting doh. Make sure dey don't git her. Dat's Preacher's baby girl. She got dat special blood da vampires want. She sees dem. But dey see her, too." She peers at Eli. "You don't want her blood, do you boy? Preacher Man, he kill you good if you bother his baby."

"No, ma'am," Eli answers. "I'd never hurt her."

Darling grunts her approval.

I rise. "Darling, if they—"

At that point, Darling has obviously experienced enough of me and Eli for the night. She tips her head back, beads jingling, opens her mouth, and yells as if being murdered. A high-pitched, bloodcurdling, banshee-type holler that makes my hair stand up.

I grab Eli by the hand. "Come on. She's through with us now."

Eli glances over his shoulder as we race from the square. As soon as we step onto the cobbles, Darling ceases her squalling.

I stare in her direction. Even from that distance, I see the whites of her teeth against her pitch-black skin as she smiles. "Bye-bye, Riley Poe!" she yells. "Watch your neck!"

"That's scary," Eli says.

"You ain't kidding," I answer, and stop under the next streetlamp. I open my palm and stare down at the object Darling gave me.

"What is it?" Eli asks.

I pull it closer. "It's a flattened tourist penny," I answer. "With Bonaventure Cemetery on the front."

Eli looks at me. The shadows play across his face, and my heart leaps. "Looks like we're headed back to the graveyard."

"Let's call the others," I say. "And get the Jeep."

No sooner have we reached Inksomnia to get the Jeep do I hear glass shatter from next door. A series of Dagala expletives fall onto the night, and in the next instant the door to SoHo Boutique—Bhing's store—flies open. Bhing's husband, Ronnie, carrying their toddler and followed by their older boy, comes running out into the alley. Inside SoHo, glass is breaking. It sounds like a tornado is going through the place. Ronnie runs straight toward me, speaking in high-gear Dagala.

"Whoa!" I say, holding up my hand. "English, Ronnie!"

As of yet I haven't been bitten by a Dagala vampire, thus I cannot speak Dagala (except the few dirty words Bhing taught me). I stress the word "yet." By now, anything's possible, and I know it.

"Bhing! Something is wrong with her!" Ronnie says, breathless. He points to his eyes. "She's no longer seeing me. She came after us, growling and trying to bite!" He looks over his shoulder. "She's tearing up the shop!"

"Mommy's bad," the little toddler in Ronnie's arms says, pointing.

"Help us!" Ronnie cries. "I've locked her in the bathroom. Downstairs."

"Okay, okay, it's going to be fine," I say, and I pray it will be.

"Take them inside," Eli says. "I'll get Bhing."

"She doesn't really know you," I say, trying to convince him that I need to get her.

"Trust me," Eli says. "She doesn't know anyone right now."

I nod. "True." Grasping Ronnie by the elbow, I give his older son a comforting smile and incline my head. "Come on. Eli here will take care of Bhing."

Ronnie stops and looks up at Eli. "Don't hurt her. Please."

Eli nods. "I won't. I promise."

With that, Eli turns and heads toward SoHo. I hurry Ronnie and his sons into Inksomnia. Inside, I turn. "Go sit in there," I say, pointing upstairs to my living quarters. "Shut the door and don't open it until you hear it's me. I'm going to help Eli."

Ronnie nods and heads upstairs with the kids. The little one in his arms turns around and looks at me. His shiny black hair swings with the movement of his head. He points. "Mommy bad."

"Mommy's just . . . sick," I correct. "She'll be okay." But by the look in his dark brown eyes, he doesn't really believe me.

I hope to prove him wrong.

Just as I swing out of Inksomnia at a full run, Eli heads out of SoHo.

Bhing, kicking, screaming bloody murder, and swearing in Dagala is head-first over Eli's shoulder.

"I've got to get her to Da Island," he says. "She's out of control."

I move around his back to take a look for myself. Bhing lifts her head and stares at me. Her glasses are gone and her eyes are milky white. She snaps at me like a freaking zombie, yet her perfectly-cut black bob swings just as easily as her toddler's. A frightening sight to be sure. "Eesh," I say. "Definitely get her there. Fast."

"What are you going to tell Ronnie?" Eli asks, heading to the Jeep.

"I have no idea. I'll think of something," I say. "Hurry."

I help Eli bind Bhing's arms and legs, then strap her into the Jeep. He takes off, and I walk inside to hopefully convince Ronnie and the kids that their adorable little Bhing isn't a monster after all.

After some hasty explanations, and a promise to help his wife, Ronnie and the kids head back to SoHo to start cleaning up the mess. I tell him the same thing we told Nyx when Seth was experiencing a quickening: drugs. I hated doing it, but it was better than the truth: vampires.

An hour later, Eli returns, and we continue on to bigger problems.

Scaling the fence at Bonaventure seems much easier now. One leap and I'm over. No more showing my ass to wind, or clinging for dear life to the metal. Up and over. Gotta love the tendencies.

I shine my flashlight to a discarded pile of items half buried in the dirt. A finger of dread inches across my spine. "This is not good."

"A hairbrush, plate, coffee mug, a toothbrush. A remote control. A plastic container with—a box of cigarettes and lighter?" Eli says, noting the items. "What the hell?"

I draw a breath and stand. "Wow."

"A Gullah grave," Eli says. "Strange. It's an old tradition, one that's not practiced much anymore. Especially here on the mainland."

I reach for the remote.

"No," Eli says. "Don't touch it."

I think a moment, then remember Preacher's teachings. "The Gullah believe that in order to guarantee the safety of the living, they must placate the dead." I point to the items. "They leave the deceased person's favorite personal belongings behind, to keep them from returning and bothering the living."

Eli pulls me away. "To touch any of it would be . . . bad."

"You're right," I agree.

Eli peers over the edge of the grave. "Looks like they didn't make it all the way down."

I look. They hadn't even reached the coffin. "Good thing, too."

"No doubt," he answers.

I glance around. "I'm not sure why Darling sent us here, but I got a bad feeling, Dupré. Let's go. Bad juju being this close to a desecrated Gullah grave."

"Where are Luc and the others?" Eli asks, looking behind him. "I thought they were heading over here?"

I glance around. "I don't know but I don't wanna stick around for them."

"Let's go," Eli says.

I turn off the flashlight and we head back to the Jeep, through the lengthened shadows that distort perception, make everything seem . . . surreal.

But the familiar pungent scent of nearby salt marsh remains steady, and it wafts through the darkened Bonaventure and penetrates my sensitive senses. Crickets chirp, a deafening chorus of melodies echoing through the oaks and magnolia trees. Still no cicadas, though. Not even one since this whole mess started.

As quickly as I noticed it, everything stopped. *Dead, deafening silence.* Not one strand of moss moved. Not one frog croaked. Quiet.

Too quiet.

Eli stares down at me, his eyes glistening in the moonlight.

A rotting stench, however, masks the brine from the salt marsh.

"Vampires," I whisper. "Newlings. Damn, they stink."

Eli senses it too and moves his body close.

I slide a look around. Although subtle, the lengthened shadows shorten inch by inch, stretching gray fingers over the milky white headstones and twisting around them. The longer I stare, the more discombobulated things become. I resist rubbing my eyes. It'll do no good. I steady the irregular breaths that puff out of my lungs and for once, I'm grateful for my sluggish heart rate. Adrenaline, though, pumps rapidly through my veins.

I blink.

In that fraction of a second it takes for my lashes to brush my cheek and lift again, newlings drop from the mossy shadows above, landing in a gap-toothed crescent around us. All punks—at least, they at one time were. Now they are punks with powers.

Eli tenses and moves a muscular arm across my chest, shielding me. "Get behind me, Ri."

His voice lowers with a lethal resonance.

He's got to be kidding.

I stay to his left, curve slightly around his backside, but I don't cower behind him. We just had this discussion. Eligius Dupré has about the hardest freaking head I've ever encountered.

Lifting my ankle, I retrieve a knife and palm the handle. My eyes pan left to right.

Seven against two. Where the frig are Luc and the others?

"Steady, woman," Eli whispers.

I palm another blade and brace myself.

Eli's strong presence comforts me. Pisses me off, too. I press my head against his shoulder. "Here they come—"

Shrill yells echo throughout Bonaventure. Out of the shadows, moonlight illuminates the newlings moving toward us. Great. Fucking great.

"Ready to die, bitch?" the one closest to me says. "You won't be leaving this graveyard alive—"

My arm shoots out, lightning fast, and a whizzing noise rushes the night as my silver cuts the air. Twice.

Two newlings, on their knees now, grip their throats, a gurgled, sputtering choke of a scream breaking from their throats. Within seconds, both fall over, face to the dirt. They begin to seize. A rumble runs through the others.

"Five left," I say, palming two more blades.

Then all hell breaks loose.

More newlings surge from the shadows, and I break away from Eli, blades in hand. "Don't watch me," I warn him. "Just fight!"

The words barely leave my mouth when two newlings run toward me. Three more are already on Eli. Christ, where have they all come from? Legs braced wide apart, I shift my weight and ready myself. This won't be easy.

One reaches me first, and with an in-air, roundhouse kick, I land a foot against the newling's throat, then shove my blade deep into its heart. As it drops to its knees and screams, I land and slam my fist into the other newling's face, sending it backward and down. The crunch of bone and cartilage mixes with the gurgle of fluid as I shove my blade into its throat. Crouching, I palm two more blades.

Another newling grabs me from behind. *Shit.*

Lifting my foot, I bang it down on the newling's instep, but it doesn't turn me loose. Strong fingers squeeze my biceps and push my elbows awkwardly together. I curse and explode. Too late, though.

The force of another newling barreling into my gut comes unexpectedly, and the air whooshes from my lungs. For a moment, I'm dazed.

"Riley!" Eli shouts.

I want to shout back and tell him to just take care of the ones he has, but I can't speak. What's wrong with me? Why am I so freaking weak?

The newling behind me pushes my elbows together, and the pain forces my hands to open, dropping both blades. The newling in front of me smiles, his face contorting into his vampiric form, that convoluted mouth lifting, jaw dropping, exposing several jagged fangs. I shoot a glance at Eli. He has no fewer than five newlings on him. Damn it!

With a closed fist, the newling in front of me slams into my left eye. My head swings hard right, and stars flitter behind my lids. "That's for Charleston, bitch," the newling says. "But I've more for you."

I shake my head, trying to gather myself. "Fuck off—"

Like a flash of light, his arm shoots out and fists my other eye, then my ribs.

I fall forward, feeling the bone give in my side, but the newling holding me jerks me back up. "No, no, not done yet, Fight Club."

Ah, so that's it. A couple of disgruntled fighters.

I gather myself. I feel the energy inside me grow. *I've got this . . .*

Then, the one in front disappears as a flying hulk of muscle tackles him to the ground.

I wheeze, draw in as much air as I can, and lift both knees to my chest. That rib is digging into my lung or something because it's hard to breathe. I ignore it and push. The shift in my weight throws the newling holding me from behind off balance, and I twist one arm free. I turn, ignore the blinding pain in my ribs and rear back my foot, then sink it deep into the vamp's groin. Even vampires have sensitive peckers, so it seems. Another chilling, high-pitched scream breaks Bonaventure's silence.

I'm finally free and I double over, catching my breath. I scan the ground, find my blades, and lunge for them. With both firmly in each hand, I throw one at the newling holding its crotch. The silver buries to the hilt. The other vamp—a short, stocky punk with a shaved head and a tattoo on his throat, hurls himself straight at me. I roundhouse kick and land him flat on his back. I follow him down, straddling his chest in one move. With my knees, I pin his arms by his side. I press the blade to his thick, muscular neck. Jaw unhinged, fangs dropped, eyes white and pupils pinpoint red, he glares at me. Hisses, even. Hisses!

Then, Eli is beside me. "Riley, move off."

"No. I got it." I press the blade deeper, and the newling's eyes bulge.

"Get the . . . fuck . . . off me!" it says between gasps of air.

"Did Valerian send you?" I ask, already knowing the answer. Wonder where the coward was anyway?

"None of your fu—"

I find myself off the newling and on my backside. I shake my head as my equilibrium takes a twirl. I focus on Eli.

He has the newling by the throat, suspended in the air by one muscled arm. The newling's legs dangle inches from the ground.

"Who?" Eli asks, giving it a hard shake.

I slide a quick glance around. Nine downed and very dead newlings lie motionless on the ground.

"I've never seen him," the young vamp grinds out. "I've never fucking seen him. Keeps to himself."

I push myself up, holding my side, and walk closer. "A name. A place to find the name." I press my blade to the newling's testicles. "Or I swear to God, I'll cut your balls off before I stick this in your heart."

A swear tears from the newling's misshapen mouth. "Okay, okay," it says in a voice a bit higher pitched than before. "Drummond. He calls himself Drummond."

"Where are the others like you hiding out?" I press the blade deeper. A trickle of white oozes out, the fading light from the moon glinting off the milky liquid as it trails down one leg.

"Fuck!" he yells, trying to squirm away. "Crazy bitch—get off me!"

Eli squeezes harder and gives it another shake. "Speak, or I'll cut them off myself."

"Some experiment," he chokes out. "Goddamn witch doctor potions. Drummond's research—has something to do with reversing powers or something. I don't know!"

A blade whizzes through the air and buries into the newling's heart. With a curse, Eli drops the body as it begins to seize.

I drop, too.

Eli moves beside me. I'm holding my ribs. Damn, it hurts just to draw a stinking breath.

"Riley? What's wrong?" Eli says. He's holding me now.

"I'll be okay," I say, although not with much energy. "I think I got a broken rib."

My words muffle against Eli's shoulder as I fall into him. He steadies me, then scoops me up.

"Where are we going?" I ask. "We can't just leave the bodies here."

"We can and we will," Eli says. "We're in a grave-yard, Riley."

"Oh yeah," I gasp. "Hey, I'll heal quickly, right? Getting kinda hard to breathe here, Dupré."

"Yes, you'll heal quickly," he answers as he crosses Bonaventure. "Gotta get you home and wrapped first."

"That sounds interesting," I mutter.

Just before I pass out.

So much for frickin' frackin' superpowers.

What the hell?

Part Nine

REVENGE

She's cool. I mean, not just because of what she's become, and what she can do. Yeah, all that is sick but what I like best is she treats me like I'm an adult instead of a perpetual kid. I might be in the body of a fifteen-year-old but I'm far from that. I've lived dozens of full lives. I get sick of looking like a kid. But getting treated like one? Totally lame. But Riley treats me with respect. She's like a sister to me, and I'm glad she's part of our family. She can kick some sick ass, too, and she listens to me. Like when I tell her the aim of her throw is all off, she actually listens to my advice and follows it. I think that's pretty cool. And, I'm totally in love with her brother. Lol!

—Josie Dupré

"Christ, girl. Be still."

I frown, expire a huffy breath, and continue to stare at Eli's angry face. Tense muscles flex in his jaw as he inspects my injuries. With a thumb and forefinger, he tilts my chin and examines both of my swollen eyes. Then with both hands, palms open, he runs them over my entire head.

"Lift up your arms."

I sigh. "Jesus, Eli, I've looked much worse—"

"Lift up your damn arms, Riley. Now."

With a curse, I raise my arms. Eli slides his hands over my ribs, lingering on the left side. I wince when he presses the area.

"Damn, girl," Luc says, stepping into my kitchen. "You look like shit."

I shoot daggers at him with my eyes. He laughs.

"I don't know," Noah says, sliding onto the counter beside me. "I think it's pretty hot looking."

"You think a Dalmatian in heat is hot looking," I say.

"Be still," Eli commands.

I close my mouth and glare at Noah. He wags his brow and grins.

Eli's face hardens and he gently lowers my arms. "You've cracked two ribs. Don't move. I'll be right back." He disappears down the hall, leaving me alone with my annoying audience.

"So somehow you were drugged," Phin says, leaning on the counter close to me. In his palm, a small leather pouch. "That explains why you're so banged up. Talked to Garr on the phone. He swears it's a potion he's never mixed before."

"Yeah," Luc continues. "Normally, none of these injuries would've had time to set in. Not with your tendencies."

"Especially not with your funky DNA," Noah adds.

He shakes his head, his dreads moving with him. "Sick."

"I don't understand," Gabriel says, his thick Scottish burr sounding out of place in my small Savannah apartment. "Why would they drug you, and how?"

"Her powers exceed even that of most newlings," Phin adds. "She's got strength that hasn't fully developed yet, but it will." He glances at me. "Whatever sick potion Valerian is concocting, it's potent. It knocked Riley on her ass. Rendered her almost completely helpless."

"I am far from helpless," I say. "And for the record, getting sick of all of you talking around me."

"So when did Valerian become a freaking scientist?" Luc asks.

"He studied in Spain," Victorian answers. He has stood in the corner, quiet, until now. "I always knew he was interested in science, but never did I think he'd take such an interest in Gullah potions."

"He's learned to manipulate the compounds," Phin says. "Lethal in the wrong hands."

"Well, his are definitely the wrong hands," I say.

Are you okay? You look awful.

Yes, Vic, I'm fine. I look worse than I feel. Promise.

I'm sorry.

For what?

Not killing my brother sooner.

I look at Victorian, and notice the regret in his choco-late eyes. I mouth *I'm fine*, and smile. Then I glance at the neon-green numbers on the microwave. *Four twenty a.m.* My stomach growls, a grumbly reminder of how long it's been since I've eaten.

"Damn, Riley, I can hear that all the way from over here," Noah says. "You want something to eat?"

"Yeah," I answer. "Krystals. Twelve of them. With cheese. Bread extra greasy please."

"What's a Krystal?" Lucian asks.

"Can I take your Jeep?" Noah asks.

"Please, and hurry," I say. Then I smile. "And thanks."

Noah grins. "You owe me."

"Okay, anyone want to go with?" Noah asks.

All but Phin head out.

"I'm sorry we weren't there to help," he says to me. "That gang of newlings dropped out of nowhere. Took us all by surprise." He shook his head. "You should see Darius fight. That . . . is something not human."

I smile. "Funny, coming from an ancient vampire."

Phin frowns. "I'm not ancient. But I am sorry. You could've been killed."

"Well, I wasn't," I assure him. "And you had your own fight to contend with. No worries, yeah?"

"Hey Phin," Luc says, poking his head back through

the door. "Can you drive a load? Too many to fit in the Jeep."

Phin looks at me. "Be back in a bit."

"Don't forget to pick up my brother," I say.

"Will do." Phin leaves.

Eli returns with the first-aid kit. He sets the white plastic box on the counter, next to where he'd placed me, then rests a hand on each side of my hips. He urges my knees apart with his own hip and draws close, wedging his big body between my legs.

His gaze settles first on my mouth, then lifts to my eyes, where they linger for several seconds. Heat rushes to my inner thighs. In those blue, aged depths, I see more than just anger, more than just irritation because I wouldn't be still and let him doctor me. I see regret.

And something else that doesn't make sense. Fear? It makes my stomach plunge, as though falling from an airplane. What could Eli Dupré possibly fear? A few deep breaths, which hurt like hell, purge the nagging feelings. No time for crap like that.

I'm silent as Eli digs through the first-aid kit and pulls out a bottle of antiseptic and a few cotton balls. Saturating the white balls, he angles my head with one hand and dabs at the dual cuts on each cheekbone with the other.

"Ouch-cha," I say, flinching.

His eyes flash, then he administers my care in total silence.

I let him.

When Eli finishes, he sets the cotton aside and picks up a roll of thick, white cloth wrapping tape.

"Lift your arms."

I lift a brow, then my arms.

He doesn't even crack a friggin' smile.

Grasping my tank top by the hem, he pulls it slowly over my head and drops it on the floor. Although I'm wearing a sports bra, Eli's eyes dip to my breasts, and they immediately respond, tightening into sensitive peaks beneath the cotton material.

Eli's nostrils flare and the muscles in his jaw jump. "Hold on to my shoulders, Poe."

Lifting my hands, I place them on Eli's muscular deltoids.

"Higher."

I lift my elbows a bit. "Better?"

He doesn't say a word, just lifts the edge of the tape from the roll and pulls about six inches loose, then presses it to my side, just under my breast. "This will hurt a bit."

I shrug. "No prob. I'm used to it."

He looks up then, that mysterious blue gaze unreadable, unsettling. "Take in a shallow breath and hold it."

I do, and he begins wrapping.

From just under my breasts to above my navel, he circles a tight bandage of tape. I won't lie—it pinches. Hell, it hurts. But I remain silent.

Finished, he sets the roll aside and inspects his work, running his hands down my sides.

After a moment, he pushes out a slow breath between his teeth. His eyes meet mine, only inches from my face. "I felt like my insides were being ripped out of my gut, watching you get hurt tonight. Doesn't matter that you held your own. Do you understand me, Riley?"

I shake my head. "Eli, I—"

Lifting his hand, he scrapes the pad of his thumb over my lip and uses the slightest pressure to urge my mouth open. He angles his head and presses into me, taking in a long breath as he kisses me totally senseless.

My own breath hitches and I drown in the slow, erotic brush of his lips, shoving my fingers through his silky hair and tasting him back. I gasp as my broken ribs pinch.

Eli's hands graze my taped sides, gently now, and he stills them against me. Warmth from his hands makes me sink into him, but he makes no further moves— only deep, possessive kissing. I can handle that.

"Damn. Thought you were hungry. For food."

I crack open one eye and stare at Luc, wagging a bag of Krystals. Everyone else has frozen in place behind him. How many people? Seven. Gotta love a close-knit family.

Eli kisses the tip of my nose and pulls back. "You need to eat."

The scent of deliciously greasy burgers rises from the bag and wafts my way. Suddenly, I agree. "You're right. Hand 'em over, Dupré."

You may not be able to see what I do, but I know you can hear me, Riley Poe. Know this: you're mine. You were always meant to be mine, no matter how long a time separates us. My brother isn't the only one who has watched you over the years. You now have me inside of you. Not just my brother. I was always stronger than him anyway. You'll come to me. And when I'm finished fucking you, no other will ever be able to satisfy you. Do you know what it feels like to be forever unsatisfied? No longer able to experience an orgasm? Trust me, Riley. You will gladly come to me. And you will beg to become mine forever.

My eyes flip open and I scan the room. I'm in my bed, alone. Daylight streams through the window. I glance at the clock. It's close to one p.m.

How in the holy hell is Valerian speaking to me in my head? Now he wants me for a lay? For a wife? Whatever, freak.

As I move, I notice I'm not nearly as sore as I was the night before. I'm not positive if it's the bandaging job

Eli did on my ribs, or if whatever dope I was slipped has finally worn off. Either way, I feel better. I walk to my bathroom and flip on the light. Peering at my face, I even see a difference there. Not nearly as swollen, and my eyes aren't as black as I thought they'd be. Cool. Fast healer. Good because I don't have time for bullshit. Especially don't have time for psycho vampires obsessed with me.

Oh, I'm obsessed with you, all right. I'm not psycho, though. You'll come to me. I can promise you that, my love. Just wait until you get the news. You'll come. And you'll know exactly where to find me. If you're wise, you'll come alone. Despite how Hollywoodish that sounds, it's true. Heed my words. And you should be finding out the details about. . . . now.

Eli throws open the door. His face is, believe it or not, paler than its usual color. I immediately know something's wrong.

"What?" I say, panic rushing through me. "Eli, what is it?"

"Estelle," Eli says, barely above a whisper. "She went missing about an hour ago."

I don't wait for an explanation. I ask no questions. No need to. I already know what's happened. I turn too fast and notice my ribs hurt more than I think they do. I ignore the pain though and hurry to my closet.

"What are you doing?" Eli asks.

"Finding something to wear," I say. There. A clean pair of cargos. I first go to the cabinet of blades, secure the leather sheaths, and stuff each one with silver. I ease into my cargos, find a long-sleeved shirt, and attempt to pull it over my head. Not working. Shirt too tight. I throw it in the corner.

"Riley, stop," Eli says, and reaches for me.

"I can't!" I jerk around to face him and cringe as my ribs pull at me. Anger forces the pain away. "I know where she is, Eli, and I'm going to get her."

His steely grip on my forearm stops me. "Like hell you are."

I shake him off and try another shirt, one last time. It's a little looser and I ease it over my head and slowly pull one arm in at a time. On crooked, but on. I yank on my boots and push past Eli.

He stops me.

"It's me he wants," I argue. "I can handle myself. Estelle is almost seventy. She might know how to concoct potions but she can't handle herself against a strigoi." I head out into the living room and grab my Jeep keys off the counter.

By the time I make it to the door, Eli is already there. "You're crazy if you think I'm going to let you walk out of here alone, Riley," he says. "Hell no. I'm going with you."

For a split second, I think of my dog and glance

around. It takes me a second to realize Chaz is at the Dupré House. Good. Because I didn't want to leave him again.

Just like I don't want to leave Eli. Or do what I was about to do.

There is no choice. Valerian will kill Estelle, and he'll not only enjoy it, but he'll flaunt it. And he'll have no regrets. He fears nothing.

That's about to change.

"Riley," Eli warns, his eyes locked solid onto mine. He senses something, and his nostrils flare. His body tenses. "Don't."

Before the word is out of his mouth, I use the one tendency Julian taught me to use before leaving Romania. I'd not tried it on anyone, save Julian.

Concentrating, I hold Eli's gaze. I speak to him in his mind.

Stay where you are, Eli. Don't move. Don't leave here until after I've gone. Your body is heavy, and my will is stronger than yours. You know it. You feel it. The synapses in your nervous system aren't firing. You're paralyzed. You'll stay that way until I'm gone. Until ten minutes after I'm gone.

The moment my words sink in, I can tell. Eli's eyes glaze over as he stares at me. I know he sees me, knows I've used something on him, and that he hears and knows everything around him. He'll be pissed. I can't worry about that now. I waste not even a second. I turn and run from my apartment.

Pelting rain slashes in stinging bullets as I kill the motor of the nineteen-foot skiff I borrowed from Bell's Landing and let it slide onto the deserted beach of the research facility. One of the smaller barrier islands, it was purchased years ago for the sole purpose of using it for the facility. I can't imagine what Valerian is using it for. Doesn't matter. He knew exactly what to use to get me here, and it worked just as well as if he had used mind control on me. Grabbing the rear anchor, I plop it into the water and tie it off. I pull the drain plug and jump out.

No sooner do my feet hit the sand than six newlings descend from the trees. I sense them before they drop to the ground. Crouching, I whip out two blades and down two newlings before they attack me.

Surprisingly, I'm not killed.

Ah, you trust me, Riley. That touches me deeply. It truly does. So to show you my good faith and word, I'll send your beloved surrogate grandmother back to the mainland with a trusted servant. You'll remain here. With me. Understood?

"I want to see her," I say, and I glance around, searching for Valerian. Instead, a newling emerges from the palm fronds and scrubs, leading a slow-walking Estelle.

"Baby, why you come here?" Estelle says angrily. "I told dat evil boy you wouldn't do it."

I struggle against my attackers. I have to stop and think about what's inside of me, what grows and changes daily. I'm strigoi. I'm Arcos. I'm Dupré. I'm Gullah.

A deep breath, and I summon all of my strength. Although it takes four newlings to hold me, I knock them all in different directions. I take off, send the last newling sprawling, and pull Estelle into a fierce hug. "Grandmodder," I say, checking her over. "Are you okay?"

"Yes, girl, yes," she says, and I can hear the relief in her voice. "I'm fine, now, stop all dat." She looks at me, her ebony face smooth, her eyes searching mine. "You shouldn't have come here, dat's right. You shouldn't have."

I hug her again, drawing in the familiar scent of Downy and Gullah herbs. "No way would I let them keep you out here, Grandmodder. No way."

I'm waiting, Riley. I don't like to wait.

A newling appears—young, no more than nineteen, wearing ripped destroyed jeans and a leather jacket. Although not morphed completely, his eyes are white, pupils pinpoint and fire red. He looks to be in a trance as he moves toward the skiff.

"No way am I letting my grandmother get into a boat with him," I say out loud. "Hell no, Valerian."

He's perfectly capable, Riley. Trust me. I've instructed him to take her straight to River Street. He'll help her up the dock and off to her home she can go. I give you my word.

"No, baby," Estelle says. "Come with me."

I kiss my surrogate grandmother on the cheek. "I can't." I smile at her. "But it'll be okay. I promise. Now go quietly, please. I'm begging you."

Without another word, the newling grasps Estelle by the arm and leads her to the skiff. As though he'd been around boats all his life, the newling pulls the anchor, plugs the drain, and starts the motor. Estelle's gaze stays on mine until they're out of sight.

The moment I let down my guard, something plunges into my neck. A pinprick. A needle. A dart. I don't know. But in seconds, I'm slipping to the ground . . .

Part Ten

REDEMPTION

I think Riley's tendencies have surpassed my own abilities. Doesn't bother me. I like how strong she is. The control she's learned in the short time we've been back from Romania blows my mind. It takes everything I have not to interfere. Her reflexes are scary fast. And the mind manipulation she exerts? No one is unaffected. Not even me. Especially that bastard Arcos. It'll be interesting to see if Riley can keep from killing him. For the sake of all of us, I hope she can. A war between the Duprés and Arcoses wouldn't be pretty. And I'm not willing to risk losing Riley. Without her, my existence is meaningless.

—Eli Dupré

Something hot and wet trails my cheek and rouses me from a drug-induced slumber. Forcing my eyelids to open, I squint into the near darkness. I try to move, but I'm shackled to a cot. The room is cold. Damp. Smells moldy. I turn my head.

And stare into a pair of dark eyes. Human. With tendencies.

"Awake now, are ya?" the man, apparently a guard, whispers in my ear. " 'Bout goddamn time."

My first reaction is to bite off his damn ear, then

291

head-butt him into oblivion. He can see me in the moonlight, but I can see only his shadowed shape. With my arms and legs bound, I can't budge.

Instead, I slide him a slow, sexy smile. I trace my bottom lip with my tongue. "God, you smell good," I lie. "Come closer."

The guard pauses, probably stunned from what I've said, but then his brain cells rush to the winning muscle and he leans over me, just like I ask. "Yeah? You think I smell good?"

"Um-hm," I croon, thanking God above that the man indeed didn't smell overly stinky. "I bet you taste even better."

Again, he pauses—but only briefly. His mouth moves to mine. "Why don't you find out?" Moving a hand to my breast, he squeezes it hard and shoves his tongue in my mouth.

Biting back the urge to barf, I kiss him back, a furious, fast kiss, just to turn him on. It does. He gropes at me then, lifting my shirt and pushing my bra up, ignoring the tape wrapping my ribs, and grasping my bare breast and squeezing. He moans, and starts to climb on top of me. "You're gonna like this, baby," he grunts.

Fighting back the urge to kill him now, I move my mouth to his ear. "Wait," I whisper, licking his earlobe. "Slow down." I bite the shell of his ear to get his attention. "This would be a lot more fun if I weren't tied up. Don't you think?"

The guard, silhouetted by the light coming down from the ceiling, grunts. "You might get away. Then my ass is fried." He bends his head and tries to kiss me, but I move my mouth.

"I'm just a girl. I can't possibly get away from you. Besides," I say, breathing hard, "why would I want to? I'm wet and horny as hell." I move to his ear once more and give a whispered moan. "And I want to fuck your brains out."

"Jesus God, woman," he says after a second. Fast as he can, he pulls something out of his pocket. "Hold still."

A pair of cutters clips through the thick plastic tie-wraps binding my wrists and ankles. As soon as I'm free, he throws them to the floor and falls upon me. Again, I give just enough to keep him interested, then push him away.

"Wait a minute," I say in a fake, excited breath. "Not so fast." I reach between his legs, grab his arousal, and give an even faker moan of sexual impatience. "Let me get on top."

"Kinky bitch, ain't ya?" he says. "With that weird tat on your face. What other tats you got, babe?" He chuckles. "Okay, whatever you say." He rises, allowing me to move out from under him, then he takes my spot, on his back. He gropes himself impatiently. "Hurry up. I'm about to spurt in my goddamn pants."

The moonlight spreads over him now, illuminating some of his features. Crew cut, mid-forties—an average-looking man. *A pervert. A pervert with tendencies.*

Internally repulsed by the disgusting threat of spurting, I sling one leg over his hips and straddle him, wriggling against his rising erection. He grabs my hips, shoving me harder against it.

"Yeah, baby, do me," he says, his voice thick with excitement. "Take off your shirt so I can see your tits swinging in my face." Apparently, junior here has watched one too many cheap pornos.

Grabbing the hem of my shirt, I slowly pull it off and drop it on the floor. His eyes glaze over as they lock on my dragons. "Goddamn, baby, that's hot as shit." He lifts a hand and fingers the ink markings on my arm.

Just to give the situation an added extra, I palm his crotch. "Oh, you're so hard," I say. "Are you ready for me?"

He presses my hand hard against him. "Oh yeah, bitch, I'm ready all right."

"Good."

He grunts with what I suspect is a sexually excited moan of pleasure.

Then I rise off him, stand next to the cot, and slowly unbutton my jeans.

"Hurry up, baby," he says, yanking his zipper down and groping himself. "I'm gonna come all over my– *Humph!*"

The wind leaves his lungs in a painful, gurgling gush as I raise my leg and slam the heel of my boot down hard on his crotch. He gasps a few times, ineffective little puffs of wind as he curls into a ball, hands cradling his privates.

Wasting no time, I rear my foot back again and catch him full force under the chin, sending him sprawling off the cot.

"Bitch!" he wheezes, spitting.

Another stomp to the groin sends the guard into a spasm of air sucking and cussing.

Dropping to my knees, I fish in his pocket for the tie-wraps I'd felt while straddling him. Grabbing a handful, I quickly bind his feet.

The guard reaches for something, and knowing he has tendencies makes me not trust him for a single second, or waste a single move. I dive in the same direction, my fingers brushing the cutters, knocking them across the room where they ping off a wall. "Ah-ah, shithead. No getting out of the wraps."

I stand and put my boot to his throat. "Turn onto

your stomach or you'll be whistling out of a brand new hole in your neck. Now."

He curses, then turns over.

I drop a knee right between his shoulder blades, wrench one of his arms behind him and pin it with my weight. Quickly, I grab the other arm, then tie-wrap them together. I kneel over him, close to his ear.

"You're going to tell me a few things," I say, barely above a whisper. I concentrate, envisioning in my head that I can make this prick do anything I want him to do with no resistance. "And you're going to do it quietly. Now roll over and be still."

He does and goes completely motionless. Says nothing. Doesn't move. But his eyes stay fixed on mine.

"Good boy. Now tell me where we are," I command.

"The research center," he mumbles. "Lab."

"What research?" I ask.

"Experiments," he says. "On blood."

"Whose?" I demand.

"All of ours," he mutters. "Yours. Mine. Those like us."

The picture became clearer. "Vampires."

He shrugs.

"Where's Valerian Arcos?" I ask.

The guard remains silent. I give him a mental shove without even realizing how I've done it. Apparently, it doesn't feel too good to have your brain pushed.

He screams.

I quickly back off.

"I've never seen him," he says, whimpering. "He only talks to me in my mind. Tells me what to do, whose blood to collect."

"How many others are here?" I ask.

"Not sure," he answers. "Could be two dozen, could be one. They come and go."

Just that fast, I'm tired of playing the game. I want answers.

"Where's the lab?"

"Out and left."

I pull my shirt back on and take off running, pushing through a single door that leads from the room and into a corridor. It has the feel of an old high school built in the fifties, with long halls and rooms on either side. The doors are closed, and only every other overhead light burns. Throwing open door after door, I find nothing. No one. It's like the facility is abandoned.

I'm hit from behind.

Not so abandoned.

I fly—not literally, but my body leaves the ground and smashes against the wall. I drop, roll, and leap up. My hand feels for a blade down my waistband. I palm it and look.

Four young vampires. Three males, one female.

All four leap at me at once.

With two quick releases, I fling blades and down the

two closest to me. I can tell I won't make it far—they're quick and almost on me. So I take off.

I know they'll have a hard time catching me.

Down the corridor I run. It's dim—almost pitch-black. I see a stairwell door and shove through and tear up the steps. In seconds I'm on the third-floor landing and I slam against the metal bar and open the door.

Six more young vampires are standing there, waiting.

"You ain't goin' nowhere, Poe," the one in front—a male with blond spiked hair—says. "He called you here for a reason." He takes a step toward me. "You're stayin' a while, darlin'."

I've had enough. Valerian Arcos is a danger I no longer care to have lingering in my life. He's been able to snatch Estelle right out from under our noses.

He's capable of anything.

He has to be stopped.

I leap at the leader. His jaws extend and teeth drop. The others follow. I ignore them all. I plunge a silver blade into his chest before my feet bound off his shoulder. As I land behind the group, they turn and descend on me. In one move I crouch, sweep out with one leg and take down the next. The blade I have palmed is buried into the newling's flesh. She screams and falls with the others.

Three more to go.

Use your other tendencies, Riley. You don't have to fight so hard.

Victorian's voice echoes inside my head. For a second, it throws me off. Another newling gets close—almost too close. My reflexes are fast and I take it down, land in a crouch. I don't wait.

I kill them all.

Their screams as their bodies break down chase me down the corridor as I start slamming open doors, searching for Valerian.

I know you're here, Arcos! You might as well come out! I yell in my mind to Valerian. A panic grips me—a desperation to find him, to punish him, to send his ass straight to Hell. But each room I find is an empty shell, with peeling walls and broken metal furniture. It reminds me of the tuberculosis sanatoriums they used to have at the turn of the twentieth century until the forties and fifties. An unsettled sensation creeps over me as I slip through the halls. I'm alone, frustrated, frantic. Innocent people have died at this place; I can sense it. Smell it.

Taste it.

As I move, I barely notice the speed at which I'm flying through the halls. I hear the eerie echo of my feet through the emptiness, but it's hard to register that I'm the one making the noises. I'm so goddamn fast, the walls and doors blur past me. My tendencies are many, and apparently they are as close to vampiric as a human can have.

In the next second, no fewer than a dozen newlings burst from the stairwell. They surround me, and I know then I'm beaten. No way can I concentrate long and hard enough to manipulate all of their minds; just like I can't possibly fight them all. They descend upon me.

I let them.

One grabs me by my arm and pulls me along. We leave the third floor, down the stairwell, to the second floor. At the end of the corridor, a door stands open. I'm shoved inside, and even though I stumble, I catch myself upright.

The door slams shut. The room is dark. Not one light is turned on.

I immediately sense his presence.

"I need something from you, Riley," Valerian's voice speaks from the shadows. "You have something that even I don't possess. As a matter of fact, I'm positive there isn't a soul alive—or not—who possesses it. You are . . . unique that way. Highly desirable."

I peer into the darkness until a shape, still as stone in the corner, moves. My hand palms the blade sheathed just below the waist of my cargo pants, at the back.

"All that silver won't do you any good with me," Valerian says.

"What do you want with me?" I ask. I still keep my fingers wrapped around the blade.

Valerian laughs lightly. "Ah, it's so refreshing to experience a human with tendencies who is still so . . . naïve."

His voice is closer to me now, although his shadow hasn't budged. It's almost like he's inside my head, speaking against my eardrum. I inch slowly toward the far wall, the sheath of my knife brushing my fingertips. Confidence races through me. "Why don't you come out of the shadows and see how naïve I am?" I say. He doesn't scare me.

I want to kick his ass.

Or, kill his ass.

Again, his low laugh resonates through me.

"Oh, I will certainly come out of the shadows," Valerian says. "I've been looking forward to this for far too long."

The shadows shift, and by the time I blink, and my lashes lift from my face, he's standing before me.

He looks strikingly like Victorian.

Dark, wavy hair brushes the collar of a black silk buttoned-up shirt, tucked loosely into a pair of equally dark pants. Eyes the color of espresso stare at me, weighing, calculating. Full lips and flawless skin make him appear Godlike. He grins.

I ease my blade from its sheath.

"Tsk, tsk," he says, and wags a finger at me. "Play nice. I'm not here to kill you, and we both know how easily I could have done that, had I wanted to."

I keep my eyes trained on him. Waiting.

"My brother has always had a severe obsession for you," he continues. "I have always hated him for that. You understand, don't you? Our kind should remain with . . . our kind. Uniting with a mortal just isn't feasible."

"Why not?" I ask. My guard is up, every nerve ending on alert.

He smiles a long, slow smile and holds out his hands. "You see," he begins. "Our kind exists forever. We're strong. Capable. We understand our affliction. But with you? Even with tendencies, it's not feasible to risk. You're . . . weak. Vulnerable." His smile is wistful. "I've learned too vulnerable."

My interest is piqued, but I say nothing.

He notices.

Valerian paces. Slowly. Predatorlike. "You are an exception, though," he says, and rubs his finger over the flat surface of a discarded metal cabinet. "You always have been."

My insides lurch.

He stops behind me and smells my hair, then rounds on me. "You know, Riley," he says, dragging a knuckle across my cheek. "You look very much like your mother. Well," he says, smiling. "Like she used to. Before."

Frozen inside, I lock my gaze to his. "What do you know of my mother?"

Valerian shrugs, but doesn't break his stare. His words are slow and calculating. "I know that she was fiercely protective over you, even when you rebelled." He steps away from me, then turns. "I also know she put up an impressive fight when your boyfriend killed her." He shakes his head. "Stupid boy." Then, his gaze turns white, his pupils pinpoint red. "Couldn't follow simple directions."

Inside of my body, my oddly mixed blood turns to ice.

A slow smile lifts Valerian's mouth. "Ah, I see you understand now. What you might not know is that I did it for you, Riley." He sighs. "All I ever wanted was you."

I growl and lunge at him.

I capture nothing but air.

Valerian's low laugh comes from behind me. "Ah, Riley. Don't exert yourself. Save your strength," he says, then is suddenly so close to my back, our bodies touch. His whisper brushes my ear. "You'll need it."

Rage roils inside of me. "You killed my mother," I say under my breath.

"Technically, yes," Valerian admits. "Although your young boyfriend actually did all the work." He shakes his head again. "Messy, that one. His demise was anything but a loss. He had no fucking sense."

I lunge again, and this time I don't find air. I find the wall.

Then he's behind me, pressing his body against mine. With one hand securing mine, he forces the blade from my grasp and presses his lips to my ear. *Be perfectly still, Riley. Don't move. Your limbs are weak. Your muscles frozen. Listen to me closely.*

Instantly, I am unable to move.

"Ah, perfect. My brother noticed you first, but I immediately wanted you," he says in a whisper. He drags his lips over my jaw. "Rather, I wanted your blood."

I tense. My heart slams against my ribs, but it's a slow slam. Adrenaline rushes.

Valerian licks my throat. "Relax, Riley," he says. "I'm not going to kill you. That was never my intention." With one hand, he skims my back, my hip, my ass. "Your blood was enigmatic then. Now? With that of the bloodline of my brother and me? It is irreplaceable." He nips my jaw with his teeth. "And will make an unstoppable army."

I feel his hard cock press against my lower back. I try to summon every ounce of vampiric strength I possess, yet nothing happens. He has me. I cringe.

Reach behind you and touch me.

As if my hand has a mind of its own, I do as Valerian says. I run my hand over his hip, then grope his crotch. He groans in my ear.

Inside, I scream. Where are my goddamn tendencies?

Only then do I hear a new voice.

Riley, damn it, concentrate! You're stronger than he is.

My mind races as Eli's words rush through me. *Stronger? Are you kidding me? I can't move! It's like he has me chained down. He killed my mother, Eli. He's watched me for all these years.*

You've got the DNA of three strigois, the Gullah, and Dupré. Trust me. You have more strength than he could ever think of having. Use your mind, Riley. Not your physical strength. Get a grip and concentrate. And whatever you do, don't fucking kill him.

Valerian's hands find their way beneath my shirt, my tank, and he pulls me tightly against him. "See how easy this is for us? Me, telling you what to do, and you, doing it without question? You see, once I give you the orgasm of your entire life, I'm going to take your blood." He kisses my throat. "Some for myself, of course, and some for morphing. We'll make powerful children, Riley." He wraps his arms completely around my body and embraces me. "We'll be unstoppable."

Concentrate!

Eli's single command jolts me. I don't know where he is, but it sounds as if he's right in my ear. I draw a deep breath, clear my mind, and then focus on memories. Recent. The past. They all jumble together.

I let them.

A vision of my mother, dead, naked, pale, and lifeless, crowds my mind. Her eyes stare unseeing into mine as I drag her from the bathtub and cradle her in my arms. Another vision, of Seth's vampiric eyes staring hungrily into mine. Of the bloodbath at Bonaventure. Of more in Charleston, and of the sickening fight club in the old rectory. Of a young marine, dead. Of Estelle, roughly handled by a newling.

My mind spins out of control as horrific images assault me. All fault lies at the feet of one. Valerian Arcos.

Inside, I rage.

My inhuman powers then merge; I can feel it occur in my body. A current of energy rushes through me and abruptly halts at my feet, then shoots back up and through my fingers, my eyes. Inside my veins, the blood there feels like lava.

Then, as fast as it starts, it stops.

I look up. And everything is suddenly crystal clear. Julian's advice rings inside my head. I remember.

Remember your mother, Valerian? What happened to her? Did you kill her? Get off me now, Valerian Arcos, and move away.

"You will not mention her!" he says vehemently. "Do not!"

But my body is released, and Valerian, slowly, moves backward.

I turn and meet his gaze. It's wide, white, with pin-point red pupils.

They stare at me with horror and hatred.

I give another command. It comes out of the blue, yet somehow, it's perfect.

Suffer.

Valerian's body begins to quiver, and his eyes widen farther still. His face contorts, but not into his vampiric image. He seems to contort into pain.

More.

A sob—male, throaty, and desperate—escapes from him. His body shakes uncontrollably. He drops to the floor. I stand over him, his eyes glaring up at me.

Agony. Fire. Strangulation.

Valerian's body thrashes uncontrollably; his hands fly to his neck as choking noises gurgle from his throat. Satisfaction courses through me as I watch him writhe in pain, imaginary flames licking his skin. With my mind, I force the delusion on him. Harder. Faster.

"Riley, stop!"

Although I hear the voice, I can't take my eyes off of Valerian. All the things that go along with finally finding a loved one's killer run through me. I take pleasure in watching his pain. His anguish. It must be something similar to what my mother experienced when she died. What all of those innocent people experienced. All because of selfish, pathetic Valerian.

On my thigh, a sheath is strapped. I reach for the blade, the silver turning cool in my hand. I envision the silver slipping easily through his flesh. Ending his sorry fucking existence.

"No, *chère*," the voice said calmly. "No."

A hand goes to my shoulder. Gently. Firmly. I look up. It takes a minute for my mind to register.

The first one I see is Eli.

Behind him, Noah, Phin, Jake, Darius, Gabriel, Seth, and Victorian.

"You can't kill him," Victorian says. "No matter that you want to."

I look down at Valerian. His body is still now, staring up at me. I'm holding him in some sort of weird abstraction without even trying.

"We'll take him back to my father tonight," Victorian says, then puts a hand on my shoulder. "It's over, Riley."

Eli moves close, almost between Victorian and me.

The two stare off at one another.

"My team and I will accompany you and your brother back to Romania," Jake Andorra says to Victorian.

Victorian nods, but keeps his gaze locked on to mine. "I must have a word with Riley first," he says.

"We've got him," Jake says, and grabs Valerian off the floor.

Surprisingly, Victorian looks at Eli. "Do you mind?"

My eyes flash to Eli's, and I know his answer before he says it.

"Hell yes, I mind. But she doesn't. Go ahead. And keep your hands to yourself."

Anger is surfacing inside me, and maybe it's because I already know what Victorian is about to tell me. Doesn't matter. I allow him to grasp me by the elbow and lead me out of the dingy little concrete room.

In seconds, we're outside. The moon hangs low, more than a crescent now, and the air is chilled. A light pours from a single lamp beside the entrance of the facility. It's enough to cast Victorian's beautiful face into odd planes and shadows.

"I never wanted Valerian to have you," he begins. "I tried my best to warn you away, but I was powerless in my tomb. I knew of your lover, and of Valerian's plan to have him kill your mother." Anguish forces his features into a frown. "I couldn't stop him. He's always been stronger than me. Even entombed."

He places a hand on my jaw and tilts my head

309

toward him. "I'm sorry, Riley. I wish I could change things. I wish I could bring your mother back."

My heart eases a bit. Valerian's power over Victorian is just as easily believed as his power over me. "I understand, Vic." I place my hand over his, at my jaw. "It's okay." It's not okay, but it's not Vic's fault. I know that.

"I'll make sure his punishment is delivered," he says. "I vow it."

I nod. *"Multumesc."*

Victorian cocks his head. "My native tongue sounds good"—he smiles—"on your tongue."

I softly laugh. "Perv."

His eyes soften. "I wish I could keep you," he says. "I've loved you your whole life. Ever since you were a child. I . . . wish you'd choose me over *him.*"

I sigh. "Victorian, don't."

Beneath the moonlight, he looks at me. Sincerity gleams in his inhuman eyes. "Promise me something, Riley Poe."

I look up at him. Waiting.

He smiles when I don't readily agree. "Promise me that if ever there's a time when you tire of him, you'll call me." He kisses my cheek, and pulls back and pins me with a steady gaze. "I will wait for you."

I hold my gaze to his, too. "I've always been drawn to you, Vic. I've never been able to explain it to myself,

310

but I have." I smile. "Don't take this the wrong way," I say, and wrap my arms around his neck. "Take care." I hug him hard. "E-mail me."

I feel his body quake with laughter. "We're vampires, Riley," he says, pulling back and smiling. "No need to e-mail when you can cyber chat"—he taps my temple—"here."

"As long as you stay out of the personal info," I remind him. "And no dirty talking."

Victorian shrugs. "I'm still a man. That is a promise I cannot make."

I laugh, and turn to leave. "Be careful, Vic—"

I'm grabbed by the arm and swung quickly and determinedly into Victorian's embrace. His mouth descends upon mine in a fervent kiss so fast, my head spins.

Literally.

Just as fast, he releases me.

"Sorry," he says, backing away. "I couldn't help myself."

I simply shake my head.

Valerian is tethered and within the hour is taken away by Victorian, Jake, and the others. Eli, Phin, and Seth remain behind.

"There are more out there," Phin says grimly. His eyes glisten in the light of the moon. "It'll take time to collect them."

"At least Valerian won't be able to manipulate their minds," Seth says.

"There is that," Eli says. He looks at me. "Ready?"

I glance around me, at the facility. At the island. "Yeah. I am."

Seth drapes an arm over my shoulder. "You've got some wicked tendencies, Ri," he says. "Do you even remember what you were doing to Valerian?"

I think about it. "Not really."

"That'll come," Phin says. "You'll learn more control over time."

"And flexion of your mind muscles," adds Eli. He grins. "Good thing you have more time now."

I hug my brother and look sideways at him as we walk to the skiff. It's hard to believe that a few short months ago, he was experiencing a quickening. Floating to the top of his room, for God's sake. So much has changed.

We've all changed.

The ride back to the mainland is a fast one. It's early—too early—to visit with Preacher and Estelle, or Nyx. Phin and Seth step out of the Jeep as we park on the merchant's drive behind Inksomnia. Just as we near the door, Eli pulls me to a stop.

"Wait," he says. "I've got something to show you."

I glance at Seth and Phin and shrug. "Later."

They both grin and head inside.

Eli links his fingers through mine and we get back into the Jeep.

"How tired are you?" he asks, and the tone in his voice makes me shiver.

"Not tired at all," I answer.

We take off across Bay Street and down Abercorn.

For the first time in months, I notice a particular ease in the air. The chill is right. The crisp is right. The rustle of leaves is right.

Being beside Eli Dupré is even more right.

Twenty minutes from downtown and just off Waters Avenue, across from the old white concrete Cresthill Baptist Church, Eli turns down Beckman Avenue. It's an older residential street, with houses built in the forties and fifties. Some a little newer. Some ways down, Eli turns in to a corner lot and stops the Jeep. The drive is a half circle lined with aged azalea bushes that are probably gorgeous in the spring when in full bloom. The house is an older concrete block house, single story, with several tall pine trees towering overhead. A wooden swing sits suspended between two of them. I glance at Eli.

"What's this?" I ask.

A crooked grin splits Eli's face in two, and for a moment, he's not a vampire. He's a mischievous guy up to something.

I guess he can be both.

Eli's gaze lingers on my mouth, then meets my eyes. "My new house."

I feel my eyes bug out. "Are you serious?" I glance back at the older home, then back to Eli. "Really?"

He shrugs. "I met a man once, years ago. He'd just returned from the war—as in World War Two—and had started working for the electric company. He had a sweet wife named Frances and a beautiful baby daughter named Dale. I watched him one day break up a fight between two mean-asses who'd jumped this skinny kid. Cracked the two bullies' heads together. Knocked them senseless." Eli's gaze moves from mine to a place above me, and he concentrates as he pulls the memory back. He smiles. "His name was Wimpy. He gave me a job making hush puppies." He inclines his head toward the concrete house. "He built this. Raised a family here. Had three more children. He helped build that church back there." Eli slips from the Jeep and walks around to my side. "I watched his little blond-haired granddaughter, Cindy, come here every single summer and swing on that swing." He points to where it was. "She had a little friend just down the road and they'd play together nearly every day. Cindy and Julie. They were inseparable."

I look at Eli, wondering where he was going with all of this. It sounds great to me, like I'm hearing about someone from my own family.

From the family I could've had.

Eli knows I'm perplexed, and smiles. "I'll never forget the summer of nineteen seventy-six. Cindy was ten. She ran around with a *Jaws* T-shirt on nearly the whole summer." He shakes his head and laughs. "I'll have to tell you a funny story about her later. About who she is, what she became. Maybe even take you to meet her. Later, though." He glances toward the house again. "The property runs straight down to the Vernon River. Wimpy's wife, Frances, used to go down to the dock and catch blue crabs by the basketfuls." Another winsome smile touches his lips. "He built a dock over the marsh back in the fiftes. I've had some repairs made, and . . ." He grasps my hand. "Well, come see for yourself."

I'm, for a change, speechless as Eli leads me across the yard, back toward the woods where a small worn path leads to the marsh. The brine is perfect and pungent, and just the slightest breeze rustles the saw grass. We cross the marsh on a newly repaired dock, and at the end sits a small covered screened-in dock house with a red tin roof. Eli stops, steps inside, and grabs blankets from a plastic storage bin in the corner. The screen door creaks and slams behind him as he pulls me down the plank to a small floating dock.

Without a word, he spreads two blankets on the dock, and rolls a third long-ways and places it at one end. He holds out a hand. "Sit down."

I grin and do as he asks.

Silently, he kneels and removes my boots and socks. He rolls up my jeans. Then he sits, kicks off his boots and socks, and does the same. He sticks his feet into the water, and I do the same. He sits close to me, our shoulders brushing. He looks up.

"Magnificent spray of stars, don't you think?" he says.

I turn my head and look at him. "What are you doing, Eligius Dupré?"

Eli's smile is blinding. "I love it when you use my full name."

I shake my head and wait.

He looks at me. "I always secretly wanted what Wimpy had. Family. Loving, devoted wife." He laughs softly. "They called each other *monkey*. Their pet name for each other." He shakes his head. "Funniest damn thing I'd ever heard. Wimpy made magic happen here, Riley." He smiles and shrugs. "He had a great life. I want it. And I want you to share it with me."

My heart leaps. It almost stops.

With two hands, Eli grasps my face. His gaze passes over my mouth, my nose, then to my eyes. "I want to marry you, Riley Poe. And if you don't say yes now, I'll keep asking until you do."

Even in the fading light, I can see the cerulean blue brightness of Eli's eyes sparkle. The slight scruff that perpetually remained on his jaw, the fall of dark hair over his forehead, and that crazy silver hoop he still wore in his brow—all of it Eli.

And he wants to marry me.

Suddenly, my past becomes a faint memory of someone who could've been anyone other than me. The pain of my mother's death, though still present, dulls. I feel I can accomplish anything with this unique man by my side.

"Yes," I say softly. I'm looking into his eyes. They soften. He smiles.

His kiss rocks me.

Gentle at first, his lips brush mine, linger against me, and although I know he doesn't need air to breathe, you'd never know it. He sighs against my mouth. The sweet taste of him makes my head spin. He pulls me into a tight embrace.

"Thank you," he whispers against my ear. "I love you, Riley. More than you know."

I squeeze him in return. "I love you, Eligius Dupré," I say, then pull back and look at him. "I think I have from the first moment I saw you."

He grins. "I know."

"We have a lot of work ahead of us though," I say. "Jake wants to hire us. Together. Like Turner and Hootch. *Miami Vice*. Scarecrow and Mrs. King."

Eli shakes his head. "Yeah. I know." He kisses me

again. "Good thing we have years and years to be together."

With the water lapping at our ankles, we sit. We talk. We plan.

For the night, we're a normal couple in love.

I guess this is something I'll have to get used to, and I pray to God I can one day control it. I can't just run around having people touch me, inadvertently hurling me into their bodies only for me to experience some mind/body/life altering event that I can somehow change or help. I mean seriously.

Or can I?

All I know is that Seth and Eli are my world. Preacher and Estelle are my world. The Duprés are my family, and I have a shitload of the most bizarre friends a person can have.

But I'm not a person, am I? Hell no. I'm an abomination. Human, but not. Vampiric qualities, but thankfully, not a bloodsucker. I can be killed, but I won't naturally die on my own for hundreds of years. And lucky for me, the aging process is slow. I'll look twenty-five for a helluva long time. That's a plus. No Botox for me.

I'm grateful, in a way, that Seth shares the same fate as me. Probably not to the severity, since he's only had one vampiric encounter, and me, four. But we'll have a longer life together, and that suits me. I can't imagine life without my little bro.

So, all in all, I'm adjusting. To what, exactly, I'm not sure. I still love to ink. Sketch designs. I'm proud of my work and my accomplishments. But I'm now heavily considering passing ownership over to Nyx, occasionally inking when I'm in town, and then utilize for the good these crazy ass powers I've acquired. And since Eli and Seth are in it, along with Noah and Phin? Why the hell not.

We'll see.

I'm sitting at Molly MacPhearson's. Across the room, a group of seven women has gathered, and after eavesdropping, I determine that they're celebrating a local author's new book release. Pretty cool. They all clink bottles of lager and say what I can only imagine is an inside joke, and then they all burst into laughter. They have the craziest names, too, like they've all given each other nicknames. Gma. Cinny. Oogen. Auntie Betsy. Molly MacNugget. Bunty. Walowie. One of them—Oogen—gets up at everyone's urging, heads outside, and begins to pass back and forth in front of the window in some crazy little run. They all laugh. I don't get it, even though it is pretty hilarious. They're in tears, they're laughing so hard. A group of girlfriends, a night on the town celebrating a fine success. What fun. It's something I've missed in life. But I have a family now, and a new group of friends. Sure, some of them are vampires, some werewolves, and some have been on the earth longer than dirt. But I like them. I watch the women a few minutes longer until they gather their belongings and leave. Still laughing. Calling one another vulgar names. It's so funny, I hate to see them go.

Until I notice *him*.

Eli stands beneath the awning at Belford's across the street. He sees me through the window. I see him, and I move outside toward him. My soul mate.

For now, even if for a few days, I want to enjoy my life. Live it as normal for at least one damn afternoon if possible. Eat a good meal. Have some good sex. Take a walk. A swim. Crack a few oysters on Da Island with Preacher and his family. That is, if Bhing hasn't torn the island up. Last I heard, her cleansing was pretty rocky. Mean as shit, I think I heard someone say. Poor little Bhing. Anyway. I just want to be freaking normal for a while.

Because very, very soon, I have a feeling I'll be boarding a plane for Scotland.

Jake says Edinburgh is being taken over by a band of nasty fallen angels and my tendencies just might come in handy. Ginger and Sydney seriously want me to join WUP. I'm heavily considering it. I mean, what the hell else am I going to do with all this pent-up energy?

We'll see. For now, I'm all about Eli Dupré. And thankfully, he's all about me.

I'm as content as I'll ever be.

I think my mom would be proud of how I've turned out. And somewhere deep inside me, I feel she watches me, even now. I like that. Makes me feel close to her, as if she's right beside me.

I like to think that she truly is.

Who knows? I run with a pack of vampires, werewolves, and immortals. Who says ghosts aren't real? At this point in my strange existence, I'll believe just about anything.

Also Available

from

Elle Jasper

Everdark
The Dark Ink Chronicles

When Savannah tattoo artist Riley Poe is ambushed by an undead enemy, she inherits some of the traits of her attacker—and a telepathic link with a rampaging vampire. Now, she's experiencing murder after murder through the victims' eyes. And her new powers will not be enough to stop the horror—or the unending slaughter...

**Available wherever books are sold or at
penguin.com**

S0336

ALSO AVAILABLE

FROM

Elle Jasper

AFTERLIGHT
The Dark Ink Chronicles

Savannah's most unconventional tattoo artist, Riley Poe, lives on the edge. But she's pushed over the boundary when her younger brother is taken by a sinister cult led by vampires. Her only ally is the hot-tempered vampire Eli Dupre, attracted to Riley's beauty and rare blood type. To save her brother from certain un-death, Riley faces dangers she's never dreamed of, ruthless bloodthirsty enemies, and an evil of endless hunger that wants to devour it all...

**Available wherever books are sold or at
penguin.com**

Can't get enough paranormal romance?

Looking for a place to get the latest information and connect with fellow fans?

"Like" Project Paranormal on Facebook!

- Participate in author chats
- Enter book giveaways
- Learn about the latest releases
- Get book recommendations and more!

facebook.com/ProjectParanormalBooks

Penguin Group (USA) Online

What will you be reading tomorrow?

Tom Clancy, Patricia Cornwell, W.E.B. Griffin,
Nora Roberts, William Gibson, Catherine Coulter,
Stephen King, Dean Koontz, Ken Follett, Nick Hornby,
Khaled Hosseini, Kathryn Stockett, Clive Cussler,
John Sandford, Terry McMillan, Sue Monk Kidd,
Amy Tan, J. R. Ward, Laurell K. Hamilton,
Charlaine Harris, Christine Feehan...

You'll find them all at
penguin.com
facebook.com/PenguinGroupUSA
twitter.com/PenguinUSA

*Read excerpts and newsletters, find tour schedules
and reading group guides, and enter contests.*

Subscribe to Penguin Group (USA) newsletters
and get an exclusive inside look
at exciting new titles and the authors you love
long before everyone else does.

PENGUIN GROUP (USA)
us.penguingroup.com

S0151